Buried In Her Mind

Akash Kannegulla

TRUEBORNE
PRESS

First edition 2026

ISBN 979-8-9994153-0-1

TRUEBORNE
PRESS

Dedicated to my parents, family, friends, and mentors.

Stress!

We are stressed at all stages of life.

In our youth, we are stressed about education.

In our twenties, we are stressed about dating.

In our thirties, we are stressed about financial responsibilities.

In our forties, we are stressed about children.

In our fifties, we are stressed about retirement.

Beyond that, we are stressed about death.

Throughout all these stages, we find ourselves constantly trying to run away from stress.

But remember...

"The only way out is through."
-Robert Frost

PART I: DÉJÀ VU

Present

Erica

1

I wake up abruptly, my scream echoing through the room. "Aagh!" My heart races, pounding in my chest like a wild beast.

It's been ages since I've had such a terrifying nightmare. I lie there, my eyes fixed on the ceiling, my naked body shrouded by a fleece blanket. The nightmare has left me drenched in sweat, giving the blanket a sour smell. As if that's not enough, a throbbing headache starts to pierce behind my eyes.

I sit up, propping myself against the headboard, pushing the blanket aside to cool down. I glance at the digital clock on my dresser. The time glows 2:00 AM and the date reads June 19, 2023.

It's only been a few minutes since I woke, but I'm already feeling chilly and am shivering from the combination of my nakedness and sweat. I love sleeping naked, wrapped in my fleece blanket. On nights like this, though, when my dreams are filled with fear, the sheets only create a sweaty mess. I need to clear my mind.

I get out of bed, grab a towel, and quickly wipe away the sweat. I wrap myself in a robe and make my way to the large window in my bedroom that overlooks the lake. Before sitting in my rocking chair, I open the window wide. The view of the lake always calms me. If there's one place that can help me relax, it's here. My perfect bedroom, facing a peaceful lake in one of Portland's best apartment communities.

A gentle breeze wafts in, tenderly tousling my long hair and providing a soothing massage to my head. I wish I could remember the nightmare. It's not like I was watching a horror movie before bed. I can't stand horror movies. Darkness, violence, anything negative like that—I hate it, so I shouldn't be having bad dreams. As hard as I try, I can barely recollect any of it. Well, I always strive to find the silver lining, so perhaps the bad dream served as a wake-up call to appreciate the breathtaking view of the lake.

As I relax in my chair, a chilling, monstrous sound pierces the silence. It echoes from the depths of the living room, sending shivers down my spine. With bated breath, I slowly turn my head and fix my eyes on the closed door. A mysterious glow dances beneath it, casting an eerie flickering light that seeps into the darkness. My heart pounds in my chest as I take deliberate steps forward, my senses on high alert. With trembling hands, I reach out and gently pull it open, revealing a scene that defies all logic. There, in the dimly lit room, sits my brother Vincent, completely absorbed in a virtual world. The glow of the screen illuminates his face. It's an *ungodly* hour for such an intense gaming session.

The living room is suffocating, its air heavy with the stench of decay, like a dead possum abandoned to rot. A chaotic scene unfolds before me. Discarded, sweat-soaked socks form a disheveled pile nearby. The floor, once pristine, now bears the evidence of a snacking frenzy, with Cheeto crumbs scattered like confetti. A spilled soda can, long forgotten, has transformed into a sticky mess on his pillow, releasing a putrid odor that assaults my senses.

It's as if God hates to see happy sisters, so he sends in crazy brothers. They claim to move into your apartment to foster togetherness, but their true motive becomes clear as they transform your once serene living room into a battlefield of disorder.

I even entrusted him with my credit card, believing it would be used responsibly in times of need while I toil away at work. However, my trust has been betrayed, as he shamelessly exploited it to fuel his appetite for chips and soda and adorn himself in a cap that defiantly proclaims "Leave Me Alone."

"Vincent!" I call out, my voice reverberating through the room. "Could you please lower the volume?"

But he persists as if my words were mere whispers carried away by the wind.

"Vincent!" My frustration intensifies with each passing second.

"What?" he retorts without pausing the game.

"Turn the volume down."

"Chill, dude! It's already low."

Chill, dude? What on earth does that even mean? I'm deceiving my dad by pretending Vincent is only here to spend time with me, and this is the gratitude I receive?

"Vincent!" I yell again, this time with more force. "Turn the volume down or I'll send you back to Dad."

"What? If I turn it down any further, I won't be able to hear it."

"Why don't you use those stupid noise-canceling headphones I bought you for your birthday?" I ask.

"Using headphones at volumes greater than eighty-five decibels may lead to hearing issues and deep psychological effects," he says. "Would you really want your little brother to go through such pain? Or would you rather just suck it up?"

Oh god. I'm not sure if it's just my brother who pulls out ridiculous technical facts to escape blame or if that's just how younger brothers are all over the world. Either way, enough is enough.

"Suck it up? The volume was so loud that it gave me nightmares and jolted me awake. TURN IT DOWN!"

"Alright, Mad Sis!" he says, his annoyance palpable. "Here, I'm turning it down. Happy now? Just go to sleep and let me focus on my game."

"Focus? How can you possibly concentrate with this living room in such disarray and the entire place reeking? Can you please try to be less disgusting? And for the millionth time, stop calling me 'Mad Sis'!"

He points to the words on his hat. *Argh!* Teenagers and their mindless games. I was a well-behaved girl as I grew up, but I suppose Vincent was pampered far more than I ever was. I wish I had a sister instead.

It's nearly 2:30 in the morning, and the looming thought of an early wake-up call for work weighs heavily on my mind. Thankfully, the pungent odor seems confined to the living room, while the gentle breeze that wafts through the open window brings much-needed freshness to my bedroom.

I take off my robe and make my way towards the window, drawing the curtain closed. I increase the brightness of my bed lamp; I'm afraid the darkness is going to give me more nightmares. I wish I had a boyfriend to cuddle up with every night. For now, thanks to Vincent, I can watch the flickering lights from under the door and try to drift off to sleep.

2

The sound of my Google Home wakes me at 6:55 AM. Annoyed, I bark at it to shut up as I reach for my phone to check the morning notifications. As expected, my mundane existence is met with silence in the form of no message notifications. No one messages anymore, they only share reels. I scroll through them as my headache remains, refusing to release its grip on my throbbing temples. Days like these make me contemplate taking a sick leave, but the thought of being trapped at home bores me to the core. Perhaps a refreshing shower will wash away the discomfort.

I glide into the restroom, the cool tiles under my feet providing a momentary respite. With brisk movements, I brush my teeth and let the water cascade over my body in a quick shower. I emerge from the steam and dive into the chaos of my closet.

Truth to be told, my walk-in closet has barely any space to *walk in*. It's ironic how I scold Vincent for cluttering the living room when my own walk-in closet resembles a battleground of hangers. Over two hundred of them, to be precise. Jackets and garments pile up, obscuring the floor from view. It's a constant reminder of my own hypocrisy.

I put on my clothes and walk back to the bathroom. Boy, I don't look pretty. The shower I took was supposed to rejuvenate me, but instead, I'm left with dark under-eye circles that seem to mock me. Now I need to start applying some makeup to conceal them. *Argh!* The exhaustion is killing me. Fuck it! I'll fix my face and get outside to get some fresh air.

I smooth the moisturizer onto my face with slow, upward strokes, trying to wake up skin that feels as exhausted as I do. The foundation goes on next, blending out the uneven patches and softening the shadows under my eyes. A swipe of pale lipstick brightens everything up just enough. I lean closer to the mirror. There she is. The version of me I actually *love* seeing.

I step into the kitchen, craving a steaming cup of coffee to kickstart my day. Vincent, consumed by his game, grips the joystick tightly in his hand. It's evident he's been lost in the virtual world all night.

"Vincent, I'm off to work," I say, my voice laced with a hint of urgency. "You better freshen up and grab some breakfast. And for heaven's sake, shut down that stupid game."

I deliver my instructions as I stride away, fully aware that he's heard every word. Yet, he continues to play, seemingly unaffected by my commands.

I slip on my sandals and step out of my apartment, ready for my morning walk to the bus stop. It's become a routine for me to call Abbey as soon as I leave to ensure that we arrive at the bus stop together.

"Hey, Abbey, I'm on my way out now. I should reach the bus stop in about ten minutes," I say. "Where are you?"

"Good morning to you, too! I'll start making my way there right away." Before I can end the call, Abbey interrupts with a burst of enthusiasm. "You won't believe how amazing my night was. My roommate cooked the most incredible dinner—"

"Hold on a second," I interrupt in frustration. "Aren't we supposed to meet in like, ten minutes? Can't you wait until then?"

"Okay, okay, madam, just calm down. I'll see you soon," she says, hanging up abruptly.

I know she's my childhood best friend and I need to listen to her vent, but sometimes, she really gets on my nerves. She has this knack for rambling on about her supposedly amazing night without even considering the mood of the person she's talking to. I wish she had something interesting to share, but most of the time, she just gets excited about nonsensical events.

I begin my walk towards the bus stop, which is only half a mile away from my apartment. It's a short distance, but the walk there is incredibly therapeutic, especially on these Portland summer mornings. The sun shines brightly, banishing the rainy and cloudy days that have plagued us for so long. It's a precious gift, these few months of morning sun. As the day progresses, the heat intensifies, but for now, there's a gentle breeze that brushes against my skin. The chirping of birds perched on vibrant trees lining the sidewalk fills the air, creating a symphony of nature's melodies. The scent of flowers wafts through the air, adding to the soothing atmosphere.

As I walk, I notice little toddlers strolling hand in hand with their grandparents, their innocent smiles and waves warming my heart. It's as if their pure joy has the power to chase away my headache and leave me feeling refreshed and renewed.

Finally, I arrive at the bus stop located at the edge of our community and patiently wait for Abbey to join me.

A few minutes pass before my eyes catch sight of her approaching the bus stop. Abbey's captivating beauty effortlessly surpasses mine. Her dimpled cheeks, big eyes, and flawless figure make her a vision to behold. Regret instantly floods my mind as I realize I shouldn't have let my anger get the best of me. She's going to be furious now, and rightfully so. It wasn't her fault that my night was a complete disaster. Perhaps she was trying to brighten my day with her optimism.

As she draws nearer, it becomes painfully clear that she's anything but pleased. She doesn't wave or wish me a good morning but stands beside me without speaking. I've been in this situation a million times.

"Good morning," I venture cautiously, attempting to break the ice. "Tell me about your incredible night."

A hint of annoyance taints her voice as she retorts, "Do you want to hear about my incredible night or the disappointing call I had with a crazy lady this morning?"

I laugh and turn to face her. "I apologize on behalf of the crazy lady. Now, please, tell me about your extraordinary evening."

"Sure," she replies, her voice lacking any enthusiasm. "My roommate whipped up this incredibly delicious pasta, and I couldn't get enough of it."

"And?"

"Well, that's pretty much it. I had a fantastic night's sleep. But hey, are you alright? You sounded so frustrated when we spoke on the phone."

"Yeah, I'm fine. It was just a rough night filled with haunting nightmares while Vincent blasted his games in the living room with those obnoxious loudspeakers."

"Oh no! Are you feeling better now?"

"Yeah, I'm alright now. Sorry for snapping at you earlier. It's just that I had a truly terrifying night."

"Don't worry about it. Look, our bus is finally here." She points towards the approaching vehicle.

As the bus barrels down Alder Street, I find myself mentally reviewing my daily tasks. For some reason today, I'm drawing a blank. I turn to Abbey, hoping she can fill in the gaps.

"Hey, Abbey," I inquire, "do you happen to remember what we're supposed to be working on today?"

"Well, considering we just wrapped up a project, I'm guessing Mike will assign us with onboarding new employees. But hey, let's hope we find some cute guys today," she adds with a playful wink.

"Oh gosh! Stop it already," I groan. "You're always going on about meeting guys, but then you turn into a total psycho when you actually meet one."

"Hey! I like to look around, but you know, it's important to be skeptical about people before you let them into your bedroom."

"Yeah, yeah." I dismissively wave her off. "Save the lecture for someone who needs it."

We step off the bus at Alder Street, our destination: the campus. The walk to the administrative building where we work is a mere fifteen minutes. Thankfully, our management has taken the effort to transform the path into a picturesque route so our morning stroll to work is a delightful experience. I just *love* the smell of lavender.

As Abbey and I saunter along, my eyes catch sight of a group of men huddled together across the road, their attention fixated on a crumpled piece of paper. It looks like a map, and their expressions suggest they're lost. Perhaps they're a fresh team just starting their journey today.

"Abbey," I whisper, nudging her gently, "take a look at those guys over there. It looks like they're the new recruits, and it seems they've lost their way."

"Lost? But they have a map right in their hands! That's the whole point of *not* getting lost. How foolish can they be?"

"God, Abbey! You were lost on the first day, too."

As we stand there engaged in conversation, one of the guys in the group begins to approach us.

"Hey there! My name's Kevin, and I was wondering if you could help me find something on this campus." He appears respectable, and he's dressed professionally with his hair neatly combed and his face cleanly shaven.

Abbey, with an expression of suspicion as sharp as a hawk's eye, raises an eyebrow and responds, "Hmm, Kevin, you see, there are clear signs guiding people around the campus. Yet, you choose to approach two attractive women and inquire about 'familiarity with the premises.' What exactly are your intentions here?"

I *hate it* when Abbey does this. She incessantly talks about meeting cute guys, but when guys show up, she behaves cold and psychotic and drives them away with all her distrust.

Kevin, taken aback by the sudden tension, tries to defuse the situation. "Whoa, hold on! I'm not exactly sure what you're getting at, but I want to make it clear that I mean no disrespect. My friends and I are just new hires looking for the administrative building. If you could kindly point us in the right direction, we'll be on our way."

This is getting out of hand.

"Hey, sorry about that! My friend here tends to become Sherlock Holmes whenever she gets the chance," I interject, trying to lighten the mood. "Actually, we work in the administrative building."

Abbey angrily whispers in my ear, "Why are you telling them where we work? They could be criminals trying to gather information."

"Shut up! Don't make a scene," I whisper back. I return my attention to Kevin. "Alright, just keep going straight and you'll come across some signboards leading to the administrative building." I point him in the right direction.

"Thank you. Have a nice day!" Kevin walks back to his group.

They all turn towards us, expressing their gratitude with thumbs up. My heart skips a beat as my gaze locks onto one man in particular. He wears a sharp blue suit, his hair slightly disheveled, his beard perfectly groomed. With a smile, he makes direct eye contact, and even though they stand across the road, his eyes seem to pierce mine. He resembles Harry Styles, complete with a stylish beard and trendy glasses.

A surge of desire floods through me, an unfamiliar sensation that makes me want to tear off his clothes right here, right now. I've never experienced such an intense physical reaction before. It's been a while since I've sought a romantic connection, but this raw sexual energy is something entirely new. Most women don't feel this way upon first sight, but perhaps I'm simply craving sex and the good sleep that follows. As they continue walking, he glances back, his eyes meeting mine once more.

"Should we tag along with those guys and guide them?" I ask Abbey. "They claim to be new hires, and I believe we should help them."

"I think they could be well-dressed criminals. We already assisted them, so let's mind our own business."

"You really should watch the way you speak to people, especially in the workplace. What if they're the new team that we need to train? Will you be able to face them after the way you interrogated Kevin?"

"I suppose you're right," she concedes. "On the other hand, I couldn't care less."

Argh! Typical Abbey. She smirks at me and struts away. I want to share with her that I'm badly attracted to that guy in the group. I refrain in fear that she'll mess it up.

Luckily, I have access to all the information on the new employees' onboarding, so I'll find him.

We swipe our badges, granting us access to the administrative building. We make our way through the corridors, finally arriving at the conference room. There, we find the chief operating officer Mike reclining in his chair, a laptop perched on his ample belly and a steaming cup of coffee in hand.

"Good morning, Mike!" I greet him. "What's on the agenda for today?"

A wide grin spreads across Mike's face as he rises from his seat. "Good morning, ladies!" he exclaims cheerfully. "Today promises to be quite the adventure for both of you. You'll be training a fresh team of analysts and guiding them through the onboarding process. The newbies seem eager, so be sure to keep them busy!"

Abbey's eyes widen in surprise as she looks at me. "Wait, you don't think it's those guys we saw outside, do you?"

I can't help but hope it is.

"Let me call them in and introduce you to your new recruits," Mike said.

Mike dials the receptionist's number, his voice filled with authority as he instructs her to summon the new team to the conference room. Moments later, the door swings open, revealing a group of eager faces.

Abbey turns to me, her voice barely above a whisper. "Dammit! It's them."

"Welcome, everyone!" Mike's voice resonates genuine enthusiasm. "I'm thrilled to have you all here, joining the ranks of Wise AI Career Solutions, one of the most prestigious career companies in the world. As the chief operating officer, it's my pleasure to extend a warm welcome to each and every one of you. Today marks the beginning of an incredible journey.

"I wish I could spend more time getting to know each of you personally. Fortunately, I'll be leaving you in the care of two exceptional individuals. Erica and Abigail will be your guides. They will lead you through the intricacies of our operations and will initiate your training. Once again, welcome to the Wise AI family. May fortune favor you in this exciting new chapter of your lives."

Abbey's face falls flat as she realizes the consequences of her treatment towards Kevin. It's satisfying to see her experience this discomfort, as it serves as a valuable lesson in how to interact with others.

Meanwhile, the handsome man occupies the seat directly across from me, stealing occasional glances in my direction. I can't help but wonder why he's not paying any attention to Abbey. She's always been the prettier of the two of us. Could it be that he's solely interested in me?

The longer I gaze back at him, the more intense the sexual tension between us becomes. I can't help but worry about how I'll manage to deliver the onboarding presentation today knowing that his eyes will be fixed on me throughout.

"Mike, I have a question," Kevin interjects, his hand shooting up. "If we need directions to different buildings on campus, can we turn to Erica and Abigail for help?"

"Absolutely," Mike replies, his voice confident. "They'll assist you with anything and everything. Now, I must dash off to my next meeting. I trust Erica and Abigail will lead you all in introductions."

With Mike's departure, Kevin's gaze fixates on Abbey, a wicked smile on his face.

I couldn't care less about the newborn rift between Kevin and Abbey. My focus is solely on this enigmatic man before me. I yearn to know his name, his preferences, his favorite cuisine, his taste in women, and most importantly, his opinion of me.

I reach out my hand to each person in the group, eager to learn their names. I decide to save "Harry Styles" for last, not wanting to raise any suspicions of me being infatuated with him. Or maybe I'm just overthinking things. I'll play it cool, act casual.

Finally, it's his turn. I extend my hand and introduce myself with a friendly smile. "Hi, I'm Erica! It's a pleasure to meet you."

As our hands meet, I notice the warmth of his touch. His hands are rougher than mine and he has long, slender fingers. Just like I wanted.

"Nice to meet you too, Erica," he replies, his voice filled with enthusiasm. "I'm Nolan, and I'm thrilled to be a part of this company."

His smile lingers a moment longer than necessary, his eyes locked onto mine. *Nolan.* I like the sound of his name. But his gaze feels more like admiration than infatuation. Oh God, does he think I'm older than him? I hope not. I've only been with this company for a couple of years, and he must have just graduated. I did skip a grade in school, so maybe the age difference isn't that significant. Besides, it's not the 1800s anymore—age shouldn't matter.

I need to calm down. I'm overthinking everything. It's best if we start the presentation. The silence in the room is suffocating, making my heart race.

"Alright, everyone, let's dive into the onboarding process," I assert, clicking through the slideshow.

His unwavering gaze remains fixed on me, and I relish the opportunity to prolong this interaction. However, when Abbey takes over the presentation an hour later, his eyes no longer meet mine. I can't help but wonder if he feels something for me, too. How can I feel such a profound connection while he remains unaffected? I steal glances at him every few minutes and my heartrate isn't helping.

As noon approaches, Abbey concludes, "Thank you all for your attentiveness to these details. Let's reconvene in this room tomorrow. For the remainder of the day, feel free to explore the campus or take your leave and enjoy the day. After all, it's your first day."

As everyone rises to make their way outside, Nolan turns to me and asks, "Can you help me locate and set up my cubicle? It'd be a drag to head home right away."

Seriously? I'd set up his entire house if he asked. And he specifically chose to ask me instead of Abbey. That's *gotta* mean something.

"Absolutely," I reply, nodding while desperately trying to conceal my emotions.

Abbey interjects, "The handouts have all the info you need to find the cubicles and other areas on campus. It should be a piece of cake."

Nolan shoots her a strange look.

I appreciate that she's been my friend since childhood, but sometimes she's a bit too protective. She acts like she'd kill someone to keep me safe, but she ends up just being rude to others. This is my *job*, for crying out loud.

I flash her a sheepish grin and suggest, "Why don't you take a break and enjoy a meal alone today, Abbey? I'll help Nolan here find his desk and get everything sorted."

"Sure thing!" she replies, her brow furrowing as she leaves the room.

"Come with me," I say, holding the door for him. We step out of the conference room, Nolan following as I lead the way to his cubicle.

Walking side by side, there's a tension in the air, as if we both have something to say but are unsure of how to start the conversation.

I need to say something. Say something... "So, Nolan," I begin, breaking the silence, "you seem a bit quiet. Any questions about your first day?"

Did I just ask him about his first day? Now he'll see me as some kind of mentor. I should have just stayed quiet and let him take the lead.

"It's funny you think I'm quiet," he replies. "I'm actually quite talkative. I'm just taking in the building and trying to remember the way from the conference room to my cubicle. I do have plenty of questions to chat with you about once we're done setting up."

Ahh. I thought he was silent because of some heat between us. Of course, he's just getting familiar with the surroundings. It's his first day, after all. And I'm probably not at my best either, with my tired eyes hidden under makeup and my dress not showing off my sexy curves. No wonder he's focused on the building instead of me.

I steal glances at him as we walk, but his eyes rarely meet mine.

We finally arrive at his desk, ready to assemble the workstation. The IT team has already left a colossal box filled with a desktop and a bag brimming with computer accessories, all set for the arrival of a fresh recruit. The box looms large, and the weight of the desktop is substantial.

"Whoa," Nolan exclaims, a glimmer of excitement in his voice. "Seems like I've got some new gadgets to play with."

"Sure! Looks like we've got some serious lifting ahead," I reply, eyeing the weighty system. "But this thing is a bit too much for me."

Although I'm not a strong person, I can certainly lend a hand, but I choose not to. I want him to take off that blazer and lift this heavy system onto the desk. I want to witness the strain on his body as he hoists the heavy load.

"No problem. I'll handle getting the desktop off the floor and onto the table," he assures me.

With a swift motion, he removes his blazer and hands it over to me. I hold it against my chest, inhaling the scent of his cologne. It's Versace Eros, one of my favorite scents for men.

His sweat seeps through the fabric of his shirt, making it slightly translucent. I catch glimpses of his chest hair and the defined lines of his abs. My throat tightens as he flexes his muscles, lifting the weighty system. I *so* want to taste him.

Once the desktop is securely positioned on the table, he retrieves his blazer, reclaiming his cool exterior.

"Thank you," he says, then together we set up the entire system, installing both the hardware and software.

I really want to spend more time with him. Should I ask him to join me for lunch? Maybe it's too soon. What if he's not interested? But why wouldn't he be? It's just lunch.

I should calm down and get back to work.

"Thanks a lot, Erica," he says. "You've made my onboarding experience much smoother."

"No worries," I reply, trying to sound nonchalant. "I'm always happy to help."

"Would you be interested in joining me for lunch? It's my 'thank you' treat."

Wait, did he just invite me to lunch? Or is he *asking* me out? No, that can't be right. We're at work. He wouldn't cross that line.

"Don't you have your friend Kevin waiting for you?"

"Well, he's probably already on his way home, celebrating his first day with a drink."

Great, it looks like it's just going to be the two of us.

"I would love to have lunch," I say, unable to hide my smile. "It's always good to get to know your co-workers."

"Plus, I don't have many friends in Portland," he adds, his smile widening. "It would be nice to have someone like you to hang out with."

We make our way to the cafeteria, settling down for lunch as we delve into discussions about my eventful first day at work and the inner workings of the company. It's the usual lunchtime banter among colleagues, nothing out of the ordinary.

Yet, every now and then, our gazes lock for a fleeting moment, and in those stolen seconds, my heart races. There's an undeniable electricity between us, a magnetic pull that hints at something more.

But I can't let myself get carried away. I must maintain an air of composure. As we finish our meal, we exchange a firm handshake and get back to our separate cubicles.

During the workday, my mind diverts me back to him. I know I'll see him again tomorrow, but I want to spend more time with him today. Not tomorrow, but *today*. I can ask him to join me in the conference room for additional training.

I walk to his desk, and it looks like he's gone home. I need to vent out my flurry of thoughts to Abbey. It's the only way I can maintain my sanity in this moment.

I rush over to Abbey's desk, eager to share the details of my lunchtime encounter with Nolan.

"Hey, Abbey," I exclaim, unable to contain my excitement. "Guess who I had lunch with today?"

"Someone other than me," she replies dryly.

I chuckle. "Well, you weren't there to ruin it, so I had the best time with Nolan. He's incredibly sweet and brilliant. He has a degree from MIT."

Abbey raises an eyebrow. "MIT, huh? And he's not working for some high-paying corporate giant? Maybe he's not as smart as you think."

"Come on, that's not a fair judgment. Besides, he's cute and has a muscular physique. I can't help but have a huge crush on him. I wish he would ask me out sometime."

Abbey's expression turns serious. "You must be joking, right? We're at work. This could get him fired, or worse, get you fired. It's not a good idea to pursue a romantic relationship with him. I strongly advise you to keep your distance. And if you ignore my suggestion, I'll be the one to report it and get you fired."

There she goes again. I just hate this obsessive and over-protective nature of Abbey. Sometimes I feel like strangling her because of it.

"Whoa, chill out," I retort, rolling my eyes. "I just said I have a crush on him. It doesn't mean I'm going to act on it. I'll see you later this evening."

As the work hours slip away, I finally make my way home, eager to step through the front door. And what a sight awaits me! My living room, once cluttered and stale, now gleams with cleanliness and a fresh scent. Gone are the discarded soda cans and the remnants of dirty clothes and sweaty socks.

Instead, everything has been tidied up and the clothes tossed in the dryer by the sounds of the machine. And there on the couch lies my baby brother, fast asleep.

It seems he took it upon himself to not only clean the house but also to ensure proper ventilation. I can detect faint traces of odor neutralizer discreetly dispersed in the room.

I *love* my brother. Having him stay with me, even if we don't interact much, brings a sense of companionship without sacrificing my privacy. He's become a night owl, spending his nights engrossed in video games while I go about my day. That suits us both, allowing me to have someone under the same roof while still maintaining my personal space.

I cleanse my face, preparing for the evening ahead. With dinner cooked and consumed, I retreat to the sanctuary of my room, ready for my nightly ritual — writing in my journal. Writing has always been a passion of mine, and I dream of writing a novel one day, perhaps in the genre of romance. Maybe my own personal experiences in love will serve as inspiration for the story.

I open my journal and review the entries from the past few days. Nothing particularly noteworthy, just the usual routine and the arrival of my brother for the holiday season. However, today has been a roller coaster of emotions, with its fair share of highs and lows. So, it's all going in.

After writing my journal, I take off my clothes, cover my body with my fleece blanket, and try to sleep. I usually think of something nice before I sleep; it helps me avoid nightmares. So, I keep thinking about Nolan and what it would be like to date him. It tingles me as I get further intimate thoughts about him.

25

3

*B*rrrrrrrrr. My Google Home buzzes.

"Hey, Google, stop!" I shout.

I glance at the digital clock on the dresser. It reads 6:55 AM. The date is June 20, 2023.

I hear sounds of Vincent gaming in the living room again.

I slept so well. No headaches, no frustrations. It was so refreshing, as it should be. I was thinking about a romance with Nolan while I was trying to sleep, so there was no reason to have nightmares.

Stepping into the bathroom, I take a moment to freshen up. To my surprise, my dark circles have nearly vanished. My face looks clear and rejuvenated.

I take a shower then walk into my closet to put on some clothes. Normally, I don't give much thought to what I wear, but today is different. Today, I'm determined to dress to impress. You see, tonight I plan to ask Nolan out for dinner, and I need him to say *yes*. It's a role reversal for me, as I'm accustomed to men taking the initiative. However, after the intimate thoughts that consumed me last night, I simply can't wait any longer.

I pick a pair of snug cotton pants and a collared button-up shirt, leaving a few buttons undone. It's a calculated move, knowing how men are drawn to peek into my shirt. I understand the temptation, my boobs are perfectly sized. Although sometimes, all I want is to jab a knife into their prying eyes. But with Nolan, it's different. With him, I *want* him to peek into my shirt.

I hastily slip into my clothes and swing open my door, only to be greeted by the familiar sight of my living room in disarray. I snatch a hasty bite to eat, grab my coffee, and make a beeline for the front door.

At work, Abbey and I find ourselves waiting anxiously in the conference room, anticipation hanging in the air as we prepare for the second session of onboarding.

And then, like a specter emerging from the shadows, Nolan saunters into the room. His hair is neatly combed, his pale-green long-sleeve shirt is perfectly pressed, and his navy-blue jeans are tagged with his ID card. Our eyes lock, and a surge of excitement courses through me.

"Good morning, Erica!" He greets me with a warm smile.

"Yesterday was an amazing first day. Mind if I join you for lunch again today? Kevin mentioned he might be busy exploring the campus during that time."

I think he's into me. I can *feel* it.

"Absolutely!" I reply, my own smile widening.

"Can I have your number?" he asks, his voice tinged with a hint of nervousness. "You know, for any questions about training and such."

He's asking for my *personal* number. Today, he seems particularly intrigued by me. Is it because I look better than yesterday? Or has he been interested in me since we first met? I guess it doesn't matter. I've already decided to ask him out.

We exchange our personal phone numbers while Abbey busies herself with setting up the laptop and projector. I was worried about how to invite him to lunch, but since he asked me first, I can focus on the morning training session.

As the hours tick by, we wrap up the session.

I need to shake off Abbey quickly and head out for lunch.

"Hey, Abbey! Why don't you go ahead and have your lunch at your desk?" I suggest. "I'll catch up with you later. I have some work to do."

"Oh, sure. No problem," she replies, understanding. "See you later." With that, she walks away.

Nolan and I make our way to the cafeteria, our stomachs growling with hunger. We quickly grab our food and settle down at a secluded table in the corner, tucked away from others.

The cafeteria boasts an exquisite interior, adorned with lush indoor plants and elegant fountains. The atmosphere is serene, with just the right amount of distance between tables to ensure privacy. It's no wonder that many managers choose this spot for conducting job interviews; the ambiance is perfect for fostering a sense of calm and focus.

In my present circumstances, this setting couldn't be more ideal for what I have in mind. It's the perfect opportunity to gather my courage and ask Nolan out.

We start eating in utter silence, but I want to break the ice. Summoning my courage, I decide to take the plunge. "So, how are you finding Portland?"

"It's been good so far. I'm enjoying the city," he says and continues to eat in silence.

I subtly undo the top two buttons of my shirt, but he barely looks at my chest. It's a sign he's either a gentleman or gay. I'll assume the first one.

This is uncharted territory for me — asking a man out. I find myself at a loss for words, my mind devoid of any clever ideas or smooth lines. Perhaps it's better if men take the lead in these situations.

But time is of the essence. Before he delves into work-related questions, I must seize this opportunity to ask him out. I take a deep breath, mentally preparing myself for the moment.

Alright. Three... two...

"Erica," he says, interrupting my thoughts. "Can I tell you something?"

Damn! I was *this* close to asking him out. Now he's probably going to ask me about his computer or a stupid HDMI cable.

"Sure, go ahead," I say. "Feel free to ask anything."

His voice trembles as he struggles to find the right words. "Um... there's something I need to tell you. You... You're incredibly beautiful, like no one I've ever seen before. And you've been so kind to me. I know it might sound strange since we just met yesterday, but I can't shake this feeling that there's something between us. I don't know if you feel it, too. Maybe we could grab a coffee together sometime? Phew! There, I said it."

WHAT? What the fuck just happened? Did *he* ask me out? He did, he did. He actually asked me out. Oh my god! I did *not* see that coming. Either I seriously suck at reading people, or he's been a damn expert at hiding how he feels.

Of course I want to go out with him. If I say yes, we could be having dinner tonight, and who knows, maybe I'll even end up in his arms or even his bed. But what if things don't work out? What if I end up breaking his heart, or worse, what if he breaks mine? My brain is heating up.

I need to calm down. I was prepared to take the leap and ask him out, but now that he's the one asking, I'm getting cold feet.

What if Abbey's right? What if getting involved with a co-worker is just asking for trouble? I steal another glance at him, my chest tightening with a mix of curiosity and doubt. I don't know what I'm feeling anymore, and that scares me.

"Are you there?" He waves at me with a smile. "I understand if you don't want to, or if you already have a boyfriend."

"Sorry, that was a bit out of the blue," I say. "I think you're cool, I'm just worried about going out because we're co-workers now."

Cool my ass. He's freaking hot, and I *really* want to go out with him, but Abbey's warnings are still fresh in my mind.

"Before you say no, let me explain," he insists. "We may be co-workers for now, but I have plans to move to a different group in the future. Come on, it's just coffee. If you're not interested, I'll back off immediately and we can forget this conversation ever happened."

Maybe he's right. We can keep this a secret from everyone at work, including Abbey. And if things go well, one of us can make the move to a different group. This is exciting. My journal is about to get a lot more interesting.

I can't help but wonder how badly he wants to go out with me. I want him to *beg* me. If he can do that well, I know my bedtime with him would be fun.

"Why do you want to go on a date with me?" I ask.

"Ah, so you want me to beg," he says with a mischievous smile. "Alright, let me tell you why. First of all, you're absolutely stunning. But it's not just about your looks. Yesterday, you went out of your way to make me feel comfortable in my new job. That meant a lot to me. And when we spent time together, I had such a great time. There's something special between us, like an undeniable spark. I don't want to let that slip away. Plus, going for an evening stroll and enjoying a cup of coffee with you sounds much more appealing than just watching movies by myself. I could go on and on about why I want to go on a date with you. Your smile is adorable, and your wavy hair is incredibly attractive. The movement of your hips when you walk is —"

"Alright, alright, enough with the cheesy compliments!" I interrupt, unable to contain my laughter. "Yes! I'd love to grab a coffee with you," I reply, my voice hushed. "But let's keep this between us. No sharing with Kevin, Abigail, or anyone else. We need to maintain a professional front during work hours."

"Okay... so it's a secret then. That could make it even more thrilling," he suggests, a naughty glint in his eyes. "How about I pick you up at six? We can enjoy a coffee and maybe grab a quick bite."

"Sounds good to me," I agree, trying to hide my excitement.

"Perfect! Just text me your address, and I'll see you at six."

I quickly send him my address, eager for the evening to come. As we wrap up our lunch, I make my way back to my desk, my mind buzzing with anticipation.

I can't seem to concentrate on my work right now. I'm too focused on what to wear tonight. I need to dress provocatively, revealing just enough to make his mouth water. I've been saving my most expensive perfume for a special occasion like this. Tonight, I'm going all out. I also need to come up with interesting topics to discuss over dinner.

While I definitely desire a physical connection with him, if this is going to go anywhere, I need to truly understand him. I want to know his likes, his dislikes, his choice of vacations, his favorite foods, his aspirations. Is he a sensitive person? What are his thoughts on starting a family? Does he enjoy being around children? Does he possess a good sense of humor? How many women has he been with? Is he the romantic type? Gosh, I need to breathe.

I can't reveal the depth of my feelings for him. I made that mistake in the past with someone, and he took me for granted. This time, I must position myself differently so he sees me as an equal.

If Abbey catches a glimpse of me now, she'll instantly sense my excitement and nervousness just by studying my face. She might even deduce that I have a date, as nothing else in my life could possibly thrill me at this moment.

After waiting for a few agonizing hours, I manage to accomplish some work and send Abbey a text, claiming an early departure due to a pounding headache. As her response — a simple thumbs up flashes on my screen, I make my way home.

I quietly make my way to the closet where I carefully select a captivating red dress. Its low-back design and daring hip cut will undoubtedly captivate Nolan's attention. I delicately apply a touch of makeup to enhance my features and spritz Victoria's Secret perfume on my pulse points to add a hint of attraction. With a swipe of vibrant red lipstick and a gentle curl of my lashes, I complete my transformation. I leave my hair cascading freely so he can glide his fingers through it with ease.

Around six p.m., a message from Nolan pops up on my phone. *In front of your apartment.* Without wasting a second, I slip into my high heels and dart out of the apartment, eager to meet him. Thanks to my sleeping brother, I'll be able to slip out of the house unnoticed.

Nolan's grey Toyota Corolla awaits me, and I approach the car with a deliberate catwalk, allowing him to absorb my beauty. As I slide into the passenger seat, I flash him a grateful smile. "Thank you for picking me up," I say, my voice laced with genuine appreciation.

For a moment, Nolan's gaze remains on me, and I can sense the undeniable attraction between us. "You look ravishing in this dress," he compliments. "Like a glamorous movie star. And I probably look like your chauffeur in this old Corolla."

I laugh. "That's incredibly sweet of you," I say. "Honestly, I'm not one to be swayed by fancy cars. Your Corolla is just fine to me."

I'm truly not a materialistic girl. I obviously just want to make sure the guy is hot. *Duh!* If I'm sleeping naked with someone for the rest of my life, I need to make sure they are enjoyable enough. And he needs to be smart to make a decent living. But money and cars I don't care about.

"Got it," he says, his voice steady. "Here's the plan: We head to a cozy coffee shop, savor a steaming cup of joe. Then, there's a nearby restaurant within walking distance where we can enjoy a delicious dinner. Finally, I'll give you a lift back home."

I nod and smile.

We arrive at the coffee house, the aroma of freshly brewed coffee enveloping us as we step inside. We order our drinks and settle down at a table, the atmosphere tinged with an odd sense of anticipation.

It's strange, really. Just a day ago, our conversations revolved solely around work matters. Now, we're expected to delve into personal territory. I guess dating your co-worker is, in fact, weird.

"Alright, let me break the silence," he says. "So... how long have you been living in Portland?"

"For a couple of years now. I was born and raised in eastern Oregon. After completing my undergraduate studies a few years ago, I joined Wise AI."

"Ah, I see. It must be a decent place to both work and live. Tell me, what's your ultimate dream?"

"Hmm... I thought this was supposed to be a date, not an interview."

He chuckles softly. "Well, what can I say? I'm a bit of a nerd. I'm always engrossed in work or buried in books. I never know where to begin with social endeavors."

"Well, you certainly managed to ask me out on a date quite smoothly," I tease, a playful smile tugging at my lips. "You must have picked up a thing or two from those romantic novels you must read."

"Romantic novels? I've actually never read one. All the books I immerse myself in are psychological thrillers."

I can't help but let out a small sigh. "Sorry to burst your bubble, but I'm not a fan of thrillers. They're all about murder and mayhem."

"Perhaps they are," he concedes, "but many of them also contain extremely wild romantic elements."

Now we're talking!

I wonder just how intense and *wild* he can truly be. I'm eager to wrap up dinner quickly tonight and invite him over for dessert at my place.

"Hey, how about we head out for dinner soon?" I suggest, my stomach growling in agreement.

"Absolutely! I've already chosen a spot," he replies. "It's a Thai restaurant, just a short ten-minute walk from here."

Thai cuisine happens to be my absolute favorite. It's as if we're destined to be together.

We swiftly exit the coffee house, eager to reach our destination at the restaurant. The sidewalk narrows as we approach the bustling downtown area, causing his arm hair to rub against mine with each step we take.

I can already imagine the pleasure I will feel when his body rubs against mine *tonight*.

Gradually, our fingers entwine as we walk. He breaks the silence, his voice filled with sincerity when he says, "It's incredible how connected I already feel to you. This is unlike anything I've ever experienced before."

I smile at him as I tighten my grip on his hand, finding solace in his touch. With each passing moment, a sense of ease envelops us as we walk.

We arrive at the Thai restaurant and find our way to a reserved table for two. The soft glow of candlelight dances upon the table, creating an intimate ambiance. As we sit down, our hands still intertwined, the flickering flame casts a romantic spell over us.

"Unbelievable," I remark, my voice filled with awe. "It's hard to fathom that we only met yesterday. The connection we share feels like it has existed for an eternity."

"Well, I hope that time stands still so I get to spend a lot more time with you," he says with a smile.

This is all going in my journal. Every sentence he spoke to me today. All of it.

When our dinner comes to an end, we leave the restaurant and make our way back to the car. He starts driving to my apartment with his left hand, while his right hand tangles with mine.

As we arrive near my apartment, the anticipation builds, and when we step out, the air is thick with desire. I stand there, my eyes locked on him, silently transmitting my urge to taste him.

"I really had a great evening," he says, looking deep into my eyes.

I gaze back at him. "Me too. Thanks for a lovely dinner."

He approaches me with a deliberate pace, his eyes still locked on mine as he leans in, gently brushing his lips against mine. His touch sends shivers down my spine as his fingers weave through my hair, pulling me closer. Our kiss intensifies, our lips becoming moist with lust.

With a boldness that excites me, his hand glides beneath the fabric of my top, his fingertips inching closer to the softness of my breast. I let him. I surrender to his touch willingly, craving the exquisite sensation of his fingers against my bare skin. As he pulls me closer, our bodies pressed against each other, his lips continue to explore mine with an intensity that leaves me breathless. I hope he never stops.

After more than a minute, his lips slowly part from mine and he breathes out a whisper, "Are you interested in dessert?"

I am. What kind of woman denies it after a passionate kiss like that? I'm going to take him inside, and we're gonna stay up all night.

Wait. *Fuck!* Vincent is home. And he's going to stay up all night playing video games. How the hell did I forget that?

"What do you say, Erica?" he whispers.

Spur of the moment, I say, "Sorry. Now isn't a good time."

Nolan swiftly slips his hand out of my top and takes a step back, his expression a mix of surprise and disappointment.

I *ruined* the moment.

"I mean, my brother is crashing at my place," I explain, my voice tinged with regret.

"Oh, don't worry about it. I just thought we had an amazing time," he replies, disappointment evident in his tone.

"We did. I would love to spend more time with you. How about we have dessert at your place?"

I see a hesitation in his face. "My apartment's a bit of a mess. How about a date tomorrow night? I'll cook us a delicious dinner, and you can stay longer for dessert, if you'd like."

"Absolutely. Tomorrow night sounds absolutely perfect. I didn't mean to reject your offer so abruptly."

"No worries," he reassures me with a smile. "I'll see you tomorrow." He gets into his car and waves goodbye as he drives away.

I screwed up such a perfect moment even my journal would start laughing at me. I retreat into my apartment, fully expecting to find Vincent wide awake in the living room, engrossed in his gaming console. True to form, he has already managed to turn the living room into a chaotic mess.

"Ah, well, hello there, Mad Sis," he taunts. "Not scolding today for the mess? Have you finally learned your lesson?"

I choose to ignore his snide remark as I walk to my bedroom.

After I finish writing in my journal, I lay down on my bed, hoping to receive a message from Nolan, but slowly, my eyes start to haze out.

4

*B*rrrrrrrrr. My Google Home buzzes.

"Hey, Google, stop!" I shout.

I glance at the digital clock on the dresser. It's 6:55 AM on June 21, 2023.

Curiosity tugs at me, urging me to check my phone for any messages. With a swift swipe, I unlock the screen and find a single message waiting for me. It's from Nolan. My heart skips a beat at the sight of his name. The message simply reads *Good morning*, accompanied by a kissing emoji. I love it. I've waited years for morning messages like these.

I get through my usual day, eagerly awaiting the evening for my second date with Nolan. Because tonight is *the* night.

Around 5:30 in the evening, a message from him lights up my phone screen. "Hey, I'm on my way, and I got a surprise for you."

A surprise? That's exciting! I'm guessing something *wild* for our bedroom time tonight. But why would he tell me that over a message? Perhaps it's something more traditional, like a thoughtful gift or a bouquet of flowers. The thought feels a tad cliché, but I can't help but smile at the sweetness of it all.

Before long, another message arrives, interrupting my thoughts. *I'm here.*

Without hesitation, I leave my apartment and make my way towards his car.

"Okay, lover boy, what's the surprise?"

"It's called a surprise for a reason," he replies with an ornery smirk. "I need to blindfold you so that you'll enjoy it a little better."

"Blindfold me? You're kidding, right?"

"I'm not. Do you trust me?"

I'm planning on having sex tonight, so, I think that counts as trusting him.

"Yes, I trust you."

"Then turn around and let me blindfold you," he says. "I want to make sure to give you the most memorable experience of your life."

I can't help but chuckle, a mix of nerves and anticipation bubbling within me. "Fine, go ahead and blindfold me. But remember that you don't have to kidnap me since I was going to come to your house for dinner anyway."

He laughs as he blindfolds me, then starts driving the car.

"I usually watch out the window while I'm in a car, but now that you blindfolded me, I feel bored."

"Here, let me turn the radio on for you."

The DJ on the radio says, "Hello! Thank you for tuning in to 95.5 FM. It's Wednesday, the twenty-first of June, and the weekend is tantalizingly close, just two more days away. We have a special request from our last caller, who asked for the haunting melody of 'Heathens' by Twenty-One Pilots..."

This is exhilarating! The songs on the radio keep me on the edge of my seat, but the burning question remains: Where is he taking me?

If I were to think like a man, where would I choose for a second date that would leave a lasting impression? It needs to be surprising enough to blindfold the girl.

He might have decorated his living room with lights and made the place romantic. But why would I have to be blindfolded in the car for that? Unless he doesn't want me to know the way to this mystery place.

What if he cooked Thai food for us to have as dinner near some waterfalls? But the car doesn't smell like it. If there was Thai food in here, the whole car would smell like it by now.

It has been quite some time since we last encountered a traffic light, and the road seems to twist and turn, indicating that we're not on a highway.

I need to ask him.

"Seems like we're going a little far for this surprise, unless you live somewhere far away from the city."

"Calm down, my dear! Just trust that I'll give you an extraordinary experience tonight."

"Alright, alright. No worries. I'm just excited!"

Several minutes lapse, and it seems we have arrived at a remote location. The car comes to a stop, and he swiftly makes his way around to the passenger side, opening the door to assist me in stepping out.

"Alright, mister," I speak up, my curiosity piqued. "It appears we've reached our destination. Can I finally remove this blindfold? I hope you still have your clothes on."

He chuckles. "Definitely have my clothes on. We're about seventy percent done with the blindfold. Just a few more preparations and then I'll remove it."

I can smell grass, which could mean anywhere in Oregon. The state is so green. The gentle breeze suggests we're in an expansive, open space. But what could he possibly have planned in such a location? Unless he's planning to have food here and fuck me in this public place where there are no people around.

He positions himself to my left, intertwining our fingers while his right hand securely encircles my waist, guiding me toward the right direction. He suddenly stops and requests, "Can you wait here for a moment? I need to check a few things." I can hear him walk a few feet forward and start talking to someone in a hushed voice.

So, we're not alone. Where the hell are we?

Straining my ears, I eavesdrop on their conversation. What exactly are they talking about? They're speaking in low voices. I thought we were going to be alone. Wait! I think it's Kevin. Oh my god! It's Kevin. What is he doing here? I thought we were going to keep this whole thing a secret from co-workers.

Oh god! How the *fuck* can Nolan not keep our dating a *secret*? All he had to do was take me to his house, make me dinner, have sex, and keep this whole thing a secret from co-workers.

I'm so angry at him right now. My fists clench on instinct, and for a second, I seriously picture slamming one right into his smug face.

Although I'm tempted to remove the blindfold, the last thing I want to see now is another co-worker. It's best for me to remain in this spot, pretending I haven't heard a thing, and patiently await whatever surprise Nolan has in store.

I think they finished the conversation. He's coming closer.

"Alright, my dear, we're almost there. Take this."

I reach out and feel something small brush against my fingers. "What's this? A pen?"

"Yes, it is. You just need to sign here for the sake of formality."

"Sign what exactly?" I ask in confusion. "Are you asking me to blindly sign something? I hope you're not making me marry you while wearing a blindfold."

"Haa... ha... so funny! I can assure you, marriage is not on the agenda today. This is a formality at the location for the surprise I'm giving you."

"I must admit, you're making me a bit nervous. But I'm signing it because I trust you, and partly because I seem to have no choice."

He escorts me to another location a couple hundred feet away from the car, I think.

"We need to put on a jacket for this experience," he says. "And I'm going to give you headphones with melodic music so that you'll relax a bit."

I let out a weary sigh, my skepticism evident.

"Fine, go ahead. But this better be worth it."

"Rest assured, it'll exceed your expectations." His confidence is unwavering. He assists me in putting on the jacket and says, "We need to walk and get into a vehicle. We're ninety percent there."

Oh god! My heart pounds against my chest. His meticulous planning is overwhelming. I'm a simple woman, I don't need big surprises. Some love, lust, and affection will do. But he's gone to great lengths to orchestrate this surprise, and I can't ruin this for him. I already spoiled the moment last night after that seductive kiss. All I need to do now is shut up and get through the rest of the surprise.

We get inside the vehicle.

"Alright, sweetheart, it's a tight squeeze in here. You'll have to settle on my lap for the next fifteen minutes," he murmurs, his voice laced with urgency. "I'll crank up the volume on your headphones, and when the time is up, I'll remove both the blindfold and headphones simultaneously."

"Okay, lover boy, as you say. I'll count to fifteen minutes, and I'm going to hold onto this blindfold until then."

Carefully, I lower myself onto his lap, the proximity sending adrenaline through my veins. Normally, I would have loved this intimate position, but in this moment, the excitement is overshadowed by the mystery that lies ahead.

I feel a strong shake of the vehicle as it moves. Okay... that's a lot of vibration.

I think I realize what this movement feels like. We're in a boat. The coast is not far from Portland, and we drove for enough time to reach the coast.

I also know of some romantic vacation packages where couples dine on luxurious yachts in the vast expanse of the ocean, spending the night in opulent bliss. So, it's likely that we're on a smaller vessel now, making our way towards that grand yacht awaiting us in the open sea. The reason he insisted I wear a jacket becomes clearer, it's probably a life jacket. And that form I signed? It could very well be a document of consent. It all makes sense now. Wow... Dinner on a yacht, surrounded by the boundless ocean is the closest possibility.

He thought he could keep this a surprise. I'll play along, pretending that I haven't figured it all out, just so he won't be disappointed. This is so exciting. I love the Pacific!

The boat surges forward, and my body starts to slide from his lap, the rush of speed tugging me away. I cling to him, my grip desperate to keep me close amidst the growing turbulence.

Fifteen minutes pass before he speaks loudly to overcome my headphone music. "Alright, my dear! I'm about to remove your blindfold and headphones. Don't worry! The interior of this vehicle is pitch black, so you won't have a sudden flash of light pinching your eyes."

Pitch black? What kind of boat is this?

Nolan initiates the countdown, his words echoing in my ears. "Ten... nine... eight... seven... six..."

My heart is thumping so hard I can almost hear it over the music.

"Five... four... three... two... one..."

In a single swift motion, he rips away the blindfold and headphones at same instant. As my eyes adjust, I come face to face with Kevin. I'm perched on Nolan's lap, our jackets entangled.

Holy fuck! Am I in a small aircraft which barely fits a few people at a time?

"Where the hell are we? Is this a plane? And Kevin, why are you here? What the hell is happening? Speak up, Nolan!"

"We're crammed into this tiny airplane, and in matter of seconds, we'll be skydiving, with you strapped to me! Consider it my way of showing how deeply interested I am in you."

My body freezes. A wave of panic crashes down my spine, sending shivers coursing through me. I'm on an aircraft. I'm on an aircraft. My fear of heights consumes and suffocates me. I'm going to die. I'm going to die! A throbbing pain pulses in my head, as if a migraine is about to strike.

"Are you fucking crazy?" I scream at him. "Are you seriously insane? I've been diagnosed with acrophobia, and you thought it was a brilliant idea to bring me here without even considering my mental issues?"

"I can't hear you much! We'll now go towards the door as the pilot reaches 18,000 feet." His response is lost in the deafening noise. We inch closer to the door as the pilot ascends.

"What do you mean 18,000 feet?" I cry out, tears streaming down my face. "All I want is to go home. Please, tell the pilot to land this damn plane..."

The pilot's voice echoes through the cabin, interrupting my pleas. "Ladies and gentlemen, we have reached our altitude. Kevin, it's time to open the door and make your exit. Enjoy the experience."

The door swings open, revealing the vast expanse of the planet below us, a dizzying 18,000 feet in the air. I never imagined this being how I would die.

I can't jump, I just can't. I grab the side of the plane with both of my hands. "I'm not jumping!" I scream in both fear and anger. "You asshole!" This is the most intense terror I have ever experienced.

He leans in close, his voice barely audible over the roaring wind. "Hold on tight, my love. This is my ultimate gift to you."

"Noooooo!" I scream so hard it feels as if my throat is being torn apart. The sound is swallowed by the deafening rush of air.

"We'll be free-falling for sixty seconds!" he shouts into my ear. "Then, and only then, will I open the parachute."

"I hate you! You fucking maniac!" I start to feel light-headed and can't seem to catch my breath. "Oh god, I can feel a panic attack coming. I think I'm going to die. I'm going to die!"

He urgently counts down. Three... two... And with a forceful push, I release my grip on the plane. "God, help! God, help!" I cry out as terror surges through me.

A rush of wind slams against my face, the force of gravity taking hold as we plunge into free fall. The pressure feels as though my body is being pressed against an invisible wall, and for a fleeting moment, my hearing fades away.

A minute later, I hear Nolan say, "Okay, Erica, I'm going to open the parachute now." He yanks a hook once, twice, then thrice. "Shit! This parachute isn't opening." He reaches for the satellite phone strapped to his arm and desperately cries into it, "Danger! Danger! Danger! The parachute won't open. I need help! Bad chute, bad chute."

My anger boils over, mingling with fear. "What? How could you do this to me? You irresponsible moron!" My voice trembles as tears stream down my face.

The satellite phone responds, "This is ground support. Nolan, there's a backup chute attached to your chest. But it can only carry one person. You must let go of the person you're connected to or you'll both die. I repeat, detach! I repeat, detach!"

"I'm sorry, Erica, I have to do this. If I don't detach, we'll both die."

The ground rushes closer. Visions of my family flash before my eyes, their faces in grief as they gaze upon my dead body drenched in blood.

Desperation consumes me, and I plead with him, "No! You can't! Nolan! You can't detach! You can't take my life! It will shatter my family's hearts! I beg you, hold on to me! Please, I beg of you!"

"I'm sorry," he whispers.

Immediately, I can feel his hand movements trying to unhook me.

"*Noooo!* Hold on to me! Don't detach! Don't detach! Don't—"

5

"**D**on't detach!" I scream, my voice reverberating through the room as I abruptly wake up.

With a surge of urgency, I glance at the digital clock perched on the dresser. The glowing numbers reveal the time is 4:00 AM, and the date is etched into my mind: June 19, 2023.

What just happened? Is it still the nineteenth? It can't be. Why do I feel like I've lived through the twentieth and twenty-first as well? Was it all just a nightmare? It felt so vivid, so real.

Phew! The night has taken its toll on me. As usual, I can barely recall any of it. But the emotions from the dream have left my heart pounding. Thank goodness I didn't shit my bed.

God! My head is hurting so bad.

I can't tear my eyes away from the digital clock, the seconds ticking away relentlessly. Beads of sweat trickle down my bare skin, leaving me feeling damp and uncomfortable beneath the plush fleece blanket.

With a sigh, I cast the blanket aside and make my way to the window. I slide it open and settle into the worn rocking chair, the cool night air caressing my naked body.

Choosing an apartment on the fifth floor was a decision I've never regretted; it offers a vantage point unlike any other in the area. On nights like this, I want to dry my body by facing the wide-open window. It helps me breathe comfortably, especially without my top on.

I can't fathom why this night is taking such a toll on me. Just a few hours ago, I was plagued by a terrible dream, and now I find myself trapped in another horrifying nightmare. It's peculiar how I can feel the pain of these dream incidents, yet I can't recall any of the details. If only I could unravel the enigmatic workings of the human brain.

I glance at the clock once more, and it reads 4:15 AM. My body is finally free from the clutches of sweat, but the nightmare still lingers in my mind. Faces flash before me, those of Vincent, Abigail, and countless others I've never laid eyes upon. How is it possible to encounter unfamiliar faces within a dream?

And why today of all days? What makes this *particular* day so unnerving? Why did the dream feel so achingly real? Or was it real? Maybe I should check my journal.

Nah! I'm being crazy. It was just a dream, right? Or was it? Well, no one's here to judge me, so I might as well check it out.

I spring up from the rocking chair and open the top drawer of my dresser. I pick up my journal and open it where I last bookmarked.

Obviously, I see empty pages on June 20th and 21st. I put back the journal in the drawer and stare at myself in the mirror to see if there are any wounds. Nothing, not a single blemish or bruise. My skin is clear as day.

I look at the door and can still see the flashing lights from under it. Looks like Vincent hasn't slept yet. And he obviously increased the volume again. *Gosh!* How do I make this kid more humane?

I slip into my robe, taking deliberate steps towards the door. With a sudden burst of energy, I swing it open, revealing Vincent deeply immersed in his video games, with all the mess right where it was couple hours ago.

"Vincent! I specifically asked you to lower the volume hours ago. My head is aching, and sleep feels like an impossible feat. I'm starting to suspect that the relentless sounds from your game are the cause of my nightmares."

"Okay, Mad Sis."

I'm so tired of this kid!

"What does 'okay' even mean?" I ask, my plea tinged with helplessness. "Come on, Vincent, I have to wake up early tomorrow and go to work. I barely have two to three hours left to sleep. Can you please, please turn down the volume?"

He mumbles "AFK" into his microphone and turns to me. "I'm here to enjoy my vacation at your place," he retorts. "I can lower the volume a bit. Why don't you just turn on your white noise machine and try to sleep?"

"Sure, whatever. Why can't you play during the day and sleep at night like a normal person?"

He gestures towards his hat, which reads "Leave me alone."

I let out a weary sigh, shake my head in disbelief, and firmly shut the door. There's no use in engaging with him; all I can do is hope that he matures sooner rather than later.

Returning to bed, I reach out to the dresser and switch on the white noise machine. Its soothing hum fills the room as I settle back down onto the mattress.

Curiosity gnaws at me, urging me to learn more about dream psychology. Vincent and Abigail's presence in my dream seems logical, but who are these other figures? One man, in particular, stuck in my memory. I was dating him, which is not a surprise considering I've been looking for a boyfriend for a while and sometimes I do have romantic dating dreams. But this guy... he left a mark I didn't see coming. It wasn't heartbreak, it was something sharper, stranger. Even now, just thinking about it makes my chest tighten, like I'm right back in that panic all over again.

Sleep eludes me, leaving me restless and curious. I want to know more about dream psychology. I google "How long is a typical dream?" The first article I open says a typical dream lasts about twenty to thirty minutes.

Huh! Just thirty minutes? That's crazy. It feels like I've been dreaming for a few days, which means I slept fine for more than an hour even though it feels like I slept badly all night. So weird.

I search "How to avoid dreams?" Google suggests I drink a lot of water, have a sound mind, avoid stress, etc. Why can't I get some magical solutions on the internet for all my issues?

I'm gonna do one last search to have a peaceful sleep. "Do dreams come true?"

Oh lord! Now Google starts showing articles of Martin Luther King Jr. and other philosophers saying to work hard, that dreams will come true, that you must first have a dream, etc.

Searching for answers on Google will only lead to more sleepless nights. I would rather depend on my white noise machine and try to sleep before I have to wake up again for work.

6

I awake at 6:55 AM, my Google Home blaring through the room, drowning out the soft hum of the white noise machine.

A mild ache in my head persists. But I can't dwell on that now. I have to get to work, to take my mind off the terrible night.

With a sense of urgency, I dart into the bathroom, the steam from the shower already filling the cramped space. I hastily cleanse myself, the water cascading over my body, washing away the remnants of a restless sleep. I rummage through the cluttered closet, finally settling on a pair of jeans and a crisp white shirt and apply makeup to cover the dark under-eye circles.

As I step out of the bathroom, my eyes fall upon Vincent sprawled in the living room, engrossed in his video game, the controller gripped tightly in his hands.

"Vincent, I'm off to work," I call out, my voice tinged with a mix of frustration and concern. "You should clean yourself up and grab some breakfast. And for the love of God, shut down that stupid game."

I'm not sure if he even acknowledges my words, he's so lost in his virtual world. I grab a steaming cup of coffee from the kitchen, the aroma providing a brief moment of solace, and make my way out of the apartment.

The instant I'm outside, my daily routine kicks in, and I immediately dial Abbey's number.

"Hey, Abbey! I'm on my way to the bus stop," I inform her.

"Great. I'm heading there, too," she replies excitedly. "You won't believe how incredible last night was."

A sudden sense of déjà vu washes over me. I can't shake the feeling that I've heard those exact words before. It was here, at this very spot, during this same time of day, as I made my way to the bus stop.

"What did you just say?" I ask. "You said the exact same thing yesterday, didn't you?"

Abbey sounds confused on the other end. "What are you talking about? I did have an amazing night, but I never mentioned it to you yesterday. Do you want me to tell you about it?"

"Just wait until we reach the bus stop. Something feels off," I reply, a strange unease settling in.

"Sure. I'll see you in a few minutes."

I stride towards the bus stop, her words echoing in my mind. I've dialed Abbey countless times at this time over the past few years. Yet, this particular sentence resonates with an eerie accuracy. Perhaps she did say it before. But why is it triggering a sense of déjà vu now and not earlier? I'm not sure what's happening. Am I overanalyzing?

I need to meet her as soon as possible. I abandon my leisurely pace and start jogging towards the bus stop. It helps me avoid some scary thoughts and allows me to focus on my breathing.

The day is beautiful. Just like any summer day in Portland. Vibrant flowers surround me, just as they did yesterday and the day before. Yet, none of these feels like a déjà vu. They all seem normal.

I arrive at the bus stop a few minutes earlier than usual, my breath ragged as I wipe away the sweat trickling down my face. I wait anxiously for Abbey, my heart pounding in my chest. After what feels like an eternity, she finally joins me. I jumpstart the conversation. "Tell me about your evening."

"You're really eager to know, aren't you? Well, I did manage to get a good night's sleep, but my roommate — "

"Made great pasta?" The words slip out involuntarily.

Her eyes widen in surprise. "Wow, now you're finishing my sentences? I think we just reached a new milestone in our friendship."

Wait, how did I know that? How the *fuck* could I have possibly known that? Something is wrong. Something is extremely wrong.

"Wait a minute! How did I know what you were going to say?" I blurt out, fear and confusion gripping me. "This feels like déjà vu. It's like we've had this conversation before."

"Hey, don't overthink it. It's just about food and sleep, simple stuff we talk about every morning."

I shake my head, my mind racing. "I know it's simple, but everything feels so eerily familiar. It's like I've experienced this before. I had these terrible nightmares last night, and they completely ruined my sleep. Maybe you said this in one of my dreams."

"Ouch! I thought our friendship had reached a new high. If I'm in your dream, it *has* to be a sweet dream. Not a nightmare, right?"

"No, no. I can't recall anything specific from the dream. All I know is that I got stressed out and was in a state of panic when I woke up."

"Ah, I recognize this. It's hypnagogia," she says with certainty.

"Hypna-what? Are you suddenly a psychologist?"

"Once we're on the bus and settled, I'll explain," she replies, her eyes fixed on the approaching bus.

We board and find seats, then I turn to her and inquire, "Alright, now spill. What were you talking about?"

"Hypnagogia! I remember reading about it in a psychology book a few weeks ago. It's this concept where you experience vivid dreams or hallucinations right before falling asleep or waking up. They feel so real that you can feel the stress, but you can't remember the details. Did you remember anything from your dream?"

"I saw you and some other guys." I squint, struggling to recall the fragments of the dream. "Just flashes, nothing clear. But I definitely felt pain."

"That's definitely hypnagogia," she confirms confidently. "You know what? I'm tempted to quit my job and become a full-time sleep specialist to help people with bad dreams." We both burst into laughter at the thought.

Hypnagogia might explain the haunting nightmares that grip me, their vividness almost too real to bear, but it fails to account for the eerie moment when I effortlessly completed her sentence. Could it be that she said those very words to me in a dream? It would make sense if she had spoken them yesterday and my sleepy mind simply replayed the scene. It makes no sense that I dreamt about it first and then it happened in real life afterward. I hope it's not a superpower I acquired overnight. Or what if she's toying with me?

I steal a glance at her, her AirPods firmly in place while she's lost in the depths of Instagram. She appears oblivious to the whole situation. It doesn't seem like she's playing games with me.

I need to forget this ever happened. Otherwise this will consume my entire day.

We arrive at Alder Street, the morning sun casting a golden glow on the vibrant flowers and lush gardens that adorn the Wise AI campus. Taking a leisurely stroll, we soak in the beauty around us, the scent of blooming flowers filling the air. Finally, we reach the administrative building's lobby. There, I spot Mike filling his coffee cup. He greets us with a warm smile.

"Good morning, friends," he says cheerfully.

"Good morning, Mike," I reply. "How are you today?"

"I'm doing well. It's a beautiful morning, isn't it? And we have a fresh new team to meet today. Are you both excited to meet them?"

"Definitely excited, especially if any of them look like the god of thunder," Abbey chimes in.

Mike laughs with his shaking belly, but I'm in absolutely no mood to laugh right now.

"Why don't you ladies head to the conference room and welcome the new team?" he suggests. "I'll grab my coffee and join you shortly."

Abbey and I make our way into the conference room, where we find it already half-filled with new hires. We exchange handshakes and the usual morning pleasantries.

As I set up my laptop and the projector, Mike enters the room and addresses us. "I hope you guys haven't started yet because we have one more person joining the session. Apparently, he had trouble finding the right meeting room." He beckons someone outside the room to come in quickly.

My gaze shifts towards the door, and my heart skips a beat. IT'S HIM! The man from my dream last night. He stands before me in the flesh, entering the room like a stranger, waving at everyone as if he belongs.

A jolt of electricity courses through my body as if a lightning bolt has struck my head, leaving me momentarily stunned and disoriented. How is this possible? This makes NO sense. How can the events of my dream begin to manifest in reality?

I've never encountered this person in my waking life. Or have I? No, that can't be. If I had met him before, I would surely remember. Something significant is going on.

His face from the dream is etched vividly in my mind. The only difference now is his clean-shaven appearance, contrasting the bearded man I saw in my dream. Instead of a suit, he wears a pale blue shirt with a neatly tied tie, perched spectacles resting on his nose, and Converse sneakers on his feet.

But his *face* remains the same.

I continue to stare at him in shock, unable to find my voice. He approaches me, extends his hand, and introduces himself. "Hi, I'm Nolan. It's a pleasure to meet you. And you are?"

I remain silent, my gaze fixed upon him.

"Ahem, hello?" he says again, holding my hand.

"I'm... I'm... Erica," I stammer, quickly retracting my hand. Avoiding eye contact, I hurriedly set up my laptop and projector.

I wonder if Abbey noticed the turmoil on my face. I'm sure she did. The bitch has the senses of a snake when it comes to me. I can't deal with her right now; I need to focus on my laptop screen.

"Alright, everyone!" Abbey announces. "Good morning. Let's begin the meeting. Erica, can I take over your slides for now? We can switch later in the presentation, just to mix things up."

"Um, okay. Please go ahead," I reply.

I'm in no mood to give a presentation at this moment. First the phone call in the morning, then my prediction of pasta, and now this Nolan guy turns out to be real. I hope I dream about a comet tonight just to end it all.

"Okay, my friends, Abigail and Erica will assist you with anything and everything on campus and regarding your work," Mike says. "Now, I must attend another meeting, so I'll see you all later." He exits the room.

Abbey begins the presentation, occasionally glancing at me.

I can't concentrate. Who is this guy? How did I see him in my dream last night? He's an *exact* replica. His smile, speech, and body language are all identical. I wish I could recall his voice from the dream, but all I can visualize is his face. Did *he* do something in my dream that caused me stress and restless sleep? Have I seen his picture somewhere before? Not that I can think of.

I have to look him up.

I grab my phone and quickly open Facebook and Instagram, hoping to find some connection. Nothing comes up! No mutual friends, no shared interests. It's like he doesn't exist in my world. According to his LinkedIn profile, he graduated from a college in Massachusetts. That's impossible. I've never had a friend from the East Coast. My entire family and all my friends have always been here in the west. I've never even visited the East Coast for tourism. He's a *complete* stranger, yet I remember him so vividly from my nightmare.

I shift my gaze to Abbey's presentation, doing my best to avoid looking at his face.

Right before Abbey's part ends, she pauses and asks, "Before we move on, does anyone have any questions?"

Nolan raises his hand and directs his question towards me. "Can you tell us about the key tools you'll be assisting us with?" His gaze locks onto mine, and an unexpected surge of anger courses through me. It's an instinctive reaction, one I can't control.

Without overthinking, I retort, "Why don't you focus questions to Abbey, and you can ask me when I'm the one presenting."

His head drops, his eyes fixed on his notes. "Sorry," he mutters.

I shouldn't have said that. That was rude. But the words just popped out of my mouth.

In my defense, anyone in my shoes might act this way if they saw a man from their dream come out in the flesh the next day. I'm keeping my composure and am managing to stay in the same room.

"Let's all take a breather," Abbey suggests, her voice cutting through the tension. "Ten minutes, same room." She glances at me and leans into whisper, "Care to join me in the restroom?"

Ugh! Now she's gonna go on and on!

We make our way to the restroom, and as soon as the door shuts behind us, Abbey's frustration bursts forth like a raging storm.

"What the hell was that? That was beyond rude and completely out of line."

"I'm sorry, Abbey. But you have no idea what I've been dealing with since this morning."

"I don't care." She dismisses my words with a wave of her hand. "You can't just go around yelling at new hires, no matter what you're going through."

"Come on, girl, just chill! I already said I'm sorry."

"No! You need to tell me what's really going on. It's not just that rude comment. You were looking at him all weird.

Don't you think I was watching you during the presentation?"

Of course she was!

"Okay, I'm gonna tell you. But you need to understand *my* perspective of the situation."

She nods, her hands folded against her chest. "Go on," she says, her eyes fixed on me. "I'm listening."

"This might sound insane, but it's the truth. Remember when I mentioned that awful dream I had last night? Well in that dream, I saw Nolan, along with a group of random guys. When I woke up, I was overwhelmed with stress, anxiety, and fear. Do you understand what that means?"

"Do you?" She looks at me as if I've lost my mind.

"Don't you see? Nolan is the antagonist, the villain in my dream. Something he did must have caused all the panic and ruined my sleep. And now, somehow, he's come to life. I've never seen the man before today."

I think I'm being very clear and reasonable. I have no idea what's making it difficult for her to understand. Her widened eyes remain fixed on me, her gaze filled with a mix of curiosity and concern.

"Let me see how to put this," she says. "You're being mean to a new hire since he looks like someone who hurt you in the dream."

"Yes!" I exclaim, relief flooding through me. "That's exactly what I've been trying to say."

"Okay, Erica. I'll put this as gently as I can. You've completely lost it. That man in there is one of the most qualified individuals this company has ever hired. You need to get yourself together and treat him with respect. Otherwise, I'll have no choice but to report this to HR."

"Oh, really? Since when did *you* start being so supportive of men?" I snap. "You're the one who's always skeptical about men, and now, you're defending this guy over me?"

"I may have been skeptical in general, but this man seems decent and not at all creepy. Or maybe I'm defending him because your behavior towards him is a little weird. From a psychological standpoint, our memory can be peculiar. You might have seen a completely different person in your dream, and when you encounter someone with even slight similarities, your brain reconstructs the image to match the two. Now let me ask you this: What similarities do you see between the person in your dream and Nolan?"

"Similarities? Well, they have the same face. Doesn't that count?"

"I highly doubt that."

I'm tired of explaining myself to her at this point. Aren't friends supposed to just support you no matter what?

"I don't know how else to prove it to you," I say wearily.

"Fine. You know what? It doesn't matter," she says. "That was just a dream, and you better start treating Nolan with kindness. Let's get back to the meeting."

She doesn't believe me. But this doesn't change the truth of Nolan's evil role in my dream.

We make our way back to the conference room, and I take a deep breath before starting my presentation. I do my best to avoid his gaze, but I can sense his eyes fixed on me throughout the entire session.

An hour ticks by agonizingly slowly, and finally, I declare, "Thank you all for your attention. Please enjoy your lunch and have a pleasant day. We'll reconvene tomorrow morning."

I need to get away from Nolan. I can't stand another minute around him. I lower my head, shut down all the applications on my laptop, and gather my belongings before heading towards my desk.

Nolan approaches my desk and asks, "Abigail, could you lend me a hand with setting up my desk and computer?"

Abbey swivels her gaze at me and, with a sly smile, suggests, "Hey, Erica, it seems like Nolan needs some help with his desk and computer setup. Mind giving him a hand? I've got something else to take care of."

Bitch! Is she serious right now? After the long conversation we had in the restroom?

"Of course, sure," I say, then whisper to her, "Hate you! What kind of a friend does this?"

"A best friend! See ya later, babe." She smiles at me wickedly while leaving the room.

Nolan grins at me while waiting for help with his computer setup.

Every part of this moment is eerily familiar. I'm gonna get this over with quickly and relax in the lounge for a bit.

I pick up my pace, practically sprinting towards his desk, Nolan trailing behind. I'm desperate to avoid any unnecessary conversation during our walk.

Finally, we arrive at his desk. We work in silence, moving swiftly and discreetly. I make a conscious effort to avoid any accidental eye contact with him.

With the setup complete, I inform him, "Everything's done. You should be good to go now. I need to get back to my work."

As I walk away, he sprints up behind. "Hey, Erica," he pants. "Since it's my first day on the job and you helped me with the setup, can I treat you to lunch at the cafeteria? I don't have any friends here, so it would be nice to have lunch with you."

Bullshit! No way I'm having lunch with him.

"I'm sorry," I reply, "but I really have a ton of work to do. Perhaps you could text Abigail or any of the new members of the group to join you. I must go."

"How about tomorrow for lunch?" he persists.

I shake my head.

"I'm sorry. I usually prefer to eat alone at my desk. I... I have a meeting now. I really have to go. It's nice to meet you, by the way."

Without a backward glance or a wave of farewell, I stride away, leaving him behind. This entire situation is Abbey's fault.

I rush over to her desk, my heart racing with frustration. "Are you satisfied now? It was so awkward to be near him."

"What happened?" Abbey asks with a chuckle.

"He had the audacity to invite me to lunch because he's friendless. I declined and walked away."

"Oh, the poor guy. Come on, Erica, you can't be silly over a dream and be rude to people you've just met."

"Well, it's your fault. I'm stressed and hungry, so let's grab lunch, and you're buying it for me."

"Alright, alright," she says as we make our way to the cafeteria, grabbing our food before settling down to eat.

Just when I thought I could peacefully eat, my awkwardness continues when Nolan walks into the cafeteria and locks his eyes onto mine for a moment, looking deceived, and then walks away with his meal.

I *hate* this day!

Abbey, unable to contain her amusement, glances between the two of us. I can tell she's trying to stifle her wicked laughter.

"This day couldn't get any more awkward," I groan. "I just told Nolan that I always eat alone at my desk, and now he catches me here having lunch with you."

"Why did you say that? You could have told him we had planned to eat together or even invited him to join us. It would have made the situation less awkward."

"Your presence makes it less awkward? Your presence is the one that created this issue in the first place."

Taking a sip of her drink, she says, "Hey, come on now. Take it easy. Let's finish our lunch and get back to work."

My stomach's growling, but the awkwardness makes eating feel like a chore. Still, I force my food down quickly — I know if I don't, a headache will hit later. Afterward, we head back to our desks like nothing happened.

I push myself to concentrate on the reports and presentations that need to be finished. There's a nagging guilt inside me for turning down lunch with Nolan, but I can't afford any distractions right now.

To drown out the noisy thoughts, I slip on my headphones and immerse myself in the epic soundtrack of *Interstellar*.

Just as I start to get into the rhythm of work, a tapping on my desk pulls me back to reality. I turn my head and there he is, Nolan, standing beside me.

Ugh! What does he want now?

"Hey, Erica, can you lend me a hand with some software issues?"

I instinctively dodge him.

"I'm sorry, Nolan. Can you ask Abigail instead? I'm busy with some work, and I'm sorry for not joining you for lunch, too. I really need to focus."

"Okay, now I need to ask. It's my first day here, and I feel like we started off on the wrong foot. Did I do something to stifle you? I sense that you're avoiding me, and it's making me uncomfortable. If you could give me some feedback, it would be helpful me to improve. I want to establish good connections since it's my first day."

I let out a sigh before responding, "I'm sorry if I made you feel that way. It's not about you. I just have a hard time with new people. Please don't take it personally. Maybe I'll explain it to you later."

"Can you please just tell me what's bothering you? It's clear that you're not at ease around me, and since you're supposed to be training me, it would be beneficial to address this."

He's not letting this go. I could just lie to him, but I'm such a bad liar, anyone with functioning eyes could figure it out.

"It's honestly silly," I say. "I'm sure you have better things to do than listening to my problems. I'll definitely work on it and make sure to be kind to you. You know what, tell me what software assistance you need, and I'll assist you with it."

"To be honest, I don't have any software issues. I saw you at lunch and sensed there was tension between us, so I came over to resolve it. If you have the time, you can join me in the cafeteria, and we can discuss what's bothering you."

Damn! I think he deserves to know, but he's going to think I'm crazy.

He keeps looking at me with his puppy eyes; I can't help but accept his invitation.

"Sure. Let's grab a coffee at the cafeteria. I can explain, but I have to warn you, it's extremely stupid."

"Great! I'll fasten my seatbelt and brace myself for whatever you're about to say."

Today should be called 'national awkwardness day.' I'm tired of this. I think it's better if I clear it up with him. We make our way to the cafeteria and find a table to sit at.

"Okay, truth is, I saw you in a dream last night, and it totally freaked me out when I saw you in real life today," I blurt out.

As expected, his expression changes, like he's staring at a crazy person.

"I see," he says, pausing to process. "So, you, Erica, saw me in a dream even though we've never met before, and that's why you've been acting so strangely around me. Let me try to wrap my head around this."

"Look, I know it sounds ridiculous, and you said you'd be cool about it," I reply defensively.

"No, I'm cool, really. I'm just trying to understand," he says, his tone calming. "So, let's say I believe you saw me in your dream. Why does it have to be a bad thing? Maybe you can think of it as the man of your dreams taking human form and coming to you the next day." He chuckles.

"That's the thing." At the mere thought of the dream, anxiety tightens my chest. "I woke up drenched in sweat, trembling, and completely panicked. I thought you had done something to make me feel that way. So, I started avoiding you, and I'm sorry if that ruined your first day."

"Actually, now that you've said it out loud, it's kind of funny," he says, his laughter easing the tension. "I think you explaining all of this makes up for the awkwardness earlier. So, since you only remember me from the *dream* and nothing more, can we just put it aside and be normal with each other? Please."

Guilt creeps in, heavy and sudden. Regardless of why I saw him in my dream, I shouldn't have hurt his feelings. Abbey was right.

"Sure, let's start fresh." I smile as I reach out to shake his hand. "I'm Erica."

Nolan's grip is firm as he shakes my hand. "Nice to meet you, Erica. I'm Nolan. My little quirk is that I like to visit people's dreams the night before I meet them."

We both share a laugh, and in that moment, it's as if a heavy weight of guilt has been lifted from my chest.

"So, where are you from?" I inquire, genuinely curious. "And how did you end up joining this company?"

"I actually studied at MIT," Nolan reveals, his words catching my attention. Suddenly, my interest in getting to know him grows.

The more we talk, the more it hits me, Nolan's *actually* a good guy. He didn't flinch at how I acted before, just rolled with it like it didn't bother him. That kind of patience says a lot.

Chatting with him is surprisingly enjoyable. The more time I spend in his presence, the more at ease I become.

As the day draws to a close, I give him a goodbye and join Abbey as we make our way back to the bus stop for our journey home.

"Abbey, I finally told Nolan about my dream, and you know what? You were right, he's not so bad after all. He's actually kind of cute, and he's really smart, too. I'm so glad I got that off my chest. No more awkwardness!"

Abbey rolls her eyes and pleads, "Please, for the love of God, let's put this dream behind us. We've been discussing it all day. Now that you've settled it, let's not bring it up again. Tell me, what else did you and Nolan talk about?"

"Nothing too crazy. We simply got to know each other better. He's actually a decent and kind guy. I genuinely enjoyed spending time with him."

Abbey scoffs in disbelief. "So, in less than a day, you've gone from treating him like a villain to having a crush on him? You seriously need psychiatric help."

"A crush? Is that really how it appears to you?"

"I know you better than you know yourself," she asserts, her tone filled with certainty. "So, ask yourself that question."

Huh! Do I? I don't think so. Rather, I find it creepy to think that way.

As night falls, I finish pouring my heart into my journal, capturing the whirlwind of emotions that consumed me today. Typically, I'll lie naked on my bed, ready to scroll some reels before dozing off. But tonight, I can't shake the urge to look up this Nolan guy. Abbey's comment is stuck in my mind. I don't have a crush on him. I'm just curious to know who he is. My quick search earlier in the conference room turned up nothing, but now I've got time. Google, don't fail me.

His identity card at work said Nolan K. It's weird that his last name is just an initial since we usually have full name on it. Maybe he made a request to have it printed that way. Searching for Nolan K on Google seems to be leading to many irrelevant pages.

What kind of a man has no social media? In this day and age, that's baffling. I set my phone aside, my mind consumed by thoughts of Nolan. No matter how hard I wrack my brain, I find no evidence of an evil nature lurking beneath his charming face. I keep thinking about him while I doze off to sleep.

7

The next day, Abbey and I stroll towards the administrative building, our footsteps echoing in the quiet morning air. I turn to her, my curiosity piqued. "Hey Abbey, mind if I ask you something?"

"Go ahead," she replies, her eyes focused ahead. "But if it's about another dream of yours, save it for someone else."

I chuckle, shaking my head. "No dreams today, I promise. It's something else. Do you think there are people out there who don't have a social media account?"

Abbey's brow furrows as she ponders for a moment. "Well, it's possible. Some might want to avoid the addictive nature of it all, while others could be advised by their doctors to stay away, you know, to prevent any stalking tendencies. Why do you ask?"

I take a deep breath, my mind still lingering on the events of the previous night.

"Last night, I was scrolling through my social media accounts, trying to find Nolan's profile. But there was nothing. It got me thinking, you know? Is he trying to stay immune to the online world, or could that be a sign of sociopathic behavior?"

Abbey's eyes narrow, her detective instincts kicking in. "Why were you searching for his profile, anyway?"

"I know you'll start prying if I ask you something." I try to sound casual. "I was just browsing, you know? We just met, and I wanted to get to know him a bit more and maybe be a social media friend. Plus, I was pretty rude to him yesterday."

"Not prying, my friend, just curious," she counters. "Nolan seems like the introverted type. I doubt he's into watching dancing girls or pranks on social media. He's actively avoiding those addictive behaviors that mess with your dopamine levels. That's pretty commendable, if you ask me."

"Dopamine levels? Are we back to your psychology books again? Please, spare me. Or at least let me borrow them so you don't have to lecture me."

We arrive at the conference room for the second day of training. Today, I want Nolan to feel comfortable around me, to be open to asking any questions he might have.

My presentation begins, and Nolan effortlessly fires off a barrage of questions. I'm impressed by his ease. It's strange how he seems *unaffected* by the fact that I ruined his first day at work. His kind nature shines through as he looks at me today as if nothing happened.

As the session comes to an end, Nolan approaches me with a warm smile. "Hey, Erica, would you like to grab lunch together?" he asks.

"Yes, Nolan," I reply with a smile. "I would be delighted to join you for lunch."

We make our way to the cafeteria and find an empty table.

"Okay, Erica," he says, leaning in. "Any interesting dreams last night?"

I grin and shake my head. "No specific dreams this time. It was a peaceful night. You must think I'm weird after all that dream talk and my behavior yesterday..."

He cuts me off with a reassuring wave. "Nah, not at all. It's actually kind of thrilling to know that a beautiful woman like you dreams about me. I wish I knew more about what we did in your dream."

"I wish I could tell you, but my dreams are always hazy. Just fragments of memories."

He leans back, considering my words. "You know what? Maybe it's for the best. It feels like we've become friends in such a short time."

"I agree. By the way, do you have any social media accounts?" I ask. "Maybe we should connect there as well. I spent quite some time searching yesterday but couldn't find anything."

"You were searching for me? Why?"

"Just a casual search."

"Really? Casual? Or were you hoping to dig deeper into my life?"

"Okay, you caught me. I was hoping to find a connection between us because I saw you in my dream and got curious enough to search for you on social media. I just wanted to know who you are."

"Well, I don't have any social media accounts," he replies. "I believe that if someone wants to know me, they should spend time with me instead of judging me based on a bunch of pictures. This whole dream situation made me curious about you, too. You know what? I've never asked this so early on, but I feel some sort of energy around you. Would you like to go on a date with me?"

WHAT? Did he just ask me out? I only see him as a co-worker, maybe a friend. How can I possibly go on a date with him after that nightmare?

"A date?" I stumble over my words. "Um... uh... Can Abigail come with us? Wait, no. Why did I even ask that? A date?"

"Calm down," he says with a laugh. "I really want to get to know you. The fact that you saw me in your dream and the way you asked me to clear the air has piqued my interest. So yes, a date. And no, Abigail can't join us."

"I didn't mean to suggest that we should invite Abigail, although she did say you were cute."

"Wow, I should have joined this company a long time ago. If only I knew that all the women here would think I'm attractive."

"Actually, don't you think us being co-workers makes it weird for us to go on a date?"

"Come on, Erica," he pleads, giving me a reassuring look. "It's just one dinner. That's all I'm asking. If you hate it afterwards, just think of it as free food and we can both move on."

Well, one dinner won't hurt. I suppose it's a courtesy after the pain I caused him. He *is* handsome and he seems like a smart guy, but there's an eerie feeling lingering within me.

I respond with a smile, hiding my reluctancy. "Sure. It's a date then. But nothing crazy, just dinner."

"Perfect! Nothing crazy. I want to get to know you and take it slow. So, a coffee in the evening, a walk to dinner, and I can drop you off afterwards."

I nod in agreement.

We finish our lunch and return to our work.

As the evening descends, Abbey and I make our way to the bus stop. The secret of my date with Nolan weighs heavily on me. I'm unsure how she'll react when she finds out. The thought of going on a date with Nolan still makes me uneasy.

If I share that with Abbey, I know she'll caution me against dating, as she always does when I show interest in guys. She has a million reasons why I shouldn't pursue handsome men. Maybe she can motivate me to avoid this date night.

"Hey, Abbey!" I call out, hoping to share my news. "Guess what? Nolan asked me out on a date."

Her eyes widen in surprise. "When did that happen?"

"During our lunch today at the cafeteria."

Abbey furrows her brow, deep in thought. I can tell she's racking her brain for a clever way to put an end to this date night. I hope she finds a legitimate reason. Come on, Abbey, you can do it. Think!

"That sounds cool," she finally says. "You should try that Thai restaurant downtown."

Cool? I reply in shock. "Aren't you supposed to be my superhero friend, protecting me from sleazy men?"

"What? What are you talking about?" She looks genuinely confused. "Yes, I protect you from sleazy men, but not this guy. He seems intelligent and good-natured. Why would I stop you from dating someone like him?"

Seriously? She can't come up with a *single* reason for me to avoid this date?

"What about the potential issues at work?" I inquire.

"Work? Who cares? As long as no one finds out, there's no way it'll affect anything. So just enjoy the dinner."

I nod and continue walking home.

I decide to forgo any fancy preparations for this date. That way he can find me less attractive and probably not have any interest for a second date. If he were to ask me out again, I could simply decline, but it would be easier if he doesn't ask at all.

I slip into a plain woolen t-shirt and a pair of jeans, deliberately avoiding any makeup or lipstick. At this time of summer, the woolen fabric will make me sweaty and emit an unpleasant odor that will surely repel him from getting too close. This tactic should *definitely* dissuade him from pursuing another date.

He picks me up promptly at 5:30, and we make our way to the bustling coffee house downtown. The anticipation hangs heavy in the air as we step inside.

"This is quite an adventure," he remarks, a hint of amusement in his voice. "I've never been on a date with someone who actively avoided me after dreaming of me. I've had my fair share of women avoiding me after a *date*, but this is a whole new level."

He has a good sense of humor. I can give him that. It's a rare quality these days.

"Well, maybe I possess some sort of superpower to see things through my dreams," I joke, trying to lighten the mood. "But to get serious for a moment, what are your hobbies?"

He grins, clearly excited to share. "I don't want you to think I'm a total nerd, but I love pencil sketching, strumming my guitar, and playing drums. I devour books like there's no tomorrow, and I even have plans to launch my own software company with some of the ideas I've been brewing. Oh, and I'm a massive football fan."

"Wow, you certainly keep yourself busy," I tease. "I think you just redefined the term 'nerd'!"

He chuckles, shaking his head. "I promise you, I'm not a nerd. I just have a wide range of interests. What about you?"

I smile in appreciation of his genuine curiosity.

"I'm a pretty simple gal," I say. "I just watch movies, cook, and hang out with friends."

"Well, I believe in keeping things simple," he says. "And I must say, you look absolutely stunning this evening."

Is he blind? How can I possibly look beautiful in *this*? I'll have to ask him later, maybe once the sweat kicks in and my breath starts turning gross.

"Thank you," I say, forcing a smile. "But beauty doesn't really matter, does it?"

Obviously, it matters! What kind of a woman hates a fiery body on a man? We just say it doesn't matter to be polite, to seem humble.

"Is that something you learned on social media?" he says. "Let me tell you what I think. Imagine I ask you to enter a room where two men are waiting, and you have to pick one to date. I give you no information about them, just their appearances. One is overweight, his clothes disheveled and his hair a mess. The other is impeccably dressed, physically fit, and his hair perfectly groomed. Whom would you pick?"

"Obviously, the neatly dressed guy," I reply without hesitation.

"There you go! Looks do matter. People may claim they don't, but they speak volumes about hygiene, personality, and discipline. So, when I say you look beautiful, I mean it from the bottom of my heart."

Wow! He thinks just like me. He forgot to mention great sex, but everything else he said aligns *perfectly* with my beliefs. Maybe I've been too quick to judge him based on a bad dream. Maybe Abbey is right. He's actually a good guy.

"That's an incredible perspective," I remark, genuinely impressed. "You really do put a lot of thought into things, don't you?"

"Well, people often say I'm a bit sensitive. So, I tend to think things through before taking action."

His sensitive nature is endearing.

The more we chat, the more I find myself enjoying this date. He has grand aspirations of starting multiple companies, making a positive impact on society, starting a family, and exploring the world, especially islands with great beaches. Oh, I love beaches! I've always dreamt of scuba diving with my life partner, and it's wonderful to discover that he shares similar interests.

I should have prepared better for this date. *Fucking* dream almost made me turn down the opportunity to meet this incredible guy.

"You and I have such similar thoughts," he says. "I feel a strong connection to you, even in such a short time."

He gently takes my hand and gazes into my eyes. I can sense his genuine affection for me. I like Nolan. But he might be liking me more, which only adds to my favor.

"I'm glad to spend time with you this evening," I say. "I feel closer and more comfortable with you."

"I'm enjoying this date, too," he replies with a smile. He then glances at his watch and suggests, "Let's head to the Thai place nearby for dinner."

"The new Thai place? It's like you read my mind. I was just about to suggest that."

We stroll towards the restaurant, and I reach out to hold his hand, silently conveying my enjoyment of his company.

As we cover about half a mile, a strange sense of familiarity washes over me. It's as if I've walked this path before.

"I feel like I walked here before," I say. "I have this déjà vu feeling."

"Really? Have you been to this restaurant with Abigail?"

"No, not this one," I clarify. "But we frequently visited the Thai place next door countless times. Although, we never took this particular route. "

No, it's not the path. It's the sensation of walking hand in hand at this time of day. His touch is strangely familiar, as if we've shared this experience before. But that's impossible since this is our first date.

I need to shut my mind off, else the overthinking will ruin the date.

"Maybe," I reply, determined to focus on the present as we continue our journey towards the restaurant.

As we step into the dimly lit restaurant, Nolan confidently approaches the waiter and gives his name for a previously booked reservation. The waiter obliges, leading us to a secluded spot adorned with flickering candles.

Taking our seats, a sense of anticipation fills the air. Nolan's eyes meet mine, his voice filled with a hint of excitement as he whispers, "I hope this will be a memorable evening for us." Gently, he reaches out, his warm hands enveloping mine.

While I'm eating dinner, Nolan looks at me and says, "I hope that time stands still so I get to spend a lot more time with you."

I've heard that sentence before. The *same* way he said.

"Wait, what did you say?"

"Ahm... That I hope I get to spend more time with you?" he repeats, his voice tinged with confusion.

"Can you say those things to me again by holding and looking into my eyes, just like the first time you said it?"

His expression shifts, a strange look crossing his face. But then he smiles, locks eyes with me, and gently takes my hand. "I hope that time stands still so I get to spend a lot more time with you," he says, his voice filled with sincerity.

That's it. That's exactly how I remember it. I've been here before. The flickering candlelight, the romantic atmosphere, and a guy who spoke those very words with that same voice.

It's all flooding back to me now. He said that to me in my *dream*! Oh god! What the hell is happening?

"You've said that to me before," I blurt out, unable to contain my thoughts. "You said that to me in my dream. I can remember bits and pieces. We had this exact dinner before. And then... And then something happened. I was falling, collapsing to the ground."

My body trembles with a cold sweat as fear courses through me. His bewildered gaze meets mine, but the terror remains. I strain to recall more fragments of my dream, shutting my eyes tightly in concentration.

"Give me a moment," I stammer anxiously. "You... You... You... pushed me, I think. From a high place, maybe a building. I remember bits and pieces. It felt like I died. I was falling to the ground because of you. That's why I woke up in a panic. You pushed me off a building. You're the villain in my dream."

"Erica, please calm down," he pleads. "I have no idea what you're talking about. You're here, alive, on a good date. Just relax, okay?"

I take a deep breath, overwhelmed by the intensity of it all. He's right, it was just a dream. I need to calm down.

"I'm sorry." My voice is shaky. "Yes, I'll try to relax. It's just that I remember more flashes from the dream, and it's freaking me out. I usually don't remember my dreams, just the lingering anxiety. But this time, I recall snippets. What confuses me is that I distinctly remember your face, even though we only met yesterday."

"I don't know how to make sense of that, but I *do* know that everything will be fine," he reassures me. "You're safe and alive. I've never harmed anyone, and I feel a deep connection with you. I could never bring myself to hurt you. Can we put this dream behind us and enjoy the rest of the evening?"

"Yes, I'm sorry for overreacting. I don't want you to think I'm crazy. It's just the circumstances that are affecting me like this."

"Crazy? Not at all. I'm glad you're being yourself around me. It usually takes time for people to feel comfortable with strangers, after all."

"Of course." I manage a smile. "Let's forget about the past few minutes and focus on the rest of our dinner."

My entire body continues to sweat, and my woolen shirt is certainly not helping. I look disgusting, and I'm sure there won't be a second date. I screwed this up! This is on me.

We finish our meal, and he drives me back home. We exit the car, my gaze avoiding his. I know he won't be leaning in for a goodnight kiss or asking about another date. If only I hadn't dreamt of him, maybe this date would have gone smoother.

I stand there, forcing a smile, silently urging him to leave.

"Thank you for joining me for dinner, Erica," he says.

I maintain my smile, not saying a word.

He approaches me, his arms tenderly wrapping around me. His lips graze my *sweaty* forehead, and he holds me tightly for a few moments. Guys usually would like to devour my lips after the date night, but a kiss on forehead and a tight hug is far more necessary for me at this moment. He certainly cares about me more than he wants to fuck me. This isn't passion, it's peace. And I didn't know I was starving for that.

"Most people would be thinking about sex after a first date," he whispers, "but I want you to know that you mean more to me." He slowly pulls away. "I truly enjoyed my time with you, Erica. Can we have dinner again tomorrow?"

I nod instinctively, accepting his invitation for a second date.

As he drives away, I wave goodbye, watching his car disappear into the night.

I retreat to my journal, documenting every moment before finally surrendering to sleep.

8

The next morning, Abbey and I sit in the conference room, waiting for the next training session.

"So, spill the beans," she says, leaning in. "How was the date? Did you guys kiss? Give me all the juicy details."

I hesitate, not wanting to delve into the restaurant drama. I don't want to hear her psychological lecture now about dreams.

"The date was absolutely wonderful. He's such a sweetheart; he gave me a warm hug and kissed me tenderly on the forehead. It was so sweet!"

"Kissed on the forehead? What is he, a grandpa?"

"Shut up! He turned out to be a very caring guy."

"Boooring," she says, rolling her eyes. "Anyway, as long as you had a good time, that's all that matters."

"I had a fantastic time, and I can't wait to see him again tonight."

Nolan and his group enter the room, signaling the start of the training session.

When it comes to an end an hour later, Nolan approaches me.

"Last night was lovely," he says, a smile tugging at the corners of his lips. "I'll see you for dinner tonight. How about we avoid a restaurant and whip up some dinner at my place? You know, that way we can talk about your nightmares in private."

We both chuckle at his suggestion. "Absolutely! A cozy evening sounds perfect, and I'd be happy to lend a hand in the kitchen."

"Sounds like a plan!" he says before stepping out of the room.

On my way to my desk, I make a quick detour to Abbey's office.

"Hey, Abbey! Guess what? I've got a second date with Nolan, tonight. We're heading to his place to cook dinner and just hang out."

Abbey raises an eyebrow mischievously and teases, "Oh, I know what 'hang out' means."

"No, no, nothing like that. We're just going to spend some quality time together."

She chuckles and waves me off, saying, "Whatever you say, madam. Go have fun. I've got a call coming in, so we'll catch up later."

"See you later," I reply, continuing on my way to my desk.

After last night's events, my panic levels have finally subsided. I managed to get a good night's sleep, which has helped restore some sense of calm. With that in mind, I'm determined to enjoy this second date.

I focus on my work, and after an hour, my phone vibrates with the screen illuminating with a message notification. It's from an anonymous number. The words on the screen read "DON'T GO!"

Spam these days is beyond irritating. It's probably just some scammers from who knows where, targeting hardworking folks like me to steal their hard-earned money. Usually, they'd ask for a bitcoin and promise double the return. But this one seems vague. Maybe they're trying to get me to react to this message, as a phone number confirmation and then scam me? Hard to know.

Before I can fully process the situation, another message arrives from the same mysterious number: "This is my second warning. DON'T GO to Nolan's home. It's for your own safety."

My heart skips a beat and a chill runs down my spine. Just when I think I can try being excited for the date, something else turns up to scare me away from it. Who the hell is this? Is someone watching me? Slowly, I rise from my seat, scanning the surrounding cubicles. Nothing seems out of the ordinary, just the usual hustle and bustle of the office.

No one knows about the date apart from Abbey and Nolan. Who's sending these messages? Did Nolan share it with someone, and they're fooling around with me? Or is Abbey toying with me? Or worse, is someone stalking me?

I doubt Nolan would risk sharing this with anyone. He wouldn't cross that line. It must be Abbey. *Argh!* Has she no better job to do apart from freaking me out?

I leave my desk and stride purposefully towards her. I need to confront her about this behavior. Approaching her desk, I assertively say, "Cut it out, Abbey. It's not funny."

She removes her headphones and looks at me, clearly confused. "Cut out what?"

"That message I received from an anonymous number, warning me not to go to Nolan's place. It was you, wasn't it? Just playing a prank on me?"

"Girl, chill! Why would I do that? I'm busy, so stop messing around. We'll talk later." She turns back to her computer and puts her headphones back on.

If it wasn't her, then it *must* be Nolan. Why would he do that? I specifically told him to keep this a secret and take it slow.

Before I let my thoughts spiral, I need to get some clarification from him. I make my way over to Nolan's desk, trying to maintain a steady demeanor. "Hey, Nolan, I just have a quick question for you. Did you happen to mention to anyone that we're seeing each other? Not necessarily a co-worker, but anyone at all?"

"Not yet," he replies. "We agreed to take our time and see where this goes, so I haven't shared it with anyone. Why do you ask?"

So, it wasn't him either? How could someone possibly know such personal details about me and my plans?

"Oh, nothing," I say, forcing a smile. "Just curious. I'll see you later."

I turn away and start walking back, my mind racing. None of this makes any sense. Did I accidentally share this with someone and forget about it? I can't think of anyone I would have told. I have very few friends in my life, and Vincent has no clue about my first date last night. Unless he's been snooping around and reading my journal, there's no way he could know. My brother might have no life outside of video games, but I know he respects personal boundaries. It couldn't be him.

Someone is stalking me. That's the only logical explanation. I grab my fidget spinner and try to distract myself, but my left foot can't stop tapping the ground. Sweat's building on my forehead, sliding down my temples, and I'm too wired to care. There's no way I can focus on my work right now.

I open the messaging app once more, my eyes scanning the screen to decipher the texts. Just as I do, a third message pops up, sending a chill down my spine. "Consider this a friendly warning. Stop asking everyone how I know about your date and respond to my message that you will NOT be going."

I hurl my phone onto the desk as shivers run all over my body. I clench my fists until my fingers turn white and tap my feet anxiously. Someone's watching me, that message confirmed it. I glance around, searching for any sign of surveillance cameras, but the ceiling is devoid of any. That means someone must have witnessed me walking to Abbey's and Nolan's desks.

How could they possibly know what I discussed? I need to find this stalker, expose them. Rising from my seat, I sweep my gaze across the room once more. I make my way towards Nolan's desk, keeping a safe distance as I observe him intently to determine if he's the culprit. Yet, he appears engrossed in his work, his phone lying untouched.

Glancing over my shoulder, I find no one following me.

Hurriedly, I return to my desk and confront the stalker through my reply. "Who the hell are you? How dare you invade my privacy like this? How do you know my personal affairs? Respond immediately, or I'll report this to the police."

Almost instantaneously, a response flashes across the screen. "I'm only trying to help you. Nolan isn't who you think he is. He isn't the honorable man you believe him to be. Consider this my final warning. DON'T GO."

Summoning my courage, I respond with "You have no right to dictate what I should or shouldn't do. If you have a problem with Nolan, confront him yourself. You're the one stalking people, and you have the audacity to question *his* character? He's a good man, and you're a coward for texting me behind his back. If I receive another harassing message from you, I won't hesitate to involve the police."

The stalker replies: "Hee haa... Nolan *looks* decent, and you think he's decent? You're an idiot! Haven't you learnt anything from Ted Bundy? Maybe women like you deserve to be with men like Nolan! I'm just a nice guy saving your stupid little ass. This is my final warning. Don't go. Goodbye!"

I search for his number in the phone book app, but that number isn't registered. Is he right? If he truly wants to help me, why remain anonymous? How is he able to track my every move? Nolan is a genuinely nice guy. Or what if someone hates him and is trying to hurt him by making me cancel the date? There's only one way to know. I need to share this incident with Nolan.

I rush back to him without hesitation. "Nolan, I need to speak with you urgently. Can you step outside for a moment?" I don't wait for a response, leading the way into the dimly lit hallway.

"I just received a text from an unknown number, warning me not to go on our date today," I confess, my voice trembling. "I have no idea who it is or how they know what we've been discussing. It's truly terrifying."

Nolan's voice trembles as he exclaims, "What? I can't believe this is happening. You know, Erica, I've always been sensitive, and there were a few guys back in school who used to bully me relentlessly. They were smart jerks who hacked my phone and messed with my life. I thought they'd leave me alone after graduation, but it seems like they're still haunting me."

"Hack your phone? What do you mean?" I ask, my brow furrowing in confusion. "I get that if they hacked into my phone, they could see our messages. But we never discussed our second date plans through messaging. How do they know something we only talked about *verbally*?"

Nolan's voice fills with despair as he explains, "Well, someone could hack my phone's microphone, right? They could listen to everything happening around me and bully me virtually. I don't know when this will stop. I think I should change my phone and get a new number." He hangs his head in genuine sadness.

In this day and age, where the government can monitor people through phone cameras, it's not far-fetched to think that some nerds could hack a microphone. It all makes sense now.

"Hey, relax. I'm sorry they're bullying you, and I understand how painful that must be," I comfort him. "I didn't take it seriously, and I was still planning on going on the date. You should definitely switch up your phone to prevent this from happening. Wait, do you think they're listening to us right now?"

"You rushed me out of there so quickly I didn't even grab my phone. I left it on the desk. This could be a good opportunity to confirm that they're the ones behind this. They probably won't message you about what we just discussed since I don't have my phone."

"Probably... Anyway, I'm going to go calm myself down and try to get some work done."

"You should, Erica. I'm sorry those guys messaged you. I'll make it up to you on our date tonight." He smiles at me as I make my way back to my desk.

I keep anxiously checking my messages, but there's nothing. Nolan's words echo in my mind. Maybe he's right. Maybe those bullies are just using him, and I'm just caught in the crossfire.

I manage to make it through the rest of the afternoon, my mind racing with thoughts of the stalker. As the workday comes to an end, I prepare myself for the journey back home.

Around five p.m., a new message pops up on my phone. It's from the stalker. "Stop believing Nolan's lies about bullying. You really bought that? You fool! I warned you, and you ignored me. You have sixty minutes to change your mind. Tick, tick, tick... Time is running out."

My heart pounds in my chest as I read the message. How did this stalker know about this? Was Nolan giving me some cockamamie stories of bullying? I look around, but I don't see anyone gazing at me from outside. There's no window near my cubicle, so there's no way someone's watching me from outside. There must a stalker somewhere inside the building who's monitoring all my conversations.

Another message arrives, but this time it's from Nolan. "Can't wait to see you again, darling. Our second date will be amazing."

Oh, the poor guy! I don't know what to do. If I share this with Abbey, she'll think I've completely lost my mind, especially after all the bizarre dreams I've been having. I *want* to ignore this stalker's messages, but how can I when they make me feel the same way my dream did?

Maybe I should cancel the date. It would break Nolan's heart, but my own safety is at stake. A throbbing headache starts to form, and anxiety tightens its grip on my throat.

I ignore joining Abbey and rush home in an Uber. As soon as I step through the front door, I freshen up and make myself a steaming hot coffee, hoping it will calm my nerves.

At exactly 5:30, a message from the stalker pops up on my phone. "Thirty more minutes. Are you ready? Hehe..hahah a..."

The panic intensifies, causing me to throw my phone aside. I tiptoe through the house, careful not to wake Vincent who's peacefully asleep in his room. Maybe I should wake him and share this terrifying story with him? But he's just a young boy, too innocent to be burdened with such darkness.

Closing all the curtains, I head back to my bedroom, making sure that no one's watching me from outside.

I think I should cancel the date altogether.

No, I need to confront this stalker.

Just as the clock strikes six p.m., my phone buzzes again, signaling another message from the stalker. My hands tremble as I open it. "He's almost there. Get ready…"

Argh! That *bastard*. I won't let him get away with this.

I respond to the message: "Why are you doing this to me? Get ready for what?"

"Bleeeeed" is how he responds, with a symbol of tiger's paws.

In that very moment, Nolan's message lights up my screen. "Hey, Erica, I'm outside your building. Are you ready?"

Oh my god! What do I do? Should I go? Or call it off for tonight?

Nolan is waiting patiently outside, his car idling. I don't want to cancel my date with him. I take a deep breath, summoning the courage to step out of my apartment. My heart pounds against my chest, but I force a fake smile as I climb into the car beside him.

"Are you okay?" he asks.

"Yes, yes, I'm fine."

He shifts into drive and we begin our journey to his home for dinner. I wish he would ask about the stalker's messages, but he remains silent. Perhaps he assumes I've moved on, but I hope he brings it up.

As we drive further away from the city, I realize Nolan's home seems to be in a remote location. I can't help but ask, "You live pretty far?"

"Kinda," he replies, a hint of excitement in his voice. "I love nature, so I rented a small ranch home away from the city. I'm sure you'll love it."

I nod and force another smile, though my anxiety grows with each passing mile.

There's complete silence for fifteen minutes. We're surrounded by trees the whole time. I can barely see any cars around.

After a few more miles, Nolan turns onto an unpaved, one-way road that disappears into the depths of the woods. Gravel crunches beneath the tires and trees press closer with every bend. The sunlight thins as it's filtered through dense branches, almost like it's second-guessing whether to follow us.

"Are you sure this is the right way? It looks spooky," I say, trying to keep my voice steady, though it sounds too loud in the hush of the woods.

"Out here it might be," he says, "but my ranch home is beautiful. The rent is cheap as well."

I'm sure it is! This location isn't helping with my anxiety.

About a mile deep into the woods, we arrive at a ranch home enveloped by towering trees that cast eerie shadows. Sunlight struggles to penetrate the dense canopy, leaving our surroundings shrouded in darkness.

Exiting the car, we make our way to the front door, anticipation coursing through my veins. With a click, he unlocks the house and gestures for me to enter.

Stepping inside, I swiftly scan the interior, my senses on high alert as I search for any signs of danger. To my surprise, everything is meticulously arranged, as if untouched by time.

The door closes behind us and the atmosphere shifts. The house is bathed in warm light; the furniture, television, and carpet gleam with newness. The air carries a hint of freshness, mingling with the delicate fragrance of bonsai plants scattered throughout the space.

As I sink into the plush sofa, a sense of calm washes over me and my racing heart gradually returns to its regular rhythm. I take a moment to appreciate the cozy little ranch.

Nolan settles beside me and takes my hand in his, giving it a gentle peck.

"After a long day at work, being here with you brings me such peace," he murmurs. "All the stress simply melts away."

A small smile tugs at my lips as I respond, "I feel the same way."

With those words, he rises from the sofa and disappears into his bedroom, leaving me alone in the living room. I clutch my phone, taking in the view of the entire home.

I suddenly feel a vibration in my hands. I unlock my phone to see that there's no connection, but I still see a message from the stalker. I've no idea how that's possible, but without delay, I click to open it.

"Time's up! See you on the other side." There's an attached image of a newspaper article. It's from the esteemed newspaper *The East Coast Times*. It reads:

> *Notorious Serial Killer on the Run; Suspected to Have Fled to Oregon*
>
> *If you spot a man resembling the image below, do not think first of alerting the police. Immediately turn on your heels and flee! Get to safety and then call the authorities to apprehend him. He is a dangerous criminal who meticulously stalks his victims before murdering them. He goes by the name Nomitch, but he may be using another alias.*
>
> *The police investigation has uncovered that he graduated from Massachusetts and is a master of forging personal IDs. He has altered his identity and appearance more than twenty times, introducing himself in different cities with different identities. He fabricates documents and then relocates to a new city, seamlessly blending into the community before selecting his next target. He preys on attractive and unsuspecting women, brutally raping them before trafficking them to international locations. One of the survivors (whose identity is kept confidential for safety purposes) reported that these women were eventually killed, and their organs were sold to affluent men in the Middle East.*
>
> *Nomitch was last spotted at a domestic airport, his appearance altered, as he boarded a plane bound for Portland. His identity remains a mystery, and anyone who bears a resemblance to him is urged to contact the authorities immediately.*

I read the article and scroll down to look at the picture of this criminal. He has short, dark hair with a fair skin complexion, and his teeth look all crooked as if they were being cut to make every tooth into a canine. For some reason, the teeth were all spotted red. I look more carefully and imagine that man with longer hair, spectacles, and nicer teeth.

My heart drops. The facial features resemble Nolan's. The eerie atmosphere of this place and the very location of this house seems tailor-made for the plotting of a murder. Could it be that the stalker was actually trying to protect me?

Panic surges through me, urging me to flee this place immediately. But even if I start running, it's easy to chase me down the deserted road. I can't even run into the woods without getting completely lost. Tears well up in my eyes, but I fight hard to hold them back.

Wait, I spot his car keys resting on the center table. Perhaps I can snatch them and escape in his car while he's still in the bedroom. With caution, I rise to my feet and approach the center table, my heart racing.

Suddenly, Nolan emerges from the room, his gaze fixed on me as I reach for the keys. Our eyes meet. I force a smile, quickly pushing the keys aside and placing my phone on the table.

"Is everything alright, dear?" His voice is laced with suspicion.

"Yes, yes," I mutter, my words barely audible. "I was just setting my phone down on the table."

I fixate on his face, picturing him without glasses, with different hair, and with crooked teeth. It's him. He's Nomitch. The resemblance is uncanny.

He inches closer and encircles me with his arm. Our hands entwine like we're about to ballroom dance. He guides me in a slow, rhythmic motion, his voice a hushed whisper in my ear as he says, "I'm thrilled to be here with you tonight."

He lowers me onto the couch and I comply, unsure of what else to do. I must bide my time and wait for the perfect moment when he's out of reach so I can snatch the keys. Until then, I need to play along and shut off my building tears, shivers, and sweat.

He places his phone down next to me and offers, "You've had a tough day. How about I whip up some fresh juice and we can cook dinner together?"

I quickly nod in agreement as he rises from his seat and heads towards the kitchen. His gaze lingers on me before he grabs a knife and begins slicing the fruit. My phone and car keys rest on the table, but now is not the time to make a break for it. With a knife in his hand and his eyes fixed on me, it's clear that escape is not an option.

He tosses the fruit pieces into a blender, and a faint buzzing sound beside me catches my attention. It's Nolan's phone.

Carefully, I turn it over to check the notification. The name "Kevin" appears, and as I glimpse his profile picture, a vivid image forms in my mind. I remember seeing this man in my dream alongside Nolan. They were friends.

Oh my god! What's happening?

With trembling fingers, I tap on the notification, revealing a message that reads "Did you give her the juice yet?"

God help me! What's going on? I can see another person from my dream and he's asking about the juice. So, this is a *planned* trap. Just like what it said in the news article from stalker. I blink fast, trying to hold it together, but the burn behind my eyes won't go away. I've never been in a situation before where I needed to pretend to be calm outside but was crying so badly within. My throat tightens with a sharp pain, as if someone's strangling me.

Who are these people? According to the article, Nolan's a killer, but could they be part of a larger organization that lures and kills women? And who was the anonymous messenger behind the warnings and the countdown for my trap?

This panic is unbearable. I want to scream, to let it all out. Every part of me itches to run anywhere, even if it means fleeing into the depths of the woods. I'd rather face the danger of a wild animal tearing me apart than get raped by a man and sold piece by piece.

Maybe there's a chance of escape through the restroom window. It's my only hope now.

Without hesitation, I rise to my feet and ask, "Where's the restroom?"

He nods, gesturing towards an open door down the hall.

I hurry inside, my heart pounding in my chest. As I turn on the faucet, tears stream down my face and splash into the water. I desperately search for any sign of a window. *Fuck!* There isn't one. It's over.

I grab a towel, drench it in water, and shove it into my mouth. I scream and cry, releasing my anguish without letting a sound escape the walls of the restroom. I think God blessed me with a terrifying dream to *caution* me, but I was foolish to ignore the signs. If I step out now, Nolan — or Nomitch, will force me to drink that juice and start raping me.

There's only one way out if I want to survive. I must find something sharp in here, unlock the door, and run through the front entrance. If he tries to stop me, I'll use the weapon to defend myself. Once I'm out, I'll head into the dense woods, running as far as I can until I reach an area with phone signal. Then, I'll call 911 for help.

I search for my phone in every pocket. *Damn it!* I left it in the living room. There's no way I can grab it before making my escape through the front door.

Looks like I have no choice. I just need to run through the front door and into the woods and keep running until I find someone.

I search desperately for something lethal in the restroom. I check the drawers for any shaving blades or scissors, but they're empty.

Opening the cabinets below the sink, I come across a large glass jar filled with dentures. Nomitch's teeth were described as broken with red spots. However, Nolan's teeth appear normal, just like these identical dentures. If the similarities didn't confirm it before, this certainly does. Nolan is none other than Nomitch.

I need to think smarter. The distance from the restroom to the front door is at least twenty feet. If I run towards the door, he'll see me and catch me. I need to outsmart him.

I should walk out casually, pretending that I'm not interested in having juice. Instead, I could suggest that we both start cooking. This will give me the opportunity to grab a knife and stab him in the leg, buying me a few extra seconds to grab my phone and car keys for a quick escape. It's the only viable option.

I wash my face and wipe away any traces of doubt, ensuring that I appear calm and composed.

Here we go. Three... two... one.

I swing open the door and find Nolan standing right in front of me, my phone unlocked in his hand, the screen displaying the chilling snapshot of the news article from the stalker. He knows I've uncovered the truth.

His mouth stretches into a horrifying grin. With a sinister laugh, he tosses the phone aside. I scream and try to push him away, but he seizes my throat, his grip tightening as he hurls me to the ground. Desperately, I crawl backward towards the door, my voice echoing in a blood-curdling plea for help. "Leave me alone!"

His rage transforms him into a monstrous creature. He pulls my legs, tears my pants away, and sits on my stomach. His eyes, burning with fury, lock onto mine. He rips off my shirt and then removes his eyeglasses and dentures with a loud clatter. Finally, I see his true identity.

Tears stream down my face as I plead with a trembling voice, "Please let me go! Let me go!"

His eyes lock onto mine as he bellows, "I didn't want to do this. I wanted to be nice. I wanted to kill you first with poison and have sex with you before plucking out your parts. But you're a sneaky animal!"

His eyes dart to the ceiling as he roars, "I'm gonna kill you and then hunt your brother, too! I'll make sure your friends and family never find out and make them run around like dogs searching for pieces of you! Don't worry, I'll only rape you *after* you're dead."

As his grip tightens around my neck, I continue to sob. The pain in my head intensifies, blurring my vision.

My sight begins to fade. Nolan inches closer, his crooked teeth bared ready to maul my vulnerable neck. My voice weakens as I cry out, "Please, just let me go... Let me..."

9

"Let me go!" I scream, my voice jolting me awake.

I sit upright in bed and scan the room for any sign of the murderer. I throw off my fleece blanket and frantically check my clothes. I'm naked and sweat-soaked, but otherwise okay.

Unbelievable.

I swing my legs over the edge of the bed and make my way to the dresser, searching for any evidence of harm to my throat. There's nothing. No wounds, bruises, or scars.

The digital clock reads 6:00 AM on June 19, 2023. Another nightmare on the same day? It's impossible.

Nolan was trying to kill me. I remember it all. This can't be a dream. I lived through June 20th and 21st. This wasn't a dream. I need to prove it to myself.

I open the drawer on my dresser and grab my journal. Flipping through the pages, I search for my entries from the twentieth and twenty-first.

IT'S EMPTY! How the *fuck* is this even possible?

My anxiety skyrockets. I can't believe this is happening to me again. These nightmares are excruciatingly real and always happen on the same day.

Nolan was on the verge of raping and murdering me. There was a stalker watching my every move. I rush to the window, throwing it open and scanning the surroundings. There's no one.

None of this makes sense. I can't be trapped in a time loop or constantly plagued by nightmares that *feel* so real.

Tears stream down my face as a deep, piercing pain throbs in my throat, fueled by anxiety and fear. It's like the universe is messing with me, and I don't even know why. Is this all just a dream, or is it real?

I stumble towards the mirror, desperate for answers. Slapping myself across the face, I scream, "Wake up! Wake up! Wake up!" But nothing changes.

Frustration builds within me, but I can't pinpoint its target. Is it directed at Nolan, a man who doesn't even exist? Or perhaps at the mysterious stalker, whose identity eludes me? Maybe I'm angry at God for subjecting me to these nightmares. Or maybe, just maybe, I'm angry at myself. My own mind seems to be torturing me, driving me to the brink of madness.

I continue to stare at my reflection, consumed by a smothering rage. Adrenaline courses through my veins, causing my fist to clench involuntarily. Without thinking, I strike out at my own reflection, shattering the mirror and leaving my knuckles bloody.

The pain of glass shards stuck under my skin gets completely overshadowed by the headache and the overwhelming confusion that engulfs me. I need someone, anyone, to hold me and assure me that I'm safe, that I'm not being raped or murdered.

I hastily throw on my robe and rush towards the door, hoping that Vincent heard my screams or the sound of the mirror breaking. I need my brother *now* more than ever before.

As I open the door and peer into the living room, Vincent keeps playing with his headphones on. Did he not hear anything, or does he simply not care?

Overwhelmed by pain and loneliness, I collapse onto the floor, sobbing uncontrollably. Am I stuck in a time loop? Did I become so crazy that I can't identify the difference between real life or a dream?

I'm desperate for answers, for someone to confide in. I grab my phone from the dresser and dial Abbey's number.

"Hey, Erica," Abbey groggily answers. "Isn't it too early in the morning?"

Just hearing her tone instantly breaks me, and I can't help but sob as I try to speak.

"Whoa, whoa, whoa!" Abbey exclaims, sounding more awake now. "What happened? Are you alright?"

My voice trembles with emotion as I reply, "I've been plagued by these terrible dreams. I haven't slept a wink all night. It feels like the night has stretched on forever with these nightmares. I keep waking up every few hours, feeling like I'm suffocating."

"Take a deep breath, Erica," Abbey consoles me. "Please stop crying and explain what's going on. You had a bad dream and a sleepless night, right?"

I gulp, wiping away my tears and taking a deep breath. "It's not just any ordinary dream, Abbey. I can't remember the first dream that woke me up in agony. But the second dream, I remember faces and situations as if I'd been thrown off a skyscraper. The third dream, I remember most of, and it was the most terrifying experience of my life. It scared me so much that I started punching the mirror until my knuckles bled, just to make sure I was truly awake and not still trapped in a nightmare."

"You hurt yourself? Are you out of your mind? Okay, take a deep breath and tell me what else you saw in your dream. Let it all out, it might make you feel better."

"I keep dreaming about this guy named Nolan," I confess. "I vaguely remember interacting with him in one of the dreams. Then it felt like I woke up and met him again in reality. It was creepy, so I tried to avoid him, but somehow, I ended up being attracted to him .

"When I arrived at his house for our date, I realized he was a ruthless criminal, a predator who took pleasure in brutally raping and murdering women. Just as I pieced it all together, his true colors emerged, and he lunged at me, and he was about to mutilate my neck. The terror was indescribable. It's hard for anyone to truly believe the depth of my pain unless they've been in that same life-or-death situation."

"No, Erica. I believe you." Abbey's voice soothes me; her words are laced with empathy. "I can understand your pain, the sheer terror of facing someone who wants to kill you, someone you don't even know in real life. I get it. Take a deep breath, calm down. It was just a dream, you woke up. Don't let it haunt you. Okay?"

I nod with tears streaming down my face, grateful for Abbey's understanding.

"Okay. I wish I could tell you more about what I saw, but we need to get to work. I'm not sure if I'm up for it today."

"It's okay," Abbey reassures me. "What if we both take a sick day today and spend some time together? You need to clear your head, find some peace. Here's the plan: Brush your teeth, take a refreshing shower, tidy your room, convince Vincent to turn off his video games, clean the living room, and organize your closet. It may seem mundane, but it'll help you feel better and bring some clarity. Sounds good?"

"Sure, Abbey. I'll do whatever you say. But I need you here with me."

"Well, that's just the beginning for today. Once you've completed those tasks, I'll come over. We'll make a delicious breakfast and then treat ourselves to a day of shopping and a trip to the hair salon. A fresh look can do wonders for the soul. Trust me, it'll help clear your mind and make you feel so much better. Okay?"

"Sounds good. Thanks, Abbey."

"Shut up! Friends don't need thanks. It's my job to take care of you when you're down, and I have the right to drive you crazy if I feel like it. That's what best friends do. So, snap out of it and do as I say. I'll be there soon."

"Absolutely," I reply, forcing a smile. "I'll see you soon."

I sit my phone down and grab a pair of tweezers from the bathroom. Slowly, I extract the shards of glass embedded in my knuckles, wincing as I wash away the blood. I brush my teeth and take a quick shower, desperately trying to push away any thoughts. I slip into my clothes and cover the wound with a Band-Aid.

I swing open my bedroom door and call out to Vincent, "Vincent, can you please turn off the video games?"

Vincent, without uttering a single word, lifts his finger and points to the hat perched on his head. The words "Leave me alone" mock me silently.

I take a slow, deliberate step towards him, positioning myself directly in his line of sight. I fix my gaze on him, unblinking, until he finally pauses the game.

"Why are you staring at me like that, sis? It's creeping me out," he grumbles.

"I had a night from hell, and your gaming is only making it worse. I need you to turn it off and help clean up the living room."

He studies me for a moment, his expression a mix of annoyance and resignation. With a heavy sigh, he finally relents. "Yeah, I guess that's chill. Anything else you want me to do?"

"I would ask you to be invisible, but I don't think you'll be able to do that for me. So, cleaning up is good enough for now," I reply sarcastically.

We get to work, Vincent gathering the scattered clothes strewn across the floor while I vacuum up the tiny remnants of potato chips.

Once the living room is restored to some semblance of order, I turn to Vincent. "Why don't you take a shower while I tackle the closet? Abbey will be here soon, and we can all have breakfast together. After that, I'll head out with Abbey, and you can finally get some sleep."

He nods in agreement, clearly weary, and heads off to the bathroom.

I step into the cramped walk-in closet, bracing myself for the cleanup. The sheer number of clothes I own is mind-boggling. It's like fast fashion has cast a spell on my generation, making us addicted to buying endless amounts of cheap garments.

To tackle the chaos in my closet, I decide to bring all the clothes into my bedroom. I sort them out by season, setting the ones that no longer fit aside for donation. Before putting everything back, I plan to vacuum the closet.

With determination, I gather armfuls of clothes and create towering piles in my bedroom. Carefully, I retrieve over a hundred hangers from the closet and begin adorning each with an article of clothing. It takes me two hours of unwavering focus to successfully separate all my clothes by season and prepare the old ones to be given to charity.

Abbey was right. The chaos in my chest eases a little as the closet takes shape. I wipe down the dusty corners and realign the shoe rack like I'm fixing something more than just shelves. It actually looks new again, which is wild considering how long I've ignored it.

I grab the stick vacuum and step into the closet. As I vacuum near the wall, I noticed a crack that's tucked away in a corner just above the ground. My curiosity piques, and I kneel to examine it closer. It's a hidden safe cabinet, cleverly camouflaged to blend seamlessly with the wall, making it almost invisible.

It must have been here before I moved in. It could be some sort of electrical panel, but those are usually labeled, not painted to match the wall.

With a gentle press to the corner, the safe opens, releasing a puff of dust from its rusty hinges. Inside, I discover a small, six-by-six diary. Its brown cover bears a label that reads "Personal diary. Please respect my privacy and don't open."

My fingers trace the thread that binds it shut. It must have belonged to the previous tenant, forgotten in the rush of moving out. I set it aside and continue searching the safe, hoping to find any other clues, but all I find is dust.

I understand the intimacy of a journal. My own journal's buried deep in my nightstand, pages filled with things no one else should read. The right thing to do is to return this to its owner without invading their privacy. The longer I stare at the diary, however, the louder the questions get. What's inside? Who wrote it? Why hide it in a safe? My fingers twitch, itching to flip it open. But I don't. Not yet.

I lean back against the closet wall, legs cramping, brain spinning. There's no name, no number, no way to trace it. Unless... there's something written inside. That's the only shot I've got. But opening it still feels like crossing a line I'm not sure I should step over.

I wipe the diary clean and gently untangle the binding thread. With a deep breath, I open the front cover. The first page reveals beautiful calligraphy that reads "My time capsule gift to the love of my life."

My heart plummets as I turn to the next page. There, staring back at me, is a wedding picture of me and **Nolan**, locked in a passionate kiss. Below the picture is an inscription. "My one love, Andrew Nolan K, and our first kiss as a married couple. On this day, we vowed to each other to stick together no matter what barriers come our way. 23 March 2023."

The handwriting is *mine*.

My eyes widen in terror as my hands start to tremble and a cold sweat breaks out on my skin. I feel like an invisible force just struck me on my head. I toss the book aside and stare at it for a few minutes.

As the situation sinks in, it becomes harder for me to breathe. I scream so hard I begin to cry.

Nolan... He's... my husband? What the *fuck* is going on?

I can't believe this. I must still be in a dream. I grab a handful of my own hair and yank it painfully, hoping to wake myself up from this nightmare. I start banging my head against the wall, chanting over and over, "Wake up or die! Wake up or die!" After a minute, I don't even feel the pain anymore. Which means I'm now going to wake up.

"Erica, stop!" Vincent bursts into the closet and pulls me away from the wall. "What're you doing? Please stop."

Trembling and sobbing, I turn around and cling to Vincent, pleading, "Help me! Someone please help me!"

He wraps his arms around me, his voice a soothing whisper in my ear when he says, "I'm here now. Your baby brother is here, and I'll take care of you. Just take a deep breath and tell me what's hurting you so much."

"Vincent, please tell me I'm dreaming," I manage to say through the pain. "Look into that diary and tell me it's all just a figment of my imagination."

"Of course, calm down," he reassures me. "I'll take a look. Don't worry, okay?"

He reaches for the diary and gazes at the photograph inside. His eyes remain fixed on the image for so long that I can't help but ask, "Vincent, tell me you see what I see. Tell me I'm not going crazy."

Silence hangs in the air as he continues to study the picture.

"VINCENT! Say something!"

Slowly, he closes the diary, placing it down gently before meeting my gaze. "You should call Abigail," he suggests.

"What? Call Abbey? Why? What does she know?" I demand, my voice rising in pitch. "What are you hiding from me?"

"Stay here, Erica. I'll be back in a moment." He rushes into my bedroom, retrieves my phone and returns to the closet, dialing Abbey's number.

Abbey's voice is casual when she picks up. "Hey, Erica, what's up?"

I snatch the phone from Vincent. "Abbey! What's happening?" My voice trembles as I speak. "I was doing what you said, cleaning the closet, when I found a secret safe with a diary inside. As soon as I opened it, I saw a photo of me in a wedding dress, kissing Nolan — the same Nolan from my dream, the notorious serial killer who threatened to murder me and my family. There's a photo of him as my husband. What the hell is going on? I don't remember meeting this man before. Someone needs to explain!"

"Erica, I'll be there in ten minutes," she says, her tone guarded. "Just stay calm until then." She's clearly hiding something.

"No! I need answers now!"

"I'm on my way," she says before abruptly ending the call.

Vincent wraps his arms around me and murmurs with a gentle voice, "It's going to be all right, sis. Everything will be okay."

Ten minutes crawl by, the air heavy with tension as we both remain huddled inside the closet, our silence deafening.

Suddenly, the doorbell chimes, jolting me into action. I sprint towards the door, desperate to uncover Abbey's hidden secrets. I swing it open and receive another shock by seeing her and Nolan standing on the other side.

Momentary paralysis grips me as I lock eyes with Nolan, his presence in the flesh sending shivers down my spine. His expression remains blank as he slowly steps into my apartment. Instinctively, I begin to retreat, my steps faltering as I back away. Abbey and Nolan advance towards me, their intentions unclear.

With a surge of adrenaline, I dart into the kitchen, my hands trembling as I snatch a knife from the counter. Holding it out in front of me, I brandish it as a warning, a desperate plea for Nolan to stay away.

Vincent emerges from the bedroom and I hastily position him behind me, shielding him from the danger that looms before us.

Nolan continues his relentless approach, undeterred by my threats. "Stop! Stop right there!" I command, my voice trembling with a mix of fear and determination. "One more step and I won't hesitate to kill you. Abbey, why are you with him? Tell him to stop and sit in the corner."

My voice rises to a frantic pitch as I turn to Vincent. "Call the police! This man is a threat! Call the police!"

But Nolan remains unfazed, his gaze piercing into my soul. "You want to kill me? Your own husband?" he taunts, a chilling smile playing on his lips. "Go ahead, kill me."

I freeze.

Then I dart behind the dining table. "If you don't leave this apartment, I'll kill myself. Or maybe this is another dream, and when I kill myself, I might wake up."

Nolan snickers. "You think this is a Christopher Nolan movie where every time you die, you wake up? This is real life, sweetheart. And I'm your goddamn husband. So sit down and shut the fuck up. It's time to talk."

Abbey rushes over, wrapping her arms around me tightly. Her embrace floods me with a mix of love and security, and I can't help but break down in tears.

She shoots a stern look at Nolan. "Be kind, Nolan. She's been through so much. It's time she learns the truth."

Vincent hands me a glass of water, and we all gather around the tiny dining table. I place the knife on the table, my hands trembling as I stare at Nolan.

"Erica, I know this must be overwhelming and confusing for you," Abbey says, her voice gentle yet firm. "But you need to take a deep breath and listen. Especially to what Nolan has to say."

"What does Nolan have to say to me?" I can't help but quiver with anger and betrayal. "You knew him, Abbey. You lied to me this morning. How could you do this? I thought we were best friends."

She takes hold of my hands. Her touch is comforting. "I know, Erica. But you have to hear us out. You need to know everything."

My gaze shifts to Nolan. Tears stream down my face as I confront him. "Who are you? Why do you haunt my dreams? And where did this wedding picture come from?"

"My name is Andrew Nolan," he reveals, his voice filled with a strange mix of tenderness and intensity. "And I'm your husband, Erica. The man who loves you more than anything."

Although he says that, I don't see love or affection in his eyes. All I see is a new ploy, a new manipulation and a hidden motive.

"No!" I shake my head in disbelief. "That can't be true. I was never married. I don't know you, except as the dangerous figure in my nightmares. Please, just tell me the truth."

"Erica, please," Abbey begs. "Just try to calm down and listen to him."

"Yes, Erica," Nolan growls, his voice low and venom-laced. "I *strongly* suggest you do exactly what I say. Your friend is right — if I were you, I wouldn't dare provoke a guy like me." He smirks, his eyes gleaming with something far darker than amusement.

"I'm glad you found the journal. Considering it's *your* journal, everything in it must be true, right?" He leans closer. "Well, guess what? I brought mine, too." From his coat, he pulls out a weathered notebook, and slaps it on the table with a thud. "This is *my* story, my version of how it's been since the day I met you. Page after page of unfiltered truth. My thoughts. My nightmares. My reality."

He pushes the journal toward me as his voice tightens with restrained fury. "You think *you're* the one haunted by nightmares?" His tone sharpens. "No, Erica. **Read this**... and you'll finally understand the hell you've put me through the last six months."

His final words cut like a blade. "Now sit your ass down and read it — *out loud* — with those pretty little eyes wide the hell open." My fingers tremble as I reach for it. My breath catches in my throat, bracing for the storm buried in those pages.

PART II: THE JOURNAL OF ANDREW NOLAN K

Past

Nolan

10

December 2022:

Today marks my first day as a waiter at the newly opened Melting Fudge ice cream parlor, conveniently located near Wise AI's campus. This place has been generating quite a buzz, with rave reviews for their mouthwatering burgers and delectable desserts. It's no surprise they've earned an impressive 4.8-star rating for customer satisfaction, particularly when it comes to their ice cream creations.

But let me be clear — none of that matters to me. I couldn't care less about the people flocking to this joint, indulging in sugary treats that will surely lead them down the path of obesity. In fact, I think their lack of determination for a good health will quite possibly, lead them to a well-deserved death by diabetes. And I'm not taking up this job to learn about the functioning of a restaurant or to become a chef in the future.

No, the real reason I took this job is to gain insight into the minds of the young demographic that visits famous parlors like this. I want to delve deep into their psychology, to understand how they spend their time and the value they place on money. It fascinates me to observe how some men try desperately to impress their women while others obsessively snap pictures of their ice cream for the sake of Instagram and their despicable hunger for followers. What a narcissistic bunch of idiots!

Being a waiter allows me to observe my own generation, the millennials, in a way that no other job could. I can spend hours each day studying their behavior, their quirks, and their desires. The more I learn about them, the better equipped I'll be to shape my own business and tailor customer service to please this generation of fools.

In the mornings, I drive my trusty old Corolla for Uber and work at the ice cream parlor during the evening shift. That's when most of the people visit the parlor anyway.

I step into the parlor promptly at four p.m. and am greeted by the head chef who hands me an apron and a first day form to sign. The document outlines a few rules: no flirting with customers, be punctual, and absolutely no stealing food. I sign the piece of a shit document and toss it back at them.

I don't plan on staying here for more than a few months. My goal is to study millennial psychology and then escape this job. Dealing with the head chef's attitude every day is the last thing I need.

I tie on the apron, secure the hat on my head, grab a notepad and a handful of pens, and prepare myself for the soon-to-be-diabetic patients, the customers of expensive ice creams. As the clock strikes five, the parlor begins to fill up.

I'm assigned four tables to serve and clean up until closing time at nine p.m.

I eagerly await the arrival of millennial customers, hoping to seat them in my section. Some couples enter and place their orders, but there's nothing particularly interesting about them. Some are glued to their mobile phones while others engage in flirtatious banter. I hate seeing both types. After a long day of work, is this how they choose to spend their evenings? Sitting across from each other, scrolling their screens? I'd have more respect if they were holding laptops and still working. At least that would be productive. And then there are those who engage in the cheesiest displays of affection. I'm sure they'll be the first to divorce. I have a strong urge to spit in their food before serving it to them, but this job can help me to contain my rage and improve my patience in dealing with stupid people.

***

After a while, she enters. And just like that, everything else disappears — the noise, the people, the air, until there's only her. She's a *beauty*! Her eyes, her hair, her boobs, her body! I've never seen such a beautifully curvy body in my whole life. I can almost scan everything underneath her clothes just with my eyes.

Unfortunately, the parlor's policy prevents me from flirting with customers. Not that it matters; I hate flirting. I guess that's the reason most women are scared of my attitude to begin with. *Cowards!* But if there's anyone I would make an exception for, it would be her. She's a goddess.

Before she can be seated elsewhere, I swiftly make my way to the front and guide her to one of my tables. I hand her a menu and a glass of water, meeting her gaze as I say, "Good evening. How are you today?"

"I'm doing well," she replies, a warm smile gracing her lips. If she's any good at identifying a man who likes her, she should know that I'm interested.

"Would you like a few minutes to decide?" I inquire.

She ponders for a moment before responding, "Well, it's my first time here, and I've been craving some ice cream. Surprise me with the best flavor you got."

Of course! Just like most people. Ice cream and then what? Will she just sit there, snapping pictures and mindlessly scrolling through her phone?

"For sure," I say with a smile. I make my way to the kitchen and retrieve our most renowned treat, a hot fudge sundae.

As expected, she pulls out her phone and dives into the depths of Instagram. She could have chosen a book or a laptop, but like any other millennial, she gets immersed in scrolling reels.

Why would I consider dating someone like her? *Ah,* her body. I guess I can work around her habits considering how stunning she looks.

Returning to her side, I place the sundae on the table. "Here's your sundae. Hope you enjoy!"

Her eyes meet mine once more, and a smile graces her lips as she takes the dessert. I can't help but wonder about her. Where does she live? Where does she work? Does she have a boyfriend? These basic questions need answers if I'm to decide whether or not to follow her once she leaves the parlor.

I discreetly move away from her table, keeping a watchful eye from a distance. She pulls out her phone and begins snapping pictures. If she has a boyfriend, she must be sending these images to him. I need to know who she's sending them to.

As she sends the picture, I quickly walk past her, catching a glimpse of the recipient's name: Abbey. I continue to steal glances at her, offering a gentle smile each time. She reciprocates the smile *every time*.

Maybe she doesn't have a boyfriend. I want to know where she lives. I'll follow her home.

But what if she's not interested in me because she sees me as just a waiter? I'm more than that. Or maybe it's better if she thinks of me that way, so I can gauge her intentions. Is she interested in me or my money? I hate women who marry for money. So, if she believes I'm just a waiter and still falls for me, that will be a positive sign.

Half an hour passes, and I approach her again, asking, "Would you like anything else?"

"That will be all for today," she replies, handing me her credit card. Erica Hampton. It's a good name. Good enough for me to do some research tonight and find out more about her.

She settles the bill and gracefully exits the parlor, leaving me frozen in place, watching her back figure.

I *must* track her down. I hurriedly approach the head chef, desperately seeking sick leave. Unfortunately, my plea is denied, as it is my first day on the job. Well, if I have to scour the surrounding area for every Erica Hampton, then so be it.

After my shift ends, I lock up the parlor and make my way home. I wrap up some of my business work before taking up the task to search for her on the internet. Obviously, my work comes ahead of any woman's body, or anything else for that matter. I suppose I'm proud of myself in that aspect.

I begin my search by entering her name and city. In a matter of seconds, I uncover her social media accounts and personal information. Thanks to Mark Zuckerberg, I gather everything about her within minutes. She appears pleasant and exquisitely beautiful. She works as a data analyst at Wise AI and frequently shares photos of nature and food.

I decide to follow her. Tomorrow, I'll pick up an Uber passenger needing to be dropped off at the Wise AI campus and then I'll patiently wait for her. I guess that's the easiest way to find her.

With my laptop closed, I prepare myself to pursue Erica tomorrow and drift off to sleep.

11

As the clock strikes six a.m., I awake and swiftly freshen up, preparing for my day as an Uber driver. The early morning rush is prime time for commuters, and I aim to maximize my trips in the coming months.

After dropping off my first customer, I navigate towards the next pick-up location. As I arrive, I spot my customer already waiting. And to my surprise, it's Erica.

Unbelievable! I was hoping to stalk her and figure out where she lives, but Uber turned out to be helpful. Now I know where she lives, what her interests are, and even her full name. All that remains is to ensure she becomes intrigued by me.

Erica slides into my car, a smile gracing her lips.

"Hey there!" I greet her. "How are you today?"

"I'm good!" she replies. "You're the guy who served me ice cream at the parlor yesterday, right?"

She remembers me, huh!

"Yes, that's me. Are you following me?" I jest.

"Well, I think you're the one following me." She chuckles. "So, you're both a waiter and a taxi driver? You must be quite hardworking."

"I enjoy exploring different jobs," I explain. "Working in service-based roles allows me to understand customers and their thought processes."

"Thought processes? So, you're interested in understanding people's minds? Tell me, what am I thinking right now?"

I glance at her through the rearview mirror, catching a glimpse of curiosity in her eyes. She wants to know more about me, and I'm just as draw in by her as well.

I'll ask her out. It'll be a test, a way to see if she judges people by how much money they make. If she says no, then I'll know she's not worth my time. There are plenty of others who deserve someone of my stature.

"Let me see," I say, pretending to think harder while I'm actually just thinking what pick-up line to use. "You're thinking that you want to know more about me, and you're hoping that I'll ask you out for a date. Is that close enough?"

She hesitates, her interest evident. "Hoping for a date might be a stretch," she admits. "But I am intrigued by a man who works as hard as you do."

We arrive at Wise AI's administrative building, our destination. "Well, here we are," I say, gesturing towards the building. "And if you don't mind that I'm a mere waiter and driver, would you be interested in going on a date with me?"

Her surprise flees, replaced by a genuine smile. "Are you serious?"

I nod, my confidence unwavering. "Absolutely. Unless, of course, my occupations embarrass you. I understand if they do."

She shakes her head. "I don't judge people based on their earnings. So yes, I'd be interested in going out with you. Where should we go?"

That's all I needed to hear. A little rush of excitement hits me and I grin. "That's great to hear. How about this? I close the parlor every night, and I get free ice cream. So, after I finish work at nine, we could grab some ice cream together?"

A playful smile dances across her lips. "You'll be the first person to take me on a date with free food," she says. "Alright, I'll meet you at the parlor at nine."

As she steps out of the car, I wave her goodbye, a sense of anticipation building within me.

That was a breeze. Getting dates has always been a piece of cake for me. The real challenge is securing a second one, which, to be honest, has never happened for me. Most women I've encountered are mind-numbingly dull and completely self-absorbed. No wonder I never felt the need to call them back.

Then there are the women who are drop-dead gorgeous, but they reject going out with me, saying that I have some kind of attitude problem. I can never quite figure out what they mean. What if I told them I'm a billionaire? Would they still avoid my second date because of some "attitude problem"? NO! They would be happy to sleep with me all day.

But Erica, she's different. She's smoking hot, no doubt about it, and I have no doubt our time together will be mind-blowing. From what I gather, she's a data analyst and she's highly educated. The fact that she agreed to a first date with me knowing that I barely make any money is a good sign.

After spending the morning driving a few Uber rides, I make my way to the ice cream parlor for the evening shift.

At closing time, I flip the sign on the parlor door and begin tidying up the tables. Just as I start, Erica strolls in, her white, long-sleeved t-shirt and blue jeans giving off a simple yet alluring vibe. Her perfectly proportioned body could make anything look hot.

"You're right on time," I greet her, flashing a smile. "Please have a seat. I'll be finished with my cleanup in no time."

She settles into a chair, her eyes fixed on me as I wrap up my tasks. When everything is complete, I take a seat beside her.

"Thanks for joining me on this date!" I exclaim. "You know, with anyone else, we'd have to go to a restaurant, wait for a waiter to take our order, and then wait for the chef to prepare our meal before we can even start eating. But with me, we can have whatever we want. And the best part is, we get to make it together and have a blast!"

"Make it together?" she responds, her eyes widening.

Duh! Is she expecting me to cook for her while she barks orders like a boss?

"Why not?" I ask. "Do you really want our date to be so predictable? Who knows where this could lead? If it goes well, we'll have a more exciting story than those boring dates where two people just flirt with each other."

"Wow, you're more direct than I thought," she says. "You know what? Let's whip up some delicious desserts. But I have no idea how to make them."

"Don't worry, we have a recipe book that all the chefs use for brand consistency. We'll just follow the steps from there."

We both make our way to the kitchen, and I can sense her excitement to join me. I hand her the menu, eager to see what she'll choose. Her eyes sparkle with delight as she selects a dessert: a luscious scoop of creamy vanilla ice cream perched atop a moist chocolate cake oozing with hot fudge. It's clear that this is her favorite.

"Are you sure you want that one?" I gesture to her selection on the menu. "You can pick something more expensive if you'd like."

"I don't judge people or ice creams by their price tags. Sometimes, simplicity is the key."

I *knew* she was different. It's easy to recognize something special when you see it. Most of the women I've dated would always go for the most expensive option, just because they could get it for free. *Cheapskates!* I'm relieved that Erica isn't like them.

"Thank you for thinking that way," I say sincerely. "I can't stand being around people who are all about price tags."

I read the instructions one by one as she skillfully combines the ingredients. Together, we create the desserts with precision and artistry, then take a seat at the table.

She takes her first bite, her eyes widening in delight. "These taste divine! Somehow, they're even better than the ones I had at this parlor the other day."

"Exactly! It's not just about the taste; it's about savoring the moment. The fact that we spent time together and prepared these desserts adds to the joy of eating them. So, here's something you should know about me, I value experiences over material possessions."

"I feel the same way. I, too, am an unmaterialistic person," she says, her voice genuine.

But is she really unmaterialistic? Most women claim to be, yet they're often obsessed with clothes and jewelry. I need to find out if she's one of them.

I raise an eyebrow skeptically and ask, "Can you tell me how many pairs of clothes you have in your closet right now?"

She hesitates then mumbles, "Um... maybe more than a hundred."

"I thought you said you were unmaterialistic," I joke, trying to lighten the mood. "Just kidding. I didn't mean to offend you. Sometimes people talk about how they want to be, rather than how they *actually are.*"

"Wow! Thank you for saying that on our first date."

"Sorry, I'm just used to analyzing people. It's a habit I can't seem to break. I'll try to control myself from now on."

I'm certainly not sorry for what I said. Someone had to break it to her at some point.

"Well, I guess you're right. I'm hoping to be more and more simple moving forward. And psychological analysis, you say? I now understand why you're single." She chuckles.

Alright, so she wants to improve herself. That's a positive sign. I can assist her with that. I can burn down half her clothes without hesitation. And she's correct about my penchant for psychological analysis blocking my love life. The real question is, how comfortable is *she* with it?

"Exactly. I've been on dates before, but I've never made it to a second one," I confess.

"I understand why. Women claim they want honesty, but they often hate it when it's given. However, I appreciate honesty. So, yes, I would love to go on a second date with you."

What just happened?

"Wait, did I already ask for one?" I inquire.

"Well, you were contemplating it, so I took the liberty of giving you my answer."

She's my perfect match. I can be myself around her. No other man will ever have a chance with her. I'll make sure of it. She's *mine*.

We continue our conversation, savoring our desserts.

After an hour, I lock up the parlor and drive her back to the apartment. The building looms ahead as I bring the car to a stop. She gazes at me, anticipation clear in her eyes as she waits for a kiss.

We lean in, our lips meeting in a gentle embrace. The taste of her lingers on my tongue, intoxicating and sweet. The kiss deepens, igniting a fire within us both. I can sense her desire, her attraction to me. Slowly, my hand slips beneath her shirt, feeling the softness of her bare skin. She likes the way I touch her.

After a few minutes, we reluctantly pull away, our breaths mingling in the air. Satisfaction and longing fill the space between us.

"Would you like to come inside for coffee?" she invites.

The temptation is strong. Who wouldn't want to continue this passionate encounter? But I want her to yearn for me, to crave my presence. I want to keep the excitement alive, escalating with each date. Plus, having her desire me gives me the upper hand.

In the past, I've never reached this point. Others would bid me goodnight and leave. But tonight, I'm going to deny myself the pleasure of entering her room.

"I really want to," I say regrettably, "but I have a lot of work to do tonight before I can get some sleep. I hope you understand."

A flicker of disappointment crosses her face.

"Well, have a good night," she says, stepping out of the car.

She must be thinking, *What kind of guy prioritizes work over sex?* But this decision sends a message — nothing is more important to me than my work. Lack of efficient work will make me a failure, and that affects my ego, and I can't allow anyone or anything to affect that. Besides, from the very beginning, she needs to learn that I won't bend my schedule just to be with her.

I wave her goodbye and head home, ready to sleep.

12

The next morning, I shoot her a message: "Morning, Erica. I'll swing by tonight at 11:30 for our second date. Sound good?"

She responds: "Morning to you, too. Was hoping to hear something about last night's kiss, but I guess we're diving right into the next date."

Why waste time talking about a kiss? Seems like she's got too many expectations. I'll tune that out eventually.

I reply: "I hope you enjoyed the kiss. Because I sure did. So, where are we with the 11:30 date tonight?"

She texts back: "11:30 at night? Isn't that a bit late? And where are we going?"

"We're going for a drive. 11:30 should work fine. Got a packed schedule before that."

She probes: "Your schedule? I thought you'd be done with the parlor by 9, and there wouldn't be many Uber calls then, right? Or do you have another job?"

Ah, she wants to know my real gig. It'll take a few more dates for her to find that out. Better if she thinks I'm just an Uber driver and waiter.

I reply: "Yup, pretty busy. 11:30 okay?"

"Okay. Works for me."

I make it through the morning, juggling work and driving for Uber. Around three p.m., a message from Erica pops up on my phone. She's planning to visit the parlor today with her friend for some ice cream. Does she really think I'll fall for that? It's obvious she wants to bring someone along to judge me. *Women!*

At four p.m., I start my shift at the ice cream parlor. A couple of hours later, I spot Erica walking in with her friend. The friend has these big, owl-like eyes and a disfigured body. I don't like her at first glance. Or maybe it's just because I suspect she's here to pass judgment on me.

Erica looks at me with a smile and a blush as I approach them. "Good evening."

"Hey, Nolan," Erica says. "I want you to meet my best friend, Abigail."

I smile politely and shake Abigail's hand. She smiles back, but there's something off about it. She gives me a once-over, as if she's already analyzing me.

I lead them to one of the tables and take their orders. When the ice cream is ready, I bring them their desserts. They eat and chat while stealing glances at me. Erica's glances are mostly filled with bashful glances, but Abigail's eyes hold suspicion. Her smile seems fake and her body language looks off. It's clear she's judging me.

Every time I pass by their table, they fall silent and then resume their conversation once I'm out of earshot. I'm dying to know what they're talking about.

Finally, they finish their ice cream and prepare to leave.

"I'll see you tonight," Erica whispers with a lingering grin.

Abigail smiles at me too, saying, "See you around."

Oh, she'll see me around alright. I need to find out what she said to Erica. What kind of doubts did she plant in her mind? I have to dig deeper. If I discover even a hint of suspicion, I'll do whatever it takes to pull Erica away from her. No matter what.

As the clock inches closer to 11:30, I make my way to Erica's apartment and pick her up. The biting cold weather surrounds us, and I can't help but notice that she's not dressed warmly. What is she thinking? Does she believe that wearing extra layers would somehow deter me from undressing her later?

"So, where are we going at this hour?" she asks, her voice filled with curiosity.

I raise an eyebrow and smirk mischievously. "Where do you think we're going?"

Her eyes sparkle with anticipation as she responds, "I don't know... Somewhere cozy?"

Cozy, huh? Ever since I kissed her, she's been yearning to sleep with me. I'll let her *crave* it a little longer.

"Nope. I'll keep it a surprise."

Her smile widens, brimming with excitement as we set off towards the mountains. The drive takes us along winding roads, the darkness of the night enveloping us. After forty-five minutes, Erica breaks the silence.

"Where are we headed? Everything looks so dark, and I'm scared of the dark," she confesses, her tone tinged with genuine fear.

"Don't worry," I assure her, reaching out to hold her trembling hands. "We're almost there." Clearly, she's never experienced the thrill of being atop a mountain after nightfall.

I despise mundane dates. What's the point of simply grabbing coffee, eating, or engaging in constant sex? When the sexual heat fades, people end up fighting until they're divorced. I prefer my dates to be filled with activities and unique experiences.

As we finally reach the summit, I guide the car towards an empty parking lot and turn off the engine. We're the *only* ones here.

Suddenly, Erica's fear intensifies. Her eyes widen with terror, as if she believes I'm about to murder her.

"Just stay in the car for a moment. Come out when I tell you to step outside."

I cautiously step out into the darkness. I quickly set up a foldable bed and cover it with a plush blanket, then I motion for her to join me.

She steps out, her eyes darting around nervously. She hesitates for a moment before finally settling beside me on the bed, seeking comfort in the warmth of the blanket.

"We could have done this at my apartment," she states with a sensuous lull in her voice.

I chuckle softly. "Do you really think I drove all the way here just to sleep with you in a public area? Look up at the sky. Tonight, there's supposed to be high solar activity and a meteor shower. We might even catch a glimpse of the aurora lights. But here's the catch, you have to keep your eyes fixed on the stars."

We both gaze up at the night sky, our eyes adjusting to the darkness. The stars twinkle, creating a breathtaking sight. Gradually, the faint outline of the Milky Way becomes visible, and every few minutes, a meteor streaks across the planet. As the night deepens, we begin to see faint traces of green lights dancing in the sky.

"Thank you for this incredible date," she whispers. "You know, you speak and think differently from most guys I've dated. It's what makes you unique, and I like that about you."

Her words warm my heart, and I hold her tightly, savoring the moment. I'm loving this, especially now that I know she likes me for who I truly am.

Without realizing, the clock strikes two a.m., and my pocket erupts with the shrill sound of my alarm.

"Alright, as much as I wish we could stay longer, I have to wake up early for work," I say, "so let's head back."

She clings to me, refusing to let go of the moment. "Please, just a little while longer."

"I wish, too. But I can't afford to be late for work."

"Alright," she relents with a sigh.

We get back into the car. I can see the joy in her eyes; she truly enjoyed our time together. Despite the absence of any intimacy, she had a great evening. I think for the first time I felt a little pinch in my heart when she looked a bit disappointed that we had to leave. It doesn't sway my decision, though, as work always takes precedence. Yet, a small sense of remorse lingers within me for causing her disappointment.

This is a new sensation for me. Perhaps I'm starting to *care* about her feelings. That's the only explanation.

As we drive back, she grabs my hand and holds it tightly against her chest. The touch sends a thrill through me. She likes me!

"Can I ask you something?"

"Go ahead."

"You always talk about work and seem so disciplined. You're just an Uber driver in the morning and a waiter in the evening, right?"

She wants to investigate me at this amazing and peaceful moment? It must be her friend Abigail. She must have encouraged her to probe into me.

"Tell your friend Abigail that this question is offensive," I respond, frustration creeping into my voice. "Drivers and waiters can be disciplined, too."

"What? Abigail?" she asks, her eyes widening in surprise. "What does Abbey have to do with anything?"

"It's her, isn't it? She asked you to find out about me. Tell me I'm wrong."

"Sure, you're wrong," she says, releasing my hand.

Damn! I need to apologize now?

"I'm sorry. Your friend was giving me weird looks today, and I thought she made you probe into me."

"That's not true. Abbey really liked you," she says, her tone softening. "She was saying that you look handsome, and you were respectful when serving us."

Huh! She liked me. Maybe she wasn't that bad.

I can probably spill a little truth to Erica about my work.

"I work these service-based jobs to understand customer psychology. It helps me excel in my actual job."

"Okay, what's your actual job?"

"I'd rather not say right now," I reply cautiously. "I need some time to deepen our relationship before sharing that. Can we please let this go?"

"Are you a drug dealer?"

"No."

"Are you a smuggler?"

"No."

"Does it have anything to do with illegal activities?"

"No."

"Alright, I can let this go for now," she says and holds my hand again.

I drop her off and kiss her goodnight.

13

Months slip away like shadows as we rendezvous each evening, delving deeper into the depths of one another's souls. It seems that I'm the one unraveling her secrets, peeling back the layers of her existence. I subject her to a battery of tests, probing her honesty, her aspirations, her core beliefs, her ties to family, and more.

Remarkably, she passes each and every one of my checklists, ticking off the boxes with a grace that leaves me in awe. Well, perhaps not every box, but close enough.

She's not only a remarkable human being, but I can envision her as a phenomenal mother as well. I always try to tackle some of the world's biggest problems, and she's always into keeping a calm, serene, and stress-free life. We kind of complement each other in that aspect.

Erica has captured my heart, and I'm going to take our relationship to the next level.

Today is February 24, 2023, her birthday. It's the perfect day to finally confess the truth. As the sun begins to rise, I send her a simple text: "Good morning, dear. Any plans after work?"

She quickly responds: "Nope, nothing. What are you thinking?"

With a surge of excitement, I propose my plan: "Nothing too crazy. I'll swing by your office after work, and we can head to my place. We need to talk."

There's a delay before her response comes through: "A hmm... Okay."

I can't help but wonder how she'll react when I reveal everything. Will she be shocked? Excited? Maybe she's been wondering about the meaning behind those four words "We need to talk."

I cancel my Uber pickups for the day and call in sick at the ice cream parlor. I clean my cozy one-bedroom apartment, adding some smart lights to create a better atmosphere.

I'm not sure why I'm nervous about sharing the truth. Usually, I don't give a *damn* about what other people feel. Erica has somehow managed to impact my emotional strength.

Until now, the only thing which gave me happiness was my work. My own happiness now seems to depend on hers. I'm not sure if that's a good thing, but I fear the day when I'll have to choose between my work and her. How will that affect my mental stability? I can't afford to give up either one.

As the clock approaches five p.m., the moment of truth draws near. This is it.

I pull up to the administrative building, my heart pounding in my chest. She climbs into the car, her eyes darting around nervously. She casually takes my hands in hers, tapping her feet anxiously. Her nails are bitten down to the quick, and her whole body is fidgety. I can't help but wonder why she's so on edge. After all, I'm the one who's bursting a bubble; I'm the one who needs to be anxious. Or maybe the serious tone of my message makes her think I'm about to end things. I'm overthinking it. For the first time in my life, I spent an entire day thinking about another human instead of my work and vision.

It's okay. I'll return to my usual self soon enough.

"What do you feel like having for dinner?" I ask, trying to lighten the mood. "Depending on your answer, we might need to swing by the store for some groceries."

"Anything you already have at home is fine," she replies, her words rushed. "Let's skip the shopping for now."

Oh boy, she's in even more of a hurry than I am.

I nod in agreement and steer the car towards my home, the weight of the evening settling heavily upon us.

We step into the house, finding our way to the couch. She glances around the apartment and remarks, "Looks like you've tidied up."

"Yeah, the whole place was a mess, and the stench —"

"Okay, I can't hold it in any longer. What did you mean by 'we need to talk'? Are you breaking up with me? What did I do wrong? I've always treated you with respect, adjusted to your work schedule, and never pried into your personal life because I know you hate discussing it. I never..." Her words rush out in a torrent.

"Honey, honey, calm down," I interject, trying to soothe her. She takes a deep breath and grasps my hands, her eyes searching mine.

"Well, there are two things I need to confess today. Let's start with the simpler one," I say, my voice steady. "I've been keeping my career details a secret from you for the past several months. I prefer to keep it anonymous to most people."

"Nolan, please tell me that you're not involved in anything illegal."

I shake my head, a small smile playing on my lips. "Far from it," I reply. "My full name is Andrew Nolan *Kash*. I'm the co-founder and chairman of Wise AI career solutions. You and most of the people in this community actually work for me. I keep my identity hidden so that I can live a normal life among everyone else. It allows me to observe and gather feedback from the people who work for my company. I drive taxis exclusively for my employees, studying their body language as they commute to work. I observe if they're going to work with excitement or with stress. I also wait tables at ice cream parlors, analyzing people's reactions to customer service. All these experiences help me improve my company. Even my employees are unaware of my true identity. They only hear from my father, Michael Kash, who manages the company's operations, or the C.E.O. who reports directly to me. I've kept this secret from you for a long time, but today, I feel ready to confess."

She stares at me, her eyes wide with shock. I know she must have countless questions swirling in her mind, but for now, I'll let the weight of my revelation sink in.

A few minutes pass as she keeps silent.

"Erica, are you still here? Can you say something? I know you must have a million questions, and I'm ready to answer them all. I hope you understand why I kept this from you."

"Wow! This is not what I expected today. I have so many questions, but the one that matters most is why you kept it a secret from me."

"I had to," I reply, my voice steady and unapologetic. "Through my journey of building this company, I've learned a lot about people. I've witnessed how they treat me differently when they know about my wealth. I didn't want that to taint our relationship. So, I let you believe I was just a waiter. And honestly, it made me happy to see that you didn't care about material possessions when it came to love."

"I get it. It's so rare to find someone who is truly authentic these days. Everyone is so busy trying to impress each other with their accomplishments. But you... you kept your greatest achievement hidden just to find a real connection. That makes me incredibly happy."

She hugs me tightly, her smile radiating warmth and understanding.

"I'm grateful that you feel the same way," I say. "Given my circumstances, it's crucial for me to grasp human psychology. So, I'd prefer to keep this between us, a secret shared by only a select few in my life. If you choose to share with anyone, make sure they're trustworthy and won't spill these details elsewhere."

"Absolutely," she assures me. "I do have many questions, but knowing the answers won't change how I feel about you.

Today, you've opened up to me, revealing your deepest secret, and it has brought us closer."

"There's something else I need to confess," I say. "As I mentioned, I started with a simpler secret."

"Simpler? That revelation sent shockwaves through me, mister. What could possibly top that?" Her eyes widen with intrigue.

Here it comes!

Swiftly, I retrieve my phone, unlocking it with a swipe. With a single tap, the room transforms before our eyes. The lighting shifts, casting a soft, sun-kissed glow. Artificial candles flicker to life on the floating shelves, and gentle bossa nova starts playing from the speakers embedded in the walls, creating a romantic ambiance.

I reach into my pocket, my fingers trembling as I retrieve a small box. With a deep breath, I lower myself to one knee, the weight of the moment heavy in the air. Slowly, I open the box, revealing a sparkling ring with a diamond at its center surrounded by delicate sapphire crystals. They glisten like vanilla ice cream atop a rich chocolate cake, a sweet reminder of the first dessert we shared on our first date. Engraved on the ring are the words "The moment we remember."

I lift my gaze to meet Erica's eyes. "Erica, my love," I begin, my voice filled with a mix of nerves and excitement. "Will you marry me?"

Her expression is one of shock, but beneath it, I can see a radiant joy shining through. Tears well up in her eyes as I continue, my words pouring forth. "I know this may seem sudden, and I understand that most people prefer a longer process before making such a decision, but the connection we've forged in these past few months is unlike anything I've ever experienced. It's a bond that others might take years to cultivate. And it's not just about time, it's about how we see the world, how our fundamental principles align. That's what truly matters to me.

"We don't need to spend more time dating, going through the motions like everyone else. I believe we already know each other deeply enough to make this decision. I'm asking you to stand by my side, to face whatever challenges come our way until the end of time. I promise to be there for you, no matter what hurdles we encounter."

I *mean* every word of my statement. There's no point wasting time with dating and flirting or whatever crap other people do. I have better things to do with my life. I need to start many more companies, and I can't do it if my mind is focused on dating apps and casual relationships. Might as well get married and focus on my vision.

"So, Erica," I ask once more, my voice laced with hope and love, "will you marry me?"

Her tear-filled eyes glisten as she nods and softly murmurs a "yes," embracing me tightly with overwhelming joy. We linger in each other's embrace before settling onto the couch, our hands intertwined.

"I'll have to share the news with Abbey today before she kills me," she says. "She's been part of my journey since our childhood friendship began. After that, I can share with my dad."

We enjoy dinner together before I drop her off at Abigail's apartment. As I make my way back home, I decide to call my parents and share the incredible news. My mom's happiness radiates through the phone, but my dad's response carries a hint of concern.

"Are you sure you're ready to take care of someone else? Isn't this moving too fast? You're always so focused on your work that you neglect everything else," he says.

I sometimes feel so angry at him that I want to stab him. But I suppress it, knowing that he plays a crucial role in managing my company's operations. Does he truly think I'm narcissistic? Doesn't every man prioritize his work over family? I love Erica. This is the farthest I've ever come in a relationship, and it frustrates me to know that I don't receive any appreciation for it from my parents.

I message Erica, eager to know what Abigail, her dad, and her brother think about our engagement. "Hey, how did Abigail and your family react to our engagement?"

Erica responds: "Hello, fiancé. I just shared the news with them, and they all want to meet you."

Curiosity piqued, I ask for more details: "Tell me the specifics of their reactions."

"Well, Abbey was overjoyed. She wants to meet you and your friends at the ice cream parlor tomorrow to celebrate. My dad gave his blessing, but he had the typical dad reaction. He's happy, though."

"A typical dad reaction? Can you tell me *exactly* what he said?"

Erica replies: "Alright, I'll tell you, but don't take this personally. At the end of the day, he wants both of us to make a thoughtful decision. He thinks your busy schedule as an entrepreneur might stress me out. My dad hates to see me stressed."

What kind of moron gets unhappy to wed his daughter to a billionaire? I have all the money needed for multiple generations, and he thinks that's not going to keep his daughter happy? No wonder he's just a barber at a mediocre salon.

My irritation seeps into my fingers as I text back: "So, does he not approve of our marriage?"

Erica reassures me: "Of course, he does. He just wants us to take our time and think things through before rushing into anything. Don't worry about it. We have his blessing."

Blessing? That's not enough. I need an apology from him for doubting my ability to keep his daughter happy. I'll prove him wrong. In today's world, it's easy to manipulate people's perceptions. I'll take Erica on a vacation, post some smiling pictures, and make him eat his words. Weak minds are easily swayed. I'll make sure he apologizes, along with my own father.

I message: "Let's meet Abigail after work tomorrow at the restaurant." And I throw in a smiling emoji with it.

14

The following evening, I make preparations to meet Erica and Abigail at the restaurant. I come accompanied by Kevin. He deserves to be there, especially after suggesting the idea of an ice-cream-shaped ring. I didn't really care about the proposal methods, but I suppose that's what assistants are for. Well, technically he's my friend, but I prefer him in the role of an assistant. That way he's solely focused on serving me without any expectations of a return.

We arrive at the restaurant and make our way to a secluded corner reserved for private parties. I introduce Kevin to Erica and Abigail, and we all settle in.

"Before we dive into conversation," Abigail begins, "I want to get to know Nolan better. After all, he's going to marry my best friend. I've come prepared with a list of questions."

Kevin immediately responds, "I'll make sure Nolan tells the truth. On one condition: For every question you ask, Erica has to answer one as well."

"Deal," Abigail says, turning to Erica with an ornery smile.

Erica gives Abigail a look. "Sure. Just make sure your questions are simple, or I might have to kill you."

Abigail starts off with a simple question, "What's the funniest thing you did as a kid?"

Kevin speaks up before I can answer. "That's a bit of a snoozer. I thought there would be some spicy questions."

"Don't worry, there are spicy questions coming up. I just wanted to start with something easy." Abigail turns to me, waiting for my answer.

"Alright, I have to admit, I'm not proud of this," I begin, though deep down I am.

"When I was seven, I had a scalp issue that caused constant peeling. My dad took me to a dermatologist, and she prescribed a medication that needed to be applied directly to my scalp. Despite my pleas, my dad decided to shave my head to make the application easier. The next day at school, Kevin started mocking my new look, proudly flaunting his own hair. Anger surged through me, and during class, I discreetly used a spoon to unscrew a blade from a pencil sharpener. With careful precision, I shaved a small section of Kevin's head without him noticing. It looked so bizarre that his dad took him to a salon that evening to get his head completely shaved. It was absolutely hilarious."

Kevin shoots me an angry glare and silently mouths, "I hate you." He turns to Erica. "It's your turn, Erica. What's the funniest thing you did as a kid?"

Erica's eyes drift away from us as though she's slipping into a nostalgic flashback. "Oh, there are so many memories. But one stands out in particular. When I was young and Vincent was just a toddler, my mom was ironing clothes on the floor instead of using an ironing board. She had to quickly dash to the kitchen, leaving the iron unattended. Before she left, she warned me, 'Hey, Erica, keep an eye on Vincent. He might crawl towards the iron. It's scorching hot.' Well, when she returned, she found Vincent crying, his tiny fingers burnt from touching the iron. She scooped him up, soothing his pain. Frustrated, she turned to me and asked, 'What on earth, Erica? I asked you to watch your brother.' Innocently, I replied, 'But Mommy, I was watching him just like you told me to.' That incident still brings a smile to my face. Poor Vincent. He still has the burn marks on his fingers to this day."

"The fact that you both find shaving and burning incidents funny makes me wonder if you're two psychopaths in love," Abigail says. "I suppose it's a perfect example of what makes you the ideal couple."

Erica chuckles, her eyes sparkling with affection. "Thank you, Abbey! We truly are the best couple." She reaches out to hold my hand. Why do women behave like this in front of a group? So *cheesy*!

"Next question," Abigail says, turning to me. "Tell me about your most memorable breakup."

"To be honest, I've never been in a relationship before Erica," I say. "I'd never met a good woman who's worthy of a second date. And the one I did meet, I'm marrying her now. There were situations where I left my first date halfway through the dinner ."

"Woah! Sounds brutal," says Abigail. "Give us an example."

I guess I should avoid the example of leaving because the woman was fat and eating like a pig.

"Well, there was this woman who couldn't stop taking selfies from the moment our date started. I couldn't handle it anymore, so I snuck out to the restroom and never came back. And I don't regret it one bit."

"Wow," Abigail says, intrigued. She then gestures for Erica to share her story.

"I haven't dated many men," Erica says, "but if I had to choose a memorable breakup, it would be with this guy who was always trying too hard to please me. He was so vulnerable, desperate, and pathetic. One time, I casually mentioned that I wished I had a sister to talk about girly stuff with. The next day, he showed up to our dinner date dressed as a woman, makeup and all. When I asked him what on earth he was doing, he said he wanted to be identified as a woman for the evening so we could talk about girly stuff. It was incredibly awkward, and I immediately dumped him and ran out of the restaurant."

"Wow! So, you both have had your fair share of weirdos," Abigail remarks. "I guess that's another reason why you two belong together. Now, let's get a little more serious. Nolan, tell me why you like Erica."

Ah, there it is. She finally gets to the question she's been leading up to. She's a so-called "protective" friend.

People eat up all the cheesy, overly optimistic crap as answers to that question. It's almost too easy to feed it to them.

"Honestly, I can't pinpoint why I'm drawn to Erica. But if there's anyone who can understand my madness, it's her."

Abigail coos, "Awww, that's so sweet."

Just as I expected.

"I agree with Nolan," Erica chimes in. "It's not about reasons, it's about being like-minded. But what truly captivates me is his vision for society, his unwavering determination, and his refusal to give up. Those qualities show his commitment, and that means more to me than anything."

She's right. I'm tenacious, and I'd do anything to get what I want.

"I thought you two were rushing into this," Abigail says, "but after our conversation today, I'm convinced you're a match made in heaven!" She raises her glass and declares, "A toast to the newly engaged couple!"

Kevin and I follow suit, clinking our glasses together in a joyous chorus.

Abigail adds, "Let's celebrate this special occasion with a scoop of vanilla ice cream and a slice of hot chocolate cake!"

We spend the next hour trading stories and laughing over shared memories.

15

The next day, Erica and I hit the road, the sun casting a dazzling reflection on the car's hood as we speed towards my parents' house.

Upon arrival, I spot my parents eagerly waiting on the front porch, their anticipation palpable. My father Mike, usually a sharp-dressed man in his suit, now dons a casual ensemble of a loose-fitting t-shirt, lounge pants, slippers, and a round hat perched on his bald head. My mother, Vivian, radiates warmth in her pink shirt, beige jeans, and the golden bracelet adorning her wrists. Her short, curled hair frames her high cheekbones. Her face is aglow with a touch of makeup and the sheer delight of meeting her future daughter-in-law. She approaches Erica and envelopes her in a warm, welcoming hug.

With a smile, Erica responds, "I'm thrilled to see you both."

We settle into the cozy living room, immersing ourselves in nostalgic conversations about my childhood. We pour over old photographs and watch cherished home videos, reliving the days gone by.

As lunchtime arrives, we continue our lively chatter, and I observe Erica growing more at ease with my family, seamlessly blending into our dynamic.

After lunch, my dad suggests, "Nolan, why don't you lend your mother a hand with the dishes while I take Erica for a stroll through the garden? I'd like to share some wisdom on how to handle you once you're married."

"Handle me?" I retort, raising an eyebrow. "I'm not some machine in need of handling."

He chuckles and says, "I just want to enjoy a pleasant walk with my future daughter-in-law." They both disappear into the garden, leaving me with a sense of unease.

I always knew moments like these would arise. As a business owner, I've developed a covert system to eavesdrop on conversations of my employees and detect any disloyalty towards my company. By manipulating the C.E.O., my puppet, I ensure that those who speak against the company are fired under legitimate pretenses.

Even before considering marriage or proposing to Erica, I foresaw scenarios where my family would talk about me behind my back. To maintain control, I planted a bug in Erica's phone that I can activate from my own device, granting me access to her conversations whenever I please. It's a way for me to safeguard our relationship and manipulate her if necessary, all for the sake of our healthy future.

Who knows? Maybe someone will try to talk her into something which might affect my life, or worse, my company.

I activate the bug, which activates Erica's mobile microphone. I slip on my ear pods and begin tidying the kitchen, my focus fixed on the conversation between my dad and my future wife.

"It's a lovely garden, sir," Erica says.

"Sir? You can call me Dad now," he replies.

"So, you were telling me something about Nolan?" she asks.

"Yes, I was. Just a heads up. Nolan is a nice man and is incredibly hardworking, but there's one thing you should know about him, he's a career chaser. He's made countless sacrifices to build his company from the ground up. When his career is at stake, he becomes ruthless and detached from his family. I'll give you an example. During the early stages of his company, his mother had a fatal accident and was hospitalized. Instead of visiting her, he chose to meet with an investor. I know it sounds cold, but that's just Nolan. If his dreams are in jeopardy, he can be difficult to handle. I don't mean to scare you, but it's important you understand his career-driven nature."

Is he kidding me? I *knew* he'd try to freak her out. I'm not sure what's a big deal in that situation. It's not like my mom was going to die, she just had an accident. But if that investor meeting had been canceled, it would have set my company back by years. How can my dad be so inconsiderate?

"I getting a sense of déjà vu, as my father gave me a similar warning," she says. "And I'll tell you what I told him: I love Nolan deeply, and I want to be the backbone to his dreams. If he reaches a point where he can't be there for the family because he's focused on securing the company's success, I'm willing to make that sacrifice. Many entrepreneurs struggle to balance their personal and professional lives, and I'm willing to provide Nolan with a peaceful home so he can conquer his battles."

That's my girl. Now that's how you give a fitting response. It's funny how she believes she can be the backbone of my dreams, but I'm thrilled by her sacrificing nature.

"I hope everything will be fine, dear," he says, his voice dripping with false sincerity. "Welcome to the family."

They walk back inside, and I swiftly remove my ear pods.

"So, what did you two chat about?" I inquire, trying to sound casual.

His response is nonchalant. "Oh, just our family history and ancestors."

What a *fucking liar*!

We spend the next couple of hours engaged in superficial chatter about wedding plans, the gathering of friends and family, and the guest list.

As the afternoon starts to fade, Erica and I set off for Lake Town, an hour east of Portland — to meet Erica's father and brother.

When we arrive at Erica's home, Myles and Vincent are waiting for us at the gate. Before the car even comes to a complete stop, Erica leaps out and rushes to hug her dad, pointing towards me for an introduction.

"Dad, this is Nolan, my fiancé," she announces.

Myles, dressed in a simple shirt and cotton pants and sporting a well-groomed French beard, looks like the epitome of a perfect barber. He smiles warmly at me and extends his hand. "Welcome, son. It's a pleasure to finally meet you."

We spend the evening at his house, enjoying a pleasant dinner. As Erica and Vincent busy themselves with cleaning the kitchen, I find myself drawn to explore Myles' two-bedroom ranch home. Myles notices my curiosity and leads me towards a small library.

I scan the shelves, taking in the vast collection of books. Myles breaks the silence, his voice filled with a hint of nostalgia. "Erica used to be a bookworm," he says. "This room was her sanctuary during her difficult childhood. It's hard to believe she's getting married now. In my eyes, she'll always be that innocent little girl who's kind to everyone she meets."

Oh god, here it comes — the "father of the bride" talk. I brace myself. "She's a wonderful woman," I reply diplomatically. "I couldn't be happier to marry Erica, and my parents are thrilled to welcome her into our family."

Myles nods, his gratitude evident in his eyes. "Thank you, son. Erica is one of the most sensitive people I've ever known. She endured so much as a child, and I wish I could have done more to ease her pain, especially after her mother, Sarah, passed away."

I guess now I need to ask him what she went through. I know her mother died, but it was a long time ago. Why is he crying about it now? I hope Erica has moved on.

His voice is filled with a mix of anger and sadness as he continues. "In this room, she would always be lost in her books, never making any friends from school. Sarah and I thought it was time for her to socialize, to find companionship. That's when we heard about Chloe, a private tutor who ran an in-home learning center in our town. It seemed like the perfect opportunity for Erica to meet other kids her age and maybe make some friends.

"Little did we know the horrors that awaited her behind those closed doors. Chloe, it turned out, was a twisted egomaniac who took pleasure in inflicting physical pain on children who didn't meet her expectations. She would strip them naked and subject them to public humiliation. It was a sickening display of power that fed her twisted ego.

"Erica, always the quiet one, never spoke of her troubles at that center. She would come home with fear in her eyes, but we had no idea what she was enduring.

"One day, all the kids at the center completed their homework, and it infuriated Chloe. She couldn't stand the fact that her students were excelling, so she assigned them an impossible task. Erica locked herself in her room and toiled away on the assignment throughout the night.

"The next day, when Erica returned to Chloe, some of the other kids hadn't finished the assignment. That's when Chloe's true sadistic nature emerged. She tied those poor children to chairs and applied a highly concentrated vapor rub to their eyes. Their screams echoed through the room as Chloe laughed, reveling in their pain. She warned them not to tell their parents, threatening even worse punishments if they dared to speak up. The physical assaults continued, leaving scars both seen and unseen.

"Though Erica herself was never subjected to the same physical torture, she witnessed these horrors for years, her young mind scarred by the brutality she was exposed to. It made her sensitive, anxious, always on edge.

"One day, Chloe's drunken rage went too far. She ended up murdering her daughter, Erica's friend. The truth finally came to light, and Chloe was sentenced to life in prison. Erica, at such a tender age, bravely testified in court, ensuring that the jury understood the true monster Chloe was.

"Less than a week later, Erica's world shattered once again. Her mom died in a devastating car accident. That stressed her out to an extreme and..." Myles hesitates, wiping his mouth.

"And then what happened?" I press, knowing there's obviously more to the story.

"The bullying," he finally admits, his voice filled with pain. "It intensified at school, tormenting her relentlessly."

"What kind of bullying?" I inquire, needing to understand the depths of her suffering.

Tears well up in Myles' eyes. "The wealthy kids, they targeted her emotionally," he reveals with a trembling voice. "They reveled in her pain. They would bring pictures of their own mothers, taunting Erica with the love and support she had lost. They tore at her heart, piece by piece, every single day. When she cried for her mother, they laughed, cruelly suggesting that Sarah had intentionally caused the accident so she could get away from Erica. This torment continued for years, and she kept it all hidden, shielding me from her pain."

"Why didn't you do something about those bullies?" I demand, my anger rising.

"I had no idea what she was going through at school," he confesses. "She only shared these horrors with me after she graduated high school. She didn't want to burden me further, not after losing Sarah. So, she suffered in silence, carrying the weight of their cruelty alone."

"And? You just let it go once you found out the truth? Why didn't you take legal action or try to track them down?"

"I'm just a barber, Nolan. I barely make enough to put food on the table and provide for my kids' education. I did everything I could to step into the role of both mother and father. I learned to keep my head down and keep moving forward."

Like a coward! If I were in his shoes, I would never give up. Surrendering means admitting defeat, and I refuse to accept defeat. I am not Myles, and I never will be.

"I know what you're thinking," he says. "You believe you could have done better. But in my situation, I lost a family member, and I couldn't afford to lose another one in a quest for revenge against a bunch of bullies. So, from my perspective, I made sure to never give a stressful life to Erica."

"Why didn't Erica share these with me?"

"She never will," he replies. "She's put it all behind her. It's been over a decade since she faced any pain. I made sure to shield her from it all, and I don't regret it. Bringing up those memories would only add to her stress. And..."

He pauses again, his eyes darting away.

"And?" I press, my voice filled with anticipation of what else he's hiding.

"Nothing," he says, his tone guarded. "That's all I wanted to share."

"Well, if you believe she'll never open up to me and you don't want to remind her of those events, then why did you tell me?" I question, a touch of frustration creeping into my voice. "I had no clue about any of this, and maybe it was better that way."

"I understand," he says. "When she mentioned marrying an entrepreneur, I couldn't help but worry that her life might become stressful one day. I wanted you to know the hardships she endured as a child, hoping that her married life would be different. I'm proud of your accomplishments and dreams. All I ask is that you give her a life free from stress."

What an *absolute* coward! Instead of facing Erica's problems head-on and finding solutions, he chose to run away. And now he expects me to follow in his footsteps? I want to challenge his request, but there's no use arguing with an old man who lacks vision and courage.

"I promise you," I declare firmly, " Erica's married life will shine brighter than her troubled childhood. I will make her a strong and resilient woman."

"Thank you, son," he says. "Those words mean the world to a father giving his daughter away."

As Erica enters the room, she signals that it's time to leave. We exchange farewells with Myles and Vincent before driving back to Portland. We reach home and snuggle up in bed.

"So, did you enjoy spending time with my family? What did you and my dad talk about for so long?" she inquires, her eyes filled with curiosity.

A strong urge to spill everything overwhelms me, fueled by Myles' warning to keep quiet. But if she's going to start weeping now for losing her mother and some kids bullying, I'd lose my sleep and my morning meetings would be affected.

"Of course, I had a great time with your family." I choose my words carefully. "We mostly discussed my company, politics, and the stock market. Just your typical man-to-man conversation."

Her eyes search mine, hoping for a different answer. "Nothing about the wedding?"

I shake my head. "Nope, nothing at all."

"No worries," she murmurs, snuggling closer to my chest. "You focus on your work, and I'll take care of the wedding preparations."

She clings to me, her grip firm at first then loosening as her breath evens out and she falls asleep.

16

A week before our wedding, on March 16, 2023, I arrange a fancy dinner party at a luxurious resort. The place is stunning, with beautiful gardens and the finest cuisine the Pacific Northwest has to offer. Both our families and some of our closest friends are gathered here, ready to celebrate our upcoming nuptials in style.

I wanted to plan this evening ahead of the wedding to silence all those people who criticized us for rushing into the engagement after only a few months of dating. I know how much everyone loves a great speech, and lucky for them, I happen to be pretty good at delivering them.

I stand up, holding a glass in my hand, and everyone taps their spoons against their wine glasses as a sign of attention.

"I am incredibly grateful to have found Erica," I begin. "We may have only known each other for a few months, but the connection between us is so strong that we've decided to take the next step and get married.

"I want to share a story with all of you about our relationship. I was scared to reveal my profession and wealth to Erica, but she never cared about any of it. She loves me for who I am and treats me the same, whether I'm a taxi driver or something else entirely. She's down to earth and one of the sweetest people I know.

"I was also worried about how her family and friends would react, but meeting all of you has been a relief. Bringing our two families together has been a blessing. I know some of you were concerned about my work-life balance and how it would fare after the wedding. Well, let me tell you, if there's one thing I'm willing to sacrifice for love, it's my work — my dreams, my vision. Erica means everything to me." I raise my glass and say, "To my love, Erica, and the new bond between our families."

Everyone shouts "cheers!" and takes a sip of their wine.

I smile at them and remain standing to observe their miserable faces. It's amazing how people will believe anything as long as it's said with confidence.

We spend the rest of the evening discussing the grand wedding that awaits us in just one week's time.

17

March 23, 2023

My wedding day has finally arrived. I relinquish all control of the preparations to Kevin, Abigail, and Erica. I couldn't care less about the meticulous planning of the wedding. But this is all for Erica. I'm more than willing to write a blank check to ensure her happiness.

Family and friends flock to the picturesque resort, ready to witness the union of two hearts.

The open-air wedding arena is a large space surrounded by evergreen trees, their branches glistening in the bright sunlight. Freshly cut grass carpets the arena and water droplets twinkle in the light. The boundaries are filled with lilies, roses, and orchids, while artificial fountain vases are scattered throughout. A red carpet leads to the center stage where the ceremony will be performed. The white center stage is covered with red rose petals, and a stone arch is draped with lush creepers and fragrant flowers.

The guests glide to their seats on either side of the aisle, marveling at the exquisite decorations and the breathtaking setting. A gentle piano melody creates a serene ambiance.

I stand on the stage, side by side with Kevin, my best man. My heart pounds as Myles escorts Erica down the aisle, a rush of adrenaline coursing through me. It's a feeling I've never experienced before, a mix of excitement and awe.

Erica's beauty takes my breath away. Her white gown is a masterpiece adorned with intricate lacework and a flowing train. The setting sun casts a soft glow on her, making her look ethereal. I can't help but marvel at her radiance. As she approaches me, our eyes lock, and I can sense the emotions swirling within her.

Our vows are spoken with sincerity, promising to weather any storm that comes our way. I truly *mean* every word. Taking her delicate hand in mine, I slide the ring onto her finger, sealing our commitment. As the ceremony draws to a close, we share our first kiss as husband and wife, igniting a wave of cheers from our loved ones. Hand in hand, we walk down the aisle, a cascade of rose petals showering us with blessings.

As the night comes to an end, we step into a vintage car, stealing one last glance at the unforgettable day we shared.

As a newlywed couple, we enter a hotel room with overwhelming emotions. The honeymoon suite is tastefully appointed, with warm caramel-hued lighting, a comfortable temperature, and a bottle of wine waiting for us in the room.

We lay down together, cuddling and whispering sweet nothings to each other. We've had sex in the past few months but this time, it feels different. I truly feel that she's *mine*. I typically don't believe in the concept of marriage, but now that I'm married and in bed beside my wife, I feel closer to her than ever before.

We make love with a tenderness and intensity that only comes from a deep connection. We blissfully collapse in each other's arms and slowly doze off. My arms remain wrapped around her the entire night, absorbing the warmth of our naked bodies.

***

As the morning alarm buzzes, I slowly open my eyes and find her romantically staring at me.

"Good morning, wifey," I say, my voice filled with genuine happiness. "Waking up next to you is the best way to start the day."

A smile tugs at the corners of her lips. "You better get used to it," she replies playfully. "We have a lifetime of mornings like this ahead of us."

I draw her closer, unable to resist the magnetic pull between us. Our lips meet in a tender kiss.

"These moments with you are divine," I murmur with a heart swollen with love. "I hope we remember this feeling until the end of our days."

She nestles her head against my chest, her warmth seeping into my skin. "I wish we could stay here forever," she whispers dreamily.

"Well, we have a flight to catch in three hours."

"Flight? What flight?"

"Don't you think I planned for our honeymoon? You signed up for life to be a roller coaster, so be ready."

Her eyes sparkle with eagerness as she eagerly asks, "Where are we going?"

"It's a surprise. But I promise you, it'll be a journey you'll never forget."

"Sure, I'll know where we're going when we take our boarding pass at the airport."

"Good luck with that. We're taking my private jet for our honeymoon."

"You have a private jet?" she exclaims, her eyes widening in disbelief.

I chuckle, relishing her astonishment. "Of course, I do."

Why would I be kidding? I'm a billionaire! I don't go out on vacation on an economy flight, checking in for my boarding pass one day ahead so I can get a better seat and waiting in line alongside a bunch of losers.

Besides, this trip is more than just a luxurious getaway. It's a statement, a way to *prove* to our fathers that our love is real, that I'm capable of caring for Erica. And when they see us happy and united, their judgment will crumble before them.

We freshen up, devour our breakfast, and stride out of the hotel. A sleek limousine glides up to us, the driver unlocking the door with a flourish. I step forward, bowing deeply as I open the door for Erica.

"Your chariot awaits, your highness," I say with a smile, guiding her into the lap of luxury. The limousine whisks us away to the airport where my private jet awaits.

I love my jet. Not only for its comfort but also for the custom office cubicle nestled inside. It allows me to work undisturbed while on the move. However, today is different. Erica and I plan to snuggle on the expandable bed while gazing at the awe-inspiring views through the window.

Forests and oceans pass by, captivating my attention. Yet, each time I ask Erica to view the planet below, she clings to my hands tighter. Surprisingly, this enhances our journey. Whenever her fear of heights surfaces, I hold her close, providing a sense of security that grants me a sense of control.

We relish the exquisite food served by my crew, but Erica can't help but speculate about our destination.

As the sun dips below the horizon, the plane begins its descent, shrouding the sky in darkness. The pilot announces our imminent arrival, and Erica prepares herself to uncover our whereabouts. Obviously, I've instructed the pilots to refrain from disclosing our destination.

The aircraft touches down and the crew opens the door, allowing us to step out into the night. Erica scans her surroundings, searching for any clue that might reveal our location, but I shake my head.

"You won't find any sign indicating our whereabouts," I inform her. "I'll reveal it to you in the morning."

She pouts, but deep down, I know she's bubbling with excitement for the morning.

We make our way to a cozy cottage, get naked, and sleep.

18

As the sun rises, Erica awakens with an excitement to step outside onto the balcony to find out where we are. She slips out of bed and reaches for her robe, but I swiftly snatch it away.

"Give me my robe!"

I hold the robe tighter, a mischievous smile playing on my lips.

"You don't need clothes to step out," I tease. "You can venture out naked."

Erica's eyes widen in disbelief. "Are you crazy? Why would you suggest that? What if someone sees me?"

"Don't worry, there's no one around to look."

"Alright." She slowly opens the balcony door and steps outside. A few seconds pass and then I hear a triumphant "woohoo" echoing from the balcony.

I get off the bed and walk towards balcony. The sun makes her skin shine like gold. I hug her from behind to soak in the heat of her skin and kiss her on the neck.

"We're on a private Hawaiian island in the Pacific Ocean," I say. "I wanted to fulfill one of your bucket list items for our honeymoon."

Erica's delight bubbles over and she turns around to give me a tight hug.

"I can't believe we're on a private island! Is this really happening? Are we really going scuba diving?"

"Yes, dear. We're scuba diving today. We'll be able to see turtles, mantas, and all kinds of colorful fish sixty feet down in the ocean."

She starts kissing all over my face with a sudden rush of excitement, and we make love on the balcony.

Before losing all our energy, we head back into the cottage and start dressing for the dive.

In no time, the diving crew arrives, whisking us away to the port. We eagerly step onto the yacht, ready to embark on our thrilling journey into the vast expanse of the open sea. Equipped with cameras, Erica and I plunge into the depths and find ourselves surrounded by a mesmerizing world of coral reefs and a dazzling array of marine life.

As we explore, we encounter a multitude of tropical fish, graceful sea turtles, playful dolphins, and majestic mantas. We glide through the intricate cave formations adorned with vibrant starfish. The tranquility of the underwater realm envelops us and we savor every moment.

Returning to the yacht, a sense of relaxation and accomplishment washes over us. She turns to me, a smile lighting up her face, and says, "Thank you for this incredible surprise. I'm feeling a mix of emotions, happiness and a tinge of sadness."

"Sadness? I wanted this to be a purely joyous experience."

"I'm overjoyed by this experience, but I can't help but feel a twinge of sadness that it's come to an end so soon."

"We have a lifetime of adventures ahead of us," I assure her. "This is just the beginning, and I promise you, it only gets better from here."

I'm a man of my word. My father hates me for many reasons, but one of the few reasons he respects me is my ability to keep promises. It's one of the reasons I've become a billionaire.

As we arrive at the port, the sun gracefully sets on the horizon, casting a warm glow over us. We spend the next two days in paradise, indulging in delectable cuisine, strolling along the Pacific shoreline, and building magnificent sandcastles.

Before we know it, we find ourselves boarding the jet and soaring through the sky on our way back home. As we touch down in Portland, we return to our ordinary lives.

Within a week of our honeymoon, I move into Erica's apartment, and we celebrate the occasion with Abigail and Kevin.

19

May 22, 2023:

At seven p.m., I receive a call from the C.E.O. of my company. The weight of the COVID-19 pandemic begins to crush our revenue, with projections for the second quarter plummeting by more than half. Our once-loyal clients are now struggling financially, abandoning our software licenses in droves.

The company teeters on the edge of bankruptcy, and the C.E.O. wants to resign. He calls to break the news, and it hits me like a death sentence. Honestly, I'd rather die than watch my company die.

I end the call with no clue how I'm supposed to deliver this news to the board of directors.

I need to hire a new executive officer and make sure that my employees continue to believe in the company's future. Otherwise, the company might not even stand until the end of year.

Sweat trickles down my face, my body temperature rising as panic sets in. I allow myself a few moments to absorb the gravity of the situation, then swiftly compose an email to the board of directors, urgently summoning them for an emergency meeting.

I rush out of the bedroom, my mind consumed by thoughts of the meeting. Erica notices my haste and asks, "Are you okay? You seem like you're in a hurry."

"I have a crucial meeting and then I'll be working with the executive team. I won't be back until late," I reply, my words laced with tension.

"Why? What happened?" she inquires.

"I told you: I'm going to work. Stop nagging."

Erica's frustration is evident in her gaze, but I can't afford to deal with her right now. I slip on my shoes, preparing to leave.

"I'm not nagging," she says. "I just wanted to make sure everything is okay. Please, calm down."

"Can you shut up? The company is on the brink of collapse, and the last thing I need is your miserable ego. Don't you dare lecture me about being calm."

I storm out of the house with a forceful slam of the door.

How dumb can Erica be? Can't she read the situation?

I speed away in my car, racing towards the administrative building with urgency.

As I burst into the conference room, I find Kevin standing by my seat, clutching a resignation letter tightly in his hand. My C.E.O., a spineless coward, chose to skip the board meeting and deliver the letter to Kevin instead.

Confusion fills the room as the board of directors take their seats, trying to make sense of this sudden emergency.

With a heavy sigh, I break the silence and deliver the shocking news to the board. The chief financial officer steps forward, sharing a grim strategy to keep the company afloat, we must lay off twenty-five percent of our workforce. Desperation hangs in the air as we learn that none of the investors in Oregon are willing to invest in our company at this point in time.

My mind races, considering the gravity of the situation. After a moment of contemplation, I make a bold decision. I announce my plan to lay off a specific segment of our workforce and declare my intention to take on the role of C.E.O. It's a risky move, but I believe I can navigate the company through this recession.

With determination in our eyes, we shake hands, exchanging a glimmer of hope. We vow to keep the company alive through austerity measures, no matter the cost.

We all exit the room, and I make my way to my office, taking my time to think about the next steps. How am I supposed to break this news to the company? What if I have to let go of the less skilled employees, only to have the talented ones leave out of fear? How can I possibly retain my existing clients and attract new ones? After all the hard work I put into building this company from scratch, it kills me to see it potentially crumble so quickly.

Suddenly, a message from Erica pops up on my phone. "When will you be home?"

Is she kidding me? I stormed out of the house to make it clear that I needed some space. My fingers itch to fire off a blasting message, but I'm sure that that will only extend this conversation and waste my time. I choose not to respond and sit my phone aside.

Within moments, my phone starts vibrating with a high-pitched message tone. It's an Amber Alert. "A man has been shot just five miles away from your location. The suspect abducted a child and is on the loose. Please stay indoors and contact the police if you notice any suspicious activity." My phone is beyond frustrating. I can't focus on the hundreds of employees and their livelihoods when I keep getting interrupted.

I leave my phone on the desk and exit the building. I need to find a place where I can gather my thoughts in peace. Home is definitely not an option right now. Kevin's place is out of the question, too. He's barely competent as an assistant, let alone capable of helping me strategize for the company's survival. I decide to drive downtown, seeking solace in the garden by the river.

As hours pass, I begin to notice numerous homeless individuals with eyes glazed over from drugs wandering aimlessly like zombies. I continue my walk along the river, inhaling the crisp air, rejuvenating myself for the challenges that lie ahead as I prepare to lead the company starting tomorrow.

At around four a.m., I make my way back to the administrative building, urgency pulsing through my veins. The need to draft an email for an emergency all-company meeting weighs heavily on my mind.

As I reach my desk, I snatch up my phone, eager to review any messages that may have come through. My heart skips a beat when I see I've missed thirty calls from Erica. There's also five unread messages, all bearing the same question: "When are you coming home?"

What the *fuck* is wrong with this woman? She promised me to stay by my side during all the struggles, and the moment a struggle comes along, the moment I need my space, she's becoming a pain in my ass.

I don't care about drafting my email anymore. Right now, I need to make her understand, to teach her a lesson once and for all. I'll storm through the front door, confront her, and issue a stern warning to stay away from me. Or perhaps, a better solution would be to pack my belongings and escape to a hotel for a week. That way she'll know where she belongs.

I rush home, quickly park my car, and practically sprint to the apartment. With a surge of anger, I unlock the door and burst inside.

The living room is a mess, the blaring news channel adding to the disarray. And there, lying motionless on the floor, is Erica.

I'm not sure how to react. Is she trying to punish me for not answering her call? Or did she simply doze off while watching TV? And why is the living room in such chaos? I cautiously nudge her with my foot, but she remains still.

Oh god! She's unconscious. This can't be happening. I dash into the kitchen and grab a glass of water. I rush back and gently turn her over. Her eyes are shriveled and surrounded by dark circles. She's breathing, thank goodness, but her body is drenched in sweat, and she smells like a skunk.

I splash the water on her face hoping to rouse her, but she remains unresponsive. I can sense her body temperature spike, and I have no choice but to drive her to the emergency room. I wish Kevin were here to help, especially since I have an important meeting in the morning.

With no sign of her stirring, I gather her in my arms and sprint towards my car. I speed towards the nearest hospital, not sure how long I'd have to stay with her.

After thirty minutes, the doctor finally arrives, his face grave as he delivers the assessment. "Based on our observations, it doesn't appear to be a heart attack. However, she's unconscious and her fever was slightly above a hundred and four. Can you provide us with any details about what happened?"

I scoff inwardly. "That's all you've got? I could tell she's unconscious and running a fever just by looking at her. Why don't you run some tests, like an MRI, to figure out what's going on?"

The doctor shakes his head. "It doesn't work like that, sir. We've brought her temperature down, but we need to determine what caused it and her unresponsiveness. Any information you can provide about what might have happened could be helpful."

I wrack my brain, but nothing specific comes to mind. "I was away on business all night. When I returned home this morning, I found her unconscious."

The doctor sighs, clearly frustrated. "Well, we're still uncertain about the cause. She'll need to remain in our care unit until she wakes up. In the meantime, if you can gather her medical history, it might shed some light on the situation."

He retreats from the room, and I'm left standing there, helpless. How can they not figure this out with all their fancy machines? *Frustrating!* And how would I know about her medical history?

Myles! He would know. I'll give him a call, and I'm sure he'll come running. Once he's here, I can head back to work and start preparing for tomorrow. He's definitely better company for Erica than I am, especially after the fight we had.

I dial Myles' number and explain the horrifying discovery of Erica unconscious in our home in the dead of night. The old man starts to cry and question me about the situation. How the hell am I supposed to be responsible for this? His daughter is so weak, and he should be held accountable for that.

Without wasting a moment, he starts driving toward the hospital immediately from Lake Town. In what feels like an eternity, but is actually less than an hour — Myles arrives at the emergency room clutching a thick file. It contains a comprehensive record of Erica's medical history.

Myles' face is drenched in sweat and tears as he pleads for answers. "What happened to Erica? Can we see her?"

With a grave expression, the doctor delivers the news. "Sir, I'm afraid your daughter is trapped in a state of unconsciousness. Can you provide us with any information about her medical history?"

Myles glances at me with a guilty expression. He's hiding something. He had been hiding something the night I met him, too, but I had no idea what it was.

"Spill it, Myles," I snap.

Reluctantly, he begins to reveal the truth. "Well, she's been perfectly healthy for over a decade," he confesses. "But during her teen years, she suffered from a rare disorder. We believed she'd been cured, though, since it hasn't resurfaced in the past ten years."

The doctor's response is firm, "Sir, we can't overlook any of her previous medical conditions. Please disclose all of her past health issues."

Myles hesitates for a moment before speaking, "When Erica was thirteen, she was diagnosed with selective amnesia, a brain disorder that affected her memory."

There we go! I *knew* he was hiding something. So, I was getting married to a mentally retarded woman, and he had the audacity to hide it from me because I'm a billionaire. What a jerk!

The doctor's tone is gentle yet probing. "Sir, could you provide us with the name of the hospital and the doctor who made the diagnosis? We need to contact them to verify the medical records."

Without hesitation, Myles shares the details of the hospital where Erica received her diagnosis all those years ago. The doctor makes the necessary calls, returning with a solemn expression. "I must be honest with you, sir. After reviewing Erica's medical report, I would say that her current symptoms are indicative of the return of her psychological condition. But obviously it's way too early for us to drive to that conclusion, considering she's not awake yet. But if that turns out to be true, then that's a disorder that can't be treated with medication, and we may have to transfer her to a specialized psychiatric facility. Please bear with us, and we'll keep you informed of any updates."

I glare at Myles, my frustration boiling over. "Why the hell didn't you tell me sooner?" I growl. "Did you honestly think I couldn't handle a mad woman? I manage hundreds of employees, for God's sake."

Myles holds up his hands, trying to calm me down. "Nolan, please, just listen to me. Erica isn't mad, and I didn't want to overwhelm you before the wedding. It's been ten years since her selective amnesia first surfaced, and I thought she was cured."

I take a deep breath, trying to rein in my emotions. "Fine," I say through gritted teeth. "Tell me everything. RIGHT NOW."

He nods. "Remember when I told you about Erica's childhood?"

"Yeah, what about it?"

He takes a shaky breath before continuing. "Erica had to witness her best friend murdered by her own mother Chloe. Less than a week later, Sarah died from an accident. The trauma was too much for her. Within twenty-four hours of Sarah's funeral, Erica was found unconscious in her room, just like she was today. Her temperature spiked, and we rushed her to the emergency room."

I lean in, sensing he was going to delay the story like he did before. I prompt him to continue. "And then what happened?"

"After she woke up, she had no memory of the past week," Myles explains. "She forgot that her mother had died, and we had to break the news to her all over again. The doctors diagnosed her with selective amnesia, a condition triggered by extreme mental stress. There's no cure for it. They advised me to keep her stress-free and avoid anything that could trigger another episode. So, for the past ten years, I've done everything in my power to protect Erica from stress and keep her safe."

Wow! They all hid this from me so well. That's pure betrayal on another level.

"When she was planning to marry you, the entrepreneur who's always busy, I was worried that she would start to face stressful situations and that this might happen. But I couldn't say no to my baby." He continues to weep.

So, he's blaming *me* now?

"Are you seriously telling me you kept something this huge from me?" I seethe. "And I can't even believe she kept it hidden, too."

"She doesn't even know she has selective amnesia," he explains calmly. "Please, don't blame her for this. The real question is, what caused her so much stress?"

"I already told you. I was working late at night and found her unconscious when I returned."

"Well, you must have had security cameras in and around the apartment," he suggests. "Did you start investigating what happened?"

"No, I didn't. I had to rush to the hospital."

We sit outside the emergency room, my heart pounding as I open the camera app on my phone. I need to see what made her so stressed, so terrified.

The camera feed starts rolling.

I storm out of the front door, leaving Erica behind in the living room, tears streaming down her face. She clutches her phone, constantly checking for my messages. Anxiety courses through her, causing her to tap her feet nervously. Finally, she sends me a message and grips the phone tightly. Shortly after, she sets it down on the table and paces back and forth, her steps filled with unease.

Suddenly, the Amber Alert blares from her phone, announcing shots fired and a dangerous suspect on the loose. Erica's eyes widen with fear, and she rushes to the front door, ensuring it's securely locked. She closes all the curtains to shut out the outside world and then sinks onto the couch. With trembling hands, she turns on the local news, looking desperate for information.

The news channel displays the gruesome details of a murder. A body covered in a yellow cadaver bag is being loaded into an ambulance. Erica rises shakily from the couch with her phone still bound in her hand. She dials my number repeatedly, frustration mounting with each unanswered call. Finally, she hurls the phone onto the couch, her anger and fear consuming her. She begins to throw kitchen utensils around the living room in a chaotic display of her emotions.

Then, she turns towards the camera and pleads, "Please come home. I'm sorry if I did something wrong. Just come home. I'm scared."

Suddenly, the news channel announces that they've identified the murder victim as Andrew, a thirty-year-old man. The reporter mentions that the police will soon deliver this tragic news to the family. Erica freezes in terror, her face drained of color.

Her phone rings, the caller ID displaying "Oregon Police." In that moment, she collapses to the floor in a heap of despair.

Hours pass, and there's no movement in the living room until I finally arrive.

I end the camera feed, my gaze meeting Myles'. I don't know what to say.

"Clearly, she was stressed out," he says. "She must have thought you were shot because she never heard from you, despite calling multiple times."

In my defense, I left my phone at work. There was *no* reason for her to worry. She could have had dinner and slept peacefully.

Now I have to take all the blame? Does he really think I don't care about his daughter? I took her to my private island for our honeymoon. Doesn't that show how much I care?

I can't leave right now. If I do, he'll think he was right. I need to prove him wrong.

"Myles, she's my wife, and I'll do whatever it takes to ensure she gets better. I'll pay any amount and find the best hospital in the world for her."

"Son, some things can't be cured by money. Please understand that —"

"Sorry to interrupt, sir, but I've faced many challenges in building my company. I believe we can find a cure for simple amnesia. So, what's the big deal? She's going to wake up and lose her memory for a day. I guess that works in my favor that she forgets all of this ever happened. Maybe that's a silver lining. Sometimes we have to find the positive."

"A day?" he says. "Selective amnesia can be unpredictable. She could lose a day, a week, or even months."

"Well, I guess the difference between you and me is that I'm trying to stay positive, and you're being pessimistic."

"Nolan, I'm just trying to be realistic so we can prepare for the worst."

"Well, that's not helping," I say. "I need to make a call. Let's wait for the doctor's recommendation."

I move away from his toxic energy and dial my father's number. I instruct him to compile the list of employees who will be laid off. This will enable me to admit Erica to a renowned hospital for her recovery while peacefully focusing on my company. She thought she could be the backbone of my dreams, but in reality, she's just a roadblock.

After an agonizing hour, the doctor finally returns to the waiting room, his face etched with urgency. "Nolan and Myles, Erica is awake now. Please, hurry."

We bolt into the emergency room, my heart pounding in my chest. I approach Erica's bedside while Myles lingers a few steps behind me, his worry palpable.

The doctor leans in, his voice gentle yet probing. "How are you feeling, Erica?"

"I'm... tired," she whispers weakly. "Where am I?"

"You're in the hospital," the doctor replies. "You had a fever. But don't worry, you'll be fine. Can you tell me the date today?"

Erica furrows her brow, her eyes searching for answers. "Um... yesterday was Thanksgiving," she answers. "I guess I had food poisoning."

"I'm sorry, Thanksgiving of 2022?" the doctor clarifies.

"Obviously," Erica retorts, her tone tinged with annoyance.

The doctor gestures to me. "Do you recognize this man?"

"I'm sorry, Doctor, I don't know who he is." Erica's gaze expresses a mix of bewilderment and uncertainty.

Is she kidding me? I've given her the best six months of her life, had sex with her like a hundred times, and dropped half a million on that damn ring, and now she acts like it meant nothing?

The doctor motions for Myles to come forward, a glimmer of recognition flickering in Erica's eyes. "Dad?" she whispers. "What am I doing here?"

Myles takes her hands in his, his touch filled with tenderness. "I'm here to take care of you," he says softly.

"Oh, God! Dad, this was probably just some food poisoning. You could have stayed in Lake Town. Abbey would have taken care of me."

"You're still sick, Erica. Why don't you rest now, and we'll talk later?"

"Sounds good," Erica murmurs, nodding weakly before closing her eyes.

Confused, I step out of the emergency room alongside Myles. The doctor trails closely behind us, delivering his unsettling news. "Nolan, our suspicions were correct. Erica's selective amnesia has resurfaced, erasing the memories of the past six months. I'm sorry, sir, but there's nothing more we can do here. We'll keep her until she gets better. However, for long-term care, you'll need to consider a psychiatric facility. If you'd like, we can provide a referrals for further assistance."

As the doctor walks away, my mind spins with confusion. "So, she's forgotten the past six months? Does that mean she has no recollection of me, our wedding, or our honeymoon? All the time and money I invested — wasted?"

"Nolan, consider this: Erica has lived a stress-free life for the past ten years. Suddenly, she has a fight with you and believes you've been shot. The shock must have been overwhelming, causing her to lose several months of memories," Myles explains, his tone sympathetic.

I can't process the fact that she's forgotten me. I poured my heart and soul into building our relationship, and it all seems to be gone in a single evening.

I pause, my mind racing with thoughts of what to do next.

"Let's not give up, Myles," I say with determination. "We should consider admitting her to a psychiatric facility. Maybe it will help her recover some of her lost memories."

Myles shakes his head, his expression filled with concern. "No, son. We shouldn't rush into anything. Erica needs love and care right now. It'll be a shock for her to learn that six months have passed without her knowledge. Let's give some time to recover and eventually tell her the whole truth and maybe, just maybe, she'll be willing to rebuild a relationship with you."

I scoff, frustration bubbling up inside me. "And what happens when she gets stressed again?"

Myles sighs, his voice filled with a mix of resignation and hope. "Well, let's make sure she lives a stress-free life from now on."

"So, we're just going to run away and live in fear?"

"Son, in times like these, we need to put our egos aside and have faith in God."

Fuck you! She's my wife and *my* responsibility by the law. I can do whatever I want.

I clench my fists, my resolve hardening. "No, Myles. I won't give up. I'm going to admit her to a psychiatric facility and ensure she gets the help she needs. After that, I'll explain everything to her, and we'll move forward with our lives. That's my decision, and it's final."

The doctor approaches with papers in hand, breaking the tension. "Nolan, here's a referral for Dr. Scott. He's one of the top psychologists in the Pacific Northwest. He works at the Oregon Regional Psychiatric Facility, and he's currently accepting new patients. I suggest you visit him and see if therapy can help revive any of Erica's memories. She's exhausted and needs rest, so we'll be moving her to a non-emergency room. It's advisable for one of you to stay with her at all times. Good luck."

"Thank you, Doctor," I say. I turn to Myles. "We *have to* pursue this. We can't give up and live in fear. I'm driving to the psychiatric facility right now to prepare for her admission."

I can sense that he's not happy with my decision. But what does he know? He's just a barber.

"Alright, son," he says. "If that's the path you choose, then at least ensure she'll receive proper care at the facility. Take a tour of where she'll be staying and familiarize yourself with the treatments they'll be administering. I hope she'll be in capable hands."

"Will do. Please stay with Erica here and await my call for the next steps."

I head out and start driving to the facility. Myles was right about one thing: I need to understand the treatment methods they'll employ for Erica. Dr. Scott might be one of the best in the nation, but I want to make sure Erica gets premium care. Hopefully I'll get to admit her in a few hours and head back to work.

As I arrive at the facility nestled in central Oregon, its vastness becomes apparent. Spanning over what looks to be two hundred acres, it exudes an air of serenity.

I pull into the parking lot and stride through the walkway. The facility emanates tranquility with the melodic symphony of chirping birds and the gentle rustling of trees. I observe several individuals engaging in meditation or lounging on the lush lawn.

Entering the main building, I complete the necessary form to meet Dr. Scott. Within minutes, the receptionist calls my name, directing me to room 125 to meet him. I rise from my seat and make my way toward his office. My knuckles rap against the door, and Dr. Scott's voice calls me inside.

I step into the room, a smile on my face. "Thank you for granting me this opportunity to meet with you, Dr. Scott."

Dr. Scott nods, extending his hand. "A pleasure to meet you, Nolan. How can I assist you?"

"I must admit, before coming here, I had envisioned a mental hospital to be a rather menacing place, with all the patients scurrying about in their uniforms. I was completely wrong about it; this campus is quite peaceful."

Dr. Scott chuckles softly. "Ah, the term 'mental hospital' carries such negative connotations. This is not a prison, nor a place of despair. It's a facility for those with psychological issues, a sanctuary for healing and peace."

"I certainly trust your expertise in treating my wife."

"Yes, we've received information about her disorder. Selective amnesia triggered by mental stress. We have a few methods we can try here. However, it's important to understand that there are no guarantees when it comes to psychological treatments."

"I don't understand. What do you mean there are no guarantees?"

Dr. Scott leans back in his chair, his expression serious. "What do you expect the outcome of admitting your wife here to be?"

"I assume you have medications and techniques to treat her and restore her memories. And once that's accomplished, I hope you can help prevent any future triggers."

"I'm sorry, Nolan. If that's your expectation, I must inform you that there is *no* facility in the world that can promise what you're seeking."

"What? How can there not be medication for this? If you're worried about money, you must know that it's not a problem."

Dr. Scott chuckles again, shaking his head. "Money and medication, Mr. Nolan. Do you believe there's a pill for every ailment? Some things require compassion and understanding. If you had that in the first place, you wouldn't be here."

How *dare* he say that to me?

I rise from my seat in rage. "Dr. Scott, you can't be serious about the comment you made. I thought you were a qualified psychologist."

"There you go," he says. "You got triggered just by my simple comment. So, you have intermittent explosive disorder, and I think you need medication. Correct?"

"What? I don't need medication. You just made me angry with your naïve comment. You're just slapping a label on my anger."

"Exactly!" he exclaims. "Please, Nolan, take a seat. Your outrage was triggered by a simple comment. You don't require medication, rather you need someone to talk you through it and help you breathe. The same goes for your wife, Erica. She needs the care of our psychologists. Some disorders are more severe than others, so we approach them psychologically, not medically. There will be some medication involved but that's not meant to provide a complete cure."

"Alright, Dr. Scott, you've made your point. Now, how can you help Erica?"

"We can't guarantee the return of her memories," he admits. "When she's rested enough for conversation, she'll realize she's lost six months of her life. It'll be a difficult truth to grasp. Moreover, if she discovers she's married, it could trigger a powerful shock, potentially re-triggering her amnesia. Our primary focus will be delicately guiding her through the revelation of her disorder and her wedding, one baby step at a time. Then, we'll explore therapy options to see if any memories can be regained, and perhaps even experiment with methods to strengthen her mind."

Well, he can conduct his experiments all he wants. The longer the merrier! It gives me a chance to focus on my company.

"Alright, sir. Please do your best."

"We certainly will, Mr. Nolan. And hopefully, if things go well, we can offer you marriage counseling. Especially since the struggle occurred so early in your marriage."

"I think I'll pass," I say. "Thank you for the offer, but I can handle my marriage just fine."

"Sure," he says with a smile. I sense the sarcasm behind his face.

What an arrogant jerk! Anyway, it's already been an hour, and I need to admit Erica to this facility as soon as possible. I sign the necessary documents and stand up from my seat to leave.

"Thanks, Dr. Scott. I'll head back to the hospital and arrange for an ambulance to transport Erica to this facility."

"Sure, Nolan. Usually, the family takes a tour of the facility and the patient's room. That way you can have peace of mind at home, knowing your wife is safe here," he says. "Would you like a quick tour?"

Honestly, I couldn't care less. The sooner I get her situated here, the sooner I can get back to work. If the board finds out I'm not handling things, they might replace me as chair. I need to be back at work by noon.

"I have faith in this facility, Dr. Scott. I'd like to head back and ensure Erica arrives within the next hour or two."

I shake his hand and drive back to the hospital. Once there, I approach Myles and quickly fill him in on the urgent plan to admit her as soon as possible.

Myles fires off a barrage of questions. "Have you checked out the facility? Is it safe? What about the doctors? Have they dealt with cases like this before?"

Oh god! I can't deal with this man right now.

"Yes, I've personally toured the entire facility, and it's impressive. The rooms and buildings are stunning. The doctors seem confident in their ability to find a cure."

He nods, but I can see he barely trusts me. I *hate* him!

"Where's Erica?" I ask.

"Her body temperature dropped, and she keeps startling awake due to nightmares. The doctors decided she needed a good night's sleep, so they gave her a sleeping pill," he explains. "She won't wake up for at least twelve hours."

We hand over all the necessary documentation to the doctors and carefully transfer Erica to the psychiatric facility.

Myles sets off towards Lake Town. I, on the other hand, rush back to the office, my mind still reeling from the events of last night.

With a heavy heart, I sit down at my desk and compose an email to the company. The words feel hollow as I try to explain the austerity measures we must take. My focus is shattered as the haunting memories of the last twenty-four hours replay in my head. Unable to bear the weight of it all any longer, I send off the email, call it a day and head home. The drive is a blur, my exhaustion pulling at my eyelids. All I can think about is a peaceful sleep.

***

The next day, Mike gives me a document to sign and we execute the layoff strategy. This is one of the most painful moments for me in my career. It's not about these employees, they're at the lower end of the spectrum in skillset anyway. Imagining what the media will have to say about it is what causes me pain.

20

It's been three days since I've seen Erica. The work as a C.E.O. is daunting. Navigating the company during these times is not easy. I badly want to have sex with my wife and have a stress buster, but she's not by my bedside. I miss her body, her naked massages, the food she cooks to please me, everything about her. I'm miserable in the bed here while she's away at the facility, probably relaxing in the garden. If only I could take her home for just *one* night, but it has only been three days, and I doubt they've even informed her that she's married to me. It shouldn't be such a shock for her to digest this news. If I woke up one day to discover I was married to a billionaire, I would be thrilled. There's no need for us to take baby steps. *Argh*! Doctors and their regulations. I keep thinking about her and imagining intimate nights we had together and touch myself to sleep.

21

June 1, 2023:

It's been a week since I've been by her side, and I'm surrounded by her unwashed clothes. It's strange how the scent of her dirty laundry helps me sleep, fooling my mind into thinking she's still here with me through the night.

The clock strikes six a.m., and my phone buzzes insistently. Dr. Scott's name flashes on the screen. My heart races with anticipation. Could this be the call I've been waiting for? Is Erica finally cured? It's hard to believe that he managed to solve everything in just seven days. I thought he would be as slow as a tortoise.

I clear my throat, my hand trembling as I swipe to answer the call. "Hey, Dr. Scott."

"Nolan, I need to talk to you about an emergency situation," he says urgently.

My heart sinks. An emergency? What could have happened to Erica? "What? What happened to Erica?"

"There was... There was a..."

"Be quick about it, Doctor!"

"There was a murder at the facility a few hours ago, and Erica was found unconscious at the crime scene." His words hit me like a punch to the gut.

WHAT? What the hell is he talking about? A murder? How is this even possible?

"What the hell are you talking about?" I manage to choke out.

"Nolan, can you hear me?" Dr. Scott's voice sounds distant, as if he's struggling to reach me.

"Yes, yes, I can hear you. What do you mean by 'murder'? Was Erica attacked?"

"We're not entirely sure yet, but we have a suspect in custody. Please, hurry to the facility right now so we can discuss everything in person."

"I'm on my way," I say.

I spring out of bed, hastily brush my teeth, and rush to my car. The moment I arrive at the facility, a swarm of police cars with flashing lights greets me. I burst into Dr. Scott's office, my voice echoing through the room, "Where's Erica? I want to see her *right now*."

Dr. Scott, in the midst of a conversation with a deputy, abruptly stands up and addresses me, "Nolan, we're sorry about what happened. Please take a seat so we can discuss it calmly."

"Calmly? Don't you dare tell me to be calm. I want to know where Erica is, and I want to take her home. Your facility has proven to be utterly useless and has put my wife in danger. I will sue you for this."

"Please, try to calm down. Erica is still unconscious and under observation. The police are conducting an investigation. Once she wakes up, we can discharge her, and you can bring her home."

"Wakes up? No. I'm taking her home right now. Do you hear me, Doctor?"

"Alright, fine. You can take her home immediately. But please, try to calm down. The investigation is already underway, and we'll get to the bottom of this."

I look at him, my anger boiling over, and retort, "My lawyer will be in touch."

"Very well. I'll arrange for an ambulance," he says, attempting to placate me. "Please, have a seat and listen to me."

"I don't need to sit, and I certainly don't need an ambulance. I'll take her home in my car."

I rush outside as they bring Erica out on a stretcher, her body limp and almost lifeless. With urgency, I carefully lift her and gently place her in the back seat of the car and fire up the engine.

I'm not even sure if they made any progress on her amnesia. If she wakes up beside me, that might trigger something again. I can't trust emergency care either.

I dial Myles' number and quickly explain the dire situation. "Myles, I need Erica to stay at your home under your watchful care until I can figure out our next move."

His voice crackles with concern as he responds, "Bring her home, son. I'll do everything in my power to nurse her back to health. She needs to be in a familiar environment. I don't know what she's been through, but please, come soon."

Damn it! Now he'll be able to tell me "I told you so."

But I won't let him defeat me. I'll let him care for her temporarily while I devise a strategy. I'll prove all these doubters wrong and cure Erica myself. Then I'll look Myles in the eye and say, "I told you so."

As I arrive in Lake Town, Myles and Vincent are standing in the driveway, their anxious faces etched with worry. They rush to the car and assist me in carrying Erica's limp body to her bedroom. I ask Myles to keep me updated on Erica's condition before I head back home to prepare for the lawsuit.

22

The following day, I speed towards the psychiatric facility, clutching the papers tightly in my hands. Determination fuels my every move as I burst into Dr. Scott's office without hesitation.

With a forceful slam, I drop the file onto his desk, the sound reverberating through the room. "Dr. Scott, I'm suing you for your reckless treatment of Erica. Your career and this entire facility will crumble under the weight of your actions. See you in court."

Dr. Scott walks to me with concern and begs, "Nolan, please don't do this. We've dedicated decades to helping countless patients here. One mistake shouldn't bring down everything we've built. I beg you to retract this lawsuit. We're already investigating and addressing the issues that surfaced last night. Please, I beg you."

A sarcastic smile tugs at the corners of my lips as I respond, "Seems like you've developed a begging disorder, Dr. Scott. Looks like you need *fucking* therapy."

"Nolan, this is the first crime ever committed in this facility, and we're gathering all the evidence to uncover the truth. Please reconsider," he pleads.

"Alright, I'll reconsider, but on one condition."

"Yes, tell me what I can do."

"I want to know everything that happened to Erica in the past seven days. How did she end up at a crime scene just a week after being admitted? I need to investigate this myself and ensure the right people are held accountable. If you provide me with all the evidence, I'll drop the lawsuit," I state firmly.

"Nolan, you know I can't do that. I could go to prison for tampering with evidence," he protests.

"Oh no, Doctor. You *will* give me the evidence. I'm a wealthy man who can take this entire facility down and guarantee that you're put in prison," I warn.

"Alright," he concedes. "The best I can do is create duplicates of the evidence and share them with you. But you must keep this a secret and drop the lawsuit as soon as possible."

"Deal."

I'm going to investigate this myself. My minor in law school taught me that the stronger the evidence, the stronger the lawsuit. I'll compile a detailed report of Erica's experiences in this facility and file a more powerful lawsuit against them. If the cash is good, I can use it for my company. Plus, my personal investigation will serve as a fitting response to my father and Myles, showing them the lengths I'm willing to go for my wife. Two birds in one shot!

I wait patiently as Dr. Scott retrieves all the camera recordings of Erica's treatments and arranges them in chronological order on a flash drive. He hands it to me, and

I carefully place it in my backpack, discarding the lawsuit papers. With a determined resolve, I head back home.

23

I take the flash drive and settle in front of my computer which is connected to two monitors. I create a new Word document on one monitor and have the flash drive open on the other. I grab my coffee, put on my headphones and am all set for creating a detailed report for stronger evidence.

I open the first video file, titled "May 22, 2023: Day 1 of Admission to Oregon Regional Psychiatric Facility - Bedroom Camera."

Erica gets escorted into her bedroom by the facility staff. They lay her down on the bed, cover her with the blanket, lock the door and leave.

After a twelve-hour slumber, she stirs and slowly rises from her bed. She surveys the room, taking in all the furniture, and rubs her eyes, probably unsure if she's dreaming or truly awake. To her left, a large window to the hallway beckons, and a door stands beside it.

Erica calls out to the stillness of her room, "Hello? Is anyone there? Where am I? Hello?"

She slides out of bed and pads softly to the window, peeking out into the deserted hallway. She reaches for the door handle, only to find it locked. Turning back, she moves to the other door opposite the bed and gives it a try. It opens, revealing an attached bathroom.

She steps closer to the other window, taking in the expansive view of the lush green campus with people strolling through the gardens.

As she surveys her unfamiliar surroundings, her expression makes it clear that she's panicked. She anxiously waits for an hour, straining her ears for any sound from the hallway, but nothing breaks the oppressive silence.

After an hour, she starts banging on the door. "Open the door, please! Can anyone hear me? I'm starting to feel claustrophobic, please open the door! Is anyone there? Dad? Vincent? Where am I?"

With no response from outside, she sobs so desperately that her vocal cords seem to be shredding. She continues to slam her fists against the door until her knuckles start to throb and bruise. She sits in the corner, her gaze fixed on the window, hoping someone will pass by.

After a few hours, she hears footsteps from the hallway and looks at the door to see if someone's going to open it. There's a small shutter at the bottom of the door, which can be opened only from the outside. As she keenly tries to listen, suddenly a plate of food wrapped with a vacuum sheet is slid through the shutter.

She runs towards the door and starts banging on it. "Hello! I know someone's out there, please open the door. Where am I? Why am I here? There must be a mistake. I need to see my dad."

She peers through the window and spots someone push-ing a cart along. She raps her knuckles against the glass, calling out for assistance, yet the food delivery person fails to even glance her way, let alone respond.

Erica's anger boils over, and she hurls the plate at the wall, sending the food flying across the room. Her sobs intensify as she weakly pounds her fists against the door, her energy slowly draining away.

An hour passes and she starts to look pale and rub her belly. Clearly, she's hungry. She shuffles towards the scattered rice, gathers it into a neat pile on the floor, then collects all the fruit into a mound beside it. She sits there with tears streaming down her face as she begins to eat the food off the floor.

There's a sudden knock at the door. Startled, she rushes to the door, her voice trembling as she cries out, "Who's there? Please, open the door!"

The person outside says, "I can't open the door, but I can open the shutter, and you can pass the plate back to me."

Erica yells, "The plate? You better open the door, or else I'll kill you! Open the fucking door!"

The delivery woman replies, "I merely deliver food and collect plates. Please pass the plate through the shutter."

"I'm not passing any plate. Now open the damn door!"

"I can't open the door, only nurses can. As per the rule, if you don't return the plate, you won't receive the next meal." She then walks away from the room.

"Wait, wait, the nurse? What nurse? What is this place?"

She gets no response as the delivery woman walks away to collect plates from other rooms.

Her loneliness starts to kick in as she stares at the roof and starts talking to herself, "I had food poisoning and I'm hospitalized. Did they keep me here for recovery? The last time I talked to Dad, I vaguely remember him mentioning another treatment. But I can't think of any reason why they'd keep me here. Something must be going on. Also, what kind of hospital looks like this? With no people around and patients locked in a room? Unless I'm in a mental hospital, which makes no sense considering my stomach was sick and nothing else."

At precisely five o'clock, she hears the telltale sound of a key turning in the lock. Rising to her feet, her eyes fix on the door with anticipation. The door swings open and she finds herself face-to-face with three strangers.

"Hello, Erica. I'm Myra, your doctor," the woman with the warm smile says. "I'm glad to see you're awake. I'm here to be your best friend until you feel better. These security guards are here to help us out. Today's our first consultation, so let's take a walk and get to know each other."

Erica says, "I'm not walking anywhere until you tell me where I am."

"Oh, you don't want to walk with us? Too bad." Myra slams the door shut.

In a desperate attempt to get answers, Erica frantically pounds on the door again, her voice trembling as she cries out, "What is this place? Please, open the door! For the love of God, please release me from this loneliness!" She continues to sob while gently hitting her head against the door in a futile effort.

Exhausted and drained, she drags herself to the window in search of a savior.

Around six p.m., Myra and two security guards opens the door again. The doctor's lips curl into a sinister smile. "Well, Erica. Let's try this again. Will you walk with us, my dear?"

Erica nods, her voice barely a whisper as she agrees. She slowly gets up, her legs trembling as she takes her first steps towards the door. The two security guards stand on either side of her as she follows Myra.

Myra looks fishy. The way she enters with the guards made it seem like Erica was put in prison, and she only made the conditions worse. Or was it intentional to assess Erica's reaction? I guess it's too soon to say.

I open the second video, titled "May 22, 2023: Day 1: Myra - Erica One-on-One Consultation."

Erica enters the consultation room on the second floor. She sits on one side of the large table, and Myra sits at the other side. Both security guards stand upright and relaxed beside her.

Erica's eyes are red rimmed from hours of tears, and her body looks drained of energy. She shivers as she stares at Myra.

Smiling, Myra asks, "So, how are you doing, Erica?"

"How am I doing? You tell me how I'm doing. Why don't you start by telling me where the hell I am?"

Myra's expression turns stern. "I must caution you to watch your language. Else you'll get no answers, and I promise you'll be in your room, tied in chains all day. Since it's your first day here, I'll cut you some slack. You're in the Regional Psychiatric Facility."

"Psychiatric facility? Why? I'm a perfectly sane woman. There must be some kind of mistake. Can you call my father? He'll be able to explain everything. If you could just give me a phone, I could dial it for you."

"No, you can't. That's against our rules."

Erica glares at Myra, her fists clenched at her sides. "Against your rules? You have no right to keep me in a prison without my consent. I demand you get me a phone, and I won't take no for an answer!"

Myra looks at her seriously and replies, "That's strike two, my dear. You're losing your chances."

"I don't think I belong in a psychiatric facility. Please understand. I'm a data analyst at a software firm. I'm one of the best employees. There must be a mistake."

"Ah, I see. I think you're right, we must let you go. But only if you answer two questions: Can you tell me which month we're in?"

"Well, I got sick after Thanksgiving dinner. I was in the hospital for a few days, so it must be December."

"Wrong. This is May," says Myra. "Second question: Can you tell me what you have been up to in the last six months? If you can answer that, you can walk out that door right now."

"I had food poisoning, and I was hospitalized over the last... six months? You mean six months have passed, and I forgot everything that happened during that time? No way, I don't trust you. Cut the crap and tell me the truth."

"You never had food poisoning. You still haven't answered me about what you did in the last six months. Can you at least tell me where you were hospitalized?"

Erica shakes her head, her eyes wide with confusion. "I don't remember that," she whispers.

Myra casts a twisted pitying look upon her and says, "Well, you haven't answered me correctly, so I'm afraid I can't let you go. Not to mention, you threatened our food delivery woman that you'd kill her. What if I let you out and you end up making good on your word? I'm sorry, my dear, but you've lost the game. I can't let you go. You belong in this place until you tell me what you've been up to these last six months."

Erica's sobs echo through the room and then she explodes. "You *fucking* maniac! I want to go home. I want my dad. Let me out!" She punches the table with her fists, tears streaming down her face.

Myra's face contorts in rage as she declares, "Strike three!" She snaps her fingers at the security guards, her voice cold when she commands, "Drag this bitch back to her room."

The security guards firmly grasp Erica by her hands and drag her from the consultation room.

Myra is clearly *forcing* Erica's recollection. I thought I had something with Myra using such insensitive methods, but Erica's threats are making it harder to build an argument considering her threats could be used against her in court.

I open the next video and continue my documentation with the file titled "May 22, 2023: Day 1 of Admission to the Oregon Regional Psychiatric Facility (continued) - Bedroom Camera."

The guards march Erica back to her bedroom, thrust her inside, and slam the door shut, the lock clicking into place.

When evening falls, she watches as the food delivery woman passes her door, pushing her cart of deliciousness. She raps her knuckles against the window, calling out to the woman, but the woman continues on her way, seemingly oblivious to Erica's pleas.

With all the crying, she begins to weaken, likely also from not having eaten. She trudges to the spot where all the food had spilled and drops to her knees. She licks the floor and quenches her thirst with a few gulps of water, then takes the plate and pushes it through the door from the slot below. She moves back to the corner and licks her lips repeatedly as if they're dry. She mutters, "God, please help me!" while gazing at the ceiling.

At precisely nine o'clock, the melodic chimes of the clock tower ring out across campus. As the last note fades away, the lights in her room and the hallway flicker and dim, bathing the area in a tranquil, light-blue hue, a gentle reminder to all the patients that it's time to sleep.

Erica slips into bed, snuggling beneath her cozy fleece blanket.

Around ten p.m. faint footsteps echo in the hallway. Erica darts to the window and peers out to discover the source of the disturbance.

Under the blue lights in the dark hallway, she finds two men — one with long, curly hair and a muscular body with bent shoulders, scars on his face and some hair covering his cheeks, innocently staring at Erica as he leans on the window.

The other person looks extremely thin his wiry hair is sparsely spread on his scalp, and he smiles at her eerily with crooked teeth.

The two men stand beside each other, smiling and staring at Erica for thirty minutes. They call her towards them by gesturing with their fingers. She slowly covers her face with the blanket.

Trembling with fear and pain, she slowly opens the blanket after a while and finds that they're gone. Tears well in her eyes, and she silently weeps until she drifts off to sleep.

End of Day 1.

How could the patients of the facility slip out of the room undetected by security? This goes against all protocols, especially in a reputable facility.

Erica isn't helping either. She has a comfortable room and good food, yet she chooses to reject them. The only thing that might strengthen my lawsuit is the unsettling way the patients leered at Erica during the night. I was hoping for more evidence.

I step out of my room craving another cup of coffee.

Myles gives me an update on Erica's condition. She's still unconscious, but her temperature appears to be improving.

I still have another five to six days' worth of recordings. Hopefully I'll be able to uncover something substantial for my lawsuit.

I step back into my room and open the next video, titled "May 23, 2023: Day 2 of Admission to the Oregon Regional Psychiatric Facility - Bedroom Camera."

Erica wakes up in the morning, slowly gets out of bed, and walks all weak and wobbly by taking the support of the wall towards the bathroom.

She emerges from the bathroom, sinks to the floor in a corner and peers out into the hallway through the window. Her eyelids are puffed up and faintly pink from crying, and dark circles are present around her eyes from fatigue.

After some time, the food deliverer picks up the returned plate as Erica receives a new plate of food. She rips open the vacuum seal and hungrily devours the food, tears streaming down her face as she takes big, desperate bites.

Around two p.m., she sits in the corner, looking pale. She rises and strides towards the mirror in the opposite corner. As she gazes into its reflective depths, she speaks softly, "Hello, I'm Erica. May I know your name?" Her lips curl into a gentle smile.

For hours, she shakily keeps staring at the mirror until she hears footsteps. She crawls back to the corner where she can see through the window and finds the skinny man she saw the night before being escorted away by a nurse and a pair of security guards.

She starts banging on the window. "Nurse, please talk to me. I need to talk to someone." The skinny man looks back at her, sneering. She turns around and collapses onto the bed and continues to sob.

At four p.m., she hears the door unlocking and jumps to her feet, her eyes wide with trepidation as she stares at the door. When it opens, she finds Myra accompanied by two security guards.

"Ah, Erica! I hear you're doing well today. Care to join us?" Myra greets her warmly.

Erica nods and slowly walks towards Myra as they head to the consultation room.

I continue to run the next video, titled "May 23, 2023: Day 2: Myra - Erica One-on-One Consultation."

They walk into the consultation room and settle into their respective sides of the table before Myra asks with a grin, "So how are you doing, Erica?"

"Good. I'm doing good," Erica responds, though she sounds fearful.

"I heard you ate your lunch today and the food deliverer was very happy with you."

"I did. I want to be nice so that I can go home to my dad."

"We want you to go home, too. Now tell me, Erica, do you have any questions for us today?"

"Yes. Can you please tell me what's going on here? I honestly don't think I belong in this place. I'm a nice person, but I'm not being treated nicely."

"I understand. But first, you must accept that you're in a facility that's here to help you. We're deeply concerned about the fact that you can't recall anything from the past six months. So, as soon as we restore your memory, you're free to go. For that, we need your cooperation. You said people aren't treating you kindly. But, in truth, you must be kind to people if you wish for them to be kind to you. You threw the plate, shouted at the delivery woman, and used foul language with me yesterday. I can assure you that if you act in a manner befitting this facility and work with us, we'll take the utmost care of you. Can you do that, my dear?"

Erica's eyes fill with tears as a wave of compassion washes over her. She chokes out her next words. "When can I see my father? I miss him so much."

"It all depends on your behavior and how fast you recover. For now, all you need to do is work with us without resisting."

"I'm suffocating in here; it's like I'm in a prison cell! Can't I just go out into the garden and get some fresh air?"

Myra shakes her head. "I'm afraid not. Instead, why don't you try some meditation and breathing exercises to help you find inner peace?"

The alarm from Myra's phone buzzes and she says, "Time's up for today. I'm afraid I must bid you farewell until tomorrow."

"No, please talk to me for a little longer."

"I'm sorry. The guards will show you the way."

Erica loses her composure and shouts, "Talk to me! Talk to me, you bitch!"

Myra signals the guards to take Erica back to her room, and they take her away.

I click on the next file, titled "May 23, 2023: Day 2 of Admission to Oregon Regional Psychiatric Facility (continued) - Bedroom Camera."

The guards bring Erica back into the room and shove her into the corner. She cries hard and bangs her own head against the wall several times until she passes out on the floor. She remains unconscious through the dinner call.

At nine p.m., the bells from the clock tower ring nine times. Erica wakes up to the chime, slowly blinking her eyes and rubbing her head. She stumbles to the bed and covers herself with the blanket. She faces the window looking out into the hallway, likely hoping to see the two people again.

Around ten p.m., the footsteps of two people can be heard. Erica gets a bit excited to see them slowly walking towards her window under the blue light. The lean man stares at her with a smirk and the other man maintains an innocent look. She looks at them both with a welcoming smile instead of apprehension. She keeps staring at them for thirty minutes and then slowly turns back and walks away with an unsteady gait.

End of Day 2.

This is unbelievable, I already see an Erica that I don't recognize. I've never seen this rage and frustration in her before. She looks extremely weak due to the poor care, and at the end of the second day, it looks like she finds comfort in seeing these two freaks peering through her window. This is useful evidence in court to display the deterioration of Erica's mental stability within two days of residence.

I proceed with the next video, titled "May 24, 2023: Day 3 of Admission to the Oregon Regional Psychiatric Facility - Bedroom Camera."

Around four p.m., Myra unlocks the door and greets, "Hello, Erica. I heard you ate and were being good today as well. I have a surprise for you. There's someone here today who would like to chat with you."

With swollen eyes, Erica looks at the floor, nods, and slowly steps out of the room, following Myra towards the consultation room.

Predictably, the next file is titled "May 24, 2023: Day 3: Scott - Myra - Erica Two-to-One Consultation."

Myra sits in one chair and keeps smiling at Erica, while Erica looks at the table all weak and tired.

A few minutes later, Dr. Scott strides into the room and takes a seat beside Myra. Erica gazes at him with a longing that suggests she's hoping he might be the one to reunite her with her family.

Dr. Scott beams with delight as he greets her. "Hello, Erica! It's so wonderful to see you awake and well. How are you feeling? Is Myra taking good care of you?"

She slowly turns her gaze to Myra, who chuckles and answers for her, "Of course! Erica is absolutely thriving here. Isn't that right, Erica?" She stares at her in a forceful way, urging her to agree to it.

Erica trembles as she replies, "Yes, Myra is taking good care of me."

Dr. Scott's brow furrows. "That's very good, Erica. But you appear a bit wan and fragile. Is everything all right?"

Erica keeps staring at them without uttering a word.

Myra glances at Dr. Scott then replies, "It's a strange new place, Doctor, so Erica's having difficulty settling in. The food is unfamiliar, too, so she's still getting used to it. I'm sure she'll be fine in no time."

"Erica, is everything okay? Are you having any problems here?" Dr. Scott asks, focusing intently on Erica alone.

She responds, her voice quavering, "Yes, Doctor, but there are two men lurking outside my window at night. Their eyes fix on me for what feels like an eternity."

Dr. Scott turns to Myra, his brow furrowed in concern as he whispers, "What's going on, Myra?"

"All the doors are firmly shut, Dr. Scott. There's no way anyone could be peering into her room. My theory is that Erica isn't just suffering from memory loss — she's also delusional. These rooms are secured with sophisticated systems, and it's impossible to breach them. I believe Erica is exhibiting signs of delusional behavior. I'll work with her. You can disregard her claims."

Dr. Scott gives Myra a perplexed look and then turns to Erica, assuring her, "I understand, Erica. Myra will make sure that no one disturbs you at night."

Erica nods, her lips pressed together in a thin line.

Myra's phone buzzes, and she announces, "That's the end of our session for today. Erica, the guards will escort you to your room."

Erica strides out of the consultation room as Dr. Scott and Myra remain in conversation. "Myra, Erica is supposed to be a person with memory loss and nothing beyond, as her husband informed me. But she appears to be suffering more severely than that. Are we providing her with the necessary comforts? We must adhere to our regulations and ensure she has access to the food she desires and the ability to communicate with her family if she so wishes."

"Without a doubt, Dr. Scott. We've laid out all the options, yet she's rejected them all. The family may not have told you, but I can confidently say she's delusional, has psychotic rage, and, of course, memory loss. She needs to be under our watchful eye for a considerable amount of time — months, perhaps even years."

He shakes his head in disbelief. "This is so peculiar. Please make sure she receives the best care," he says before exiting the room.

Fantastic! I think I've got something here. Myra oversees Erica, likely monitoring her on camera daily. She must know about those freaky nighttime visitors, yet she's either hiding the fact that she knows or she's ignoring Erica's fears. Either way, this will fly in my favor in court.

The next file is titled "May 24, 2023: Day 3 of Admission to Oregon Regional Psychiatric Facility (continued) - Bedroom Camera."

The guards leave Erica in the room, and she settles in the corner, looking at herself in the mirror.

After dinner, she waits eagerly for the nine rings from the clock tower and anticipates the arrival of two men.

Around ten p.m., the two men walk towards the window and stand beside each other while staring at Erica. The skinny man who smiles at her presses his palm against the window with his fingers widespread.

She beams gleefully as she rises to her feet and strides towards them. She outstretches her arm and presses her palm against the window so her hand aligned with his. They linger there for a moment before parting ways. Erica turns back and strides into the darkness, her eyes settling on the mirror. She gazes at her reflection, her lips widening into an eerie grin.

She then lowers herself to the floor without removing her eyes from her reflection and drifts off to sleep.

End of Day 3.

She's losing her mind. She's obsessing over the mirror, whispering to her reflection, enjoying the arrival of those freaks, and smiling at herself wickedly.

I'm already halfway through the videos, but aside from Erica's odd behavior, there's not much going on. Erica looks miserable, lonely, and seems to be going crazy. She's still secured in the room, which is locked from the outside, and I have no idea how she ended up at the crime scene.

I continue with the next video, titled "May 25, 2023: Day 4 of Admission to the Oregon Regional Psychiatric Facility - Bedroom Camera."

Around ten a.m., Myra unlocks the door and walks in with the guards. She finds Erica in the corner, gazing up at her expectantly.

"Good morning, Erica! Today, we shall have a chat while looking at some beautiful patterns. Are you ready?"

Erica gazes up at Myra, her eyes conveying a silent affirmation. Together they step out of the room.

I open the next video, titled "May 25, 2023: Day 4: Erica's Hypnotherapy."

They enter the hypnotherapy room. Myra guides Erica to the chair, her hands gently securing the straps around Erica's wrists.

"May I know why I'm being bound?" Erica asks.

"You'll know soon enough."

Myra brings a metallic arm with an attached display in front of Erica's eyes and turns down the lighting in the room to a perfect ambiance. She starts a gentle melody in the background, which provides a soothing feeling.

She says gently, "Now Erica, take a deep breath and try to relax. You're in safe hands here, and everyone around you cares deeply. Look into the display in front of you and let the rest of the world blur away. Listen to the gentle music in the background; let it drown out the voices in your head. Stay focused and keep breathing."

Erica follows her commands, her gaze fixed on the images on the display. Everything else around her begins to fade away, and she seemingly feels a wave of relaxation wash over her as the soothing music and Myra's kind words lull her into a deep state of hypnosis.

After several minutes, Myra inquires in a mild, relaxing voice, "Now Erica, can you tell me who I am?"

"You are Myra."

"That's very good, Erica. Can you tell me how many siblings you have?"

"I have one brother, Vincent."

"Good. Where do you work?"

"I work at a company called Wise AI."

"Can you tell me what you last remember before waking up in your bedroom of this facility?"

"I was with my father." Tears start to roll down her cheeks.

"What else do you remember before that?"

"I don't remember. I came back from Thanksgiving dinner and slept. By the time I woke up, six months had passed and my father was in front of me in the hospital."

"Erica, I want you to focus harder and think about what happened in the past six months."

"I don't remember anything," Erica responds, sounding agitated.

Myra asks, "How does it feel when you see Myra?"

"I feel an urge to take a blade and plunge it into her throat, snuffing out her life in a single, savage stroke."

Myra's eyes widen in shock. "All right, Erica, you did a great job. Now I want you to slowly blink your eyes." She snaps Erica out of her hypnotic trance.

Myra then brightens up the lighting in the room, dimming the music to a whisper. She looks into the camera and gives a thumbs up. She then looks at Erica with rage in her eyes but manages to smile because of the camera.

I click on the next video file, titled "May 25, 2023: Day 4 of Admission to Oregon Regional Psychiatric Facility (continued) - Bedroom Camera."

Erica drifts back into her room and settles on her bed.

At noon, the security guard opens the door and invites her to the dining hall for lunch.

Erica asks, "Am I not getting lunch sent to my room?"

The security guard responds, "Well, today is the last Monday of the month. We call it Magic Monday. All the patients are allowed to go to the dining hall and eat whatever they want."

She steps out of the room in overjoyed, probably because she gets to make some friends and interact with new people.

In an hour, she returns and walks around, looking happily outside the window.

At four p.m., Myra opens the door . "We need to talk about today's hypnotherapy session. Care to join me?"

Erica nods and walks out of the room.

Around five p.m., she returns to the room and collapses in the corner, sobbing while looking at herself in the mirror. She begins talking to her reflection.

"Dad left me here because he hates me. Why would Myra do this to me? Why would she do this to my family?" She bangs her head against the wall. "What's the point of living anymore?" Another slam. "Why was I bullied during my childhood?" And again. "Why was I tortured by Chloe?" And again. "Why does Myra hate me?" Again. "I can't let her win. I can't allow her to torture me anymore."

On the sixth blow, she rams her head extremely hard. She then presses her hands against her head as if she felt a sharp sting in her brain. She continues to press her head with one hand while rubbing her eyes with the other, struggling to stay focused.

In a split second, she involuntarily rises to her feet, her body rigid, her muscles tensing and her posture stiff. Her arms quiver as her fingers spread wide and her veins bulge at her wrists. She stumbles towards the mirror, her movements jerky and uncoordinated. She stands before it, her hair veiling her eyes as she tilts her head forward. Peering into the glass, her eyes widen and roll upward as if a ghost has entered her body.

A strange sneer spreads across her face, her teeth bared, and she whispers in a high-pitched voice, "My name is Monica." She keeps looking at herself as if she's acquired a new body.

Suddenly, she switches back to her normal self and says, "Why am I standing? I was sitting. Ah... my head is bursting." She looks into the camera and says, "Someone please help me. I need help.

"Shut up!" she yells as if this "Monica" has possessed her again. She walks stiffly towards the mirror and keeps staring at herself in rage for hours.

Around ten p.m., she hears the telltale sound of footsteps. Glancing into the mirror, she whispers to herself, "They have arrived."

The two men appear at the window, and she turns around and walks towards them. She looks them in the eye and widens her grin. The skinny man observing her starts smiling back. They gradually drift away from her window.

Erica steps backward towards the mirror and collapses to the ground.

End of Day 4.

My heart plummets after watching that recording. What was that? What happened during the lunch that made her so happy? And what transpired during her consultation with Myra that pushed her to the brink of madness, causing her to behave like a deranged psychopath?

I scroll through the flash drive, desperately searching for any trace of Erica's lunch or her meeting with Myra, but there's nothing. It's as if they never even happened.

Myra did something to her. I can feel it in my bones. I need to uncover the truth before she has a chance to escape. I have to watch the videos from days five and six, but first, I need to reach Dr. Scott and share my findings with him. Together, we can stop her from fleeing.

I quickly capture screenshots of the two mysterious men who stalked Erica at night and attach them to my document. I print out the report I compiled for the first four days, grab my car keys, and race towards the psychiatric facility.

As I speed down the road, I send a message to Myles, anxiously inquiring about Erica's current state of mind. I can't help but worry about the mess she might create when she wakes up. His response comes swiftly, informing me that she's still sound asleep.

I arrive at the facility around two p.m., my footsteps echoing through the empty corridors as I make my way to Dr. Scott's office.

"Nolan," he says with astonishment as I let myself in. "What brings you back here?"

I can't contain my frustration any longer. "Enough with the games, Dr. Scott. Tell me what you're hiding."

"What do you mean?"

"Don't play dumb with me. You deliberately hid the video of Erica's consultation with Myra."

Dr. Scott's eyes widen with a hint of panic. "Nolan, I have no idea what you're talking about. I personally ensured that all the videos were delivered, and I gave you the exact duplicates."

A surge of anger courses through me. "Well, I hate to break it to you, but it seems like your guards have been compromised."

"If you can explain which video you're referring to, I can retrieve it for you right now." He reaches for his computer, readying to search the database.

We search through the recordings, finally locating the video of Myra leading Erica into the consultation room on day four.

They settle at a small table designed for four people.

"Do you recall what I asked you during the hypnotherapy session?" Myra inquires, her voice filled with anticipation.

Erica shakes her head as though her memory is failing her. "I don't remember."

Myra abruptly stands from her seat, her movements deliberate as she approaches the camera. With a swift motion, she cuts the cable, ending the recording.

Dr. Scott watches the screen, his face contorted in shock.

"What do you make of this, Dr. Scott?" I demand.

"Nolan, I had absolutely no idea. Myra is one of our most esteemed doctors. Her patients hold her in high regard," he responds, his words tinged with genuine disbelief.

"Enough with your marketing pitch. Where is Myra? I want to talk to her *right now*."

"Of course. Let's make our way to her office without delay," he agrees, motioning for a pair of security guards to accompany us as we exit his office.

We step into Myra's office, the air heavy with tension. She remains seated, her eyes fixed on her computer screen.

I want to kill her *right here, right now.*

Reluctantly, we take our seats as she gestures for us to do so. Her gaze shifts from the computer to us, her expression guarded. "Can I help you with something, Dr. Scott?" she asks, her tone laced with feigned politeness. Then, turning to me, she asks, "And you are?"

"I'm Erica's husband."

"May I ask why you're here?"

I take a deep breath to maintain my composure. "Allow me to enlighten you as to why we've brought the security guards," I say, my eyes locked with hers. "They're here to prevent your escape while we wait for the police to arrive and arrest you for assaulting Erica during her consultation with you."

Her eyes widen in apparent surprise, a mask of innocence slipping over her features. "Assaulting Erica? I'm not sure what you're talking about."

A bitter smile tugs at the corners of my lips as I reach into my pocket, retrieving my phone. I show her the beginning of the video clip, the evidence of her entering the consultation room with Erica, inquiring about hypnotherapy, then cutting the camera cable.

"You know, for a top psychologist like yourself, you aren't that smart," I sneer, locking eyes with her again. "The facility's cameras have a backup battery and memory chip. In case of a power outage, it can record up to sixty minutes. All we need is an engineer to extract the data from the chip."

I place my backpack on the table while she stares at me, her expression unreadable.

"I have the camera from that consultation room right here," I reveal. "Now, Myra, you've got two choices. Option one: Spill every detail about what happened in that consultation room, and maybe, just maybe, I might destroy this camera and let you walk away. Dr. Scott might still suspend your sorry ass, but at least you won't end up behind bars. Option two: The police are on their way. We'll slip this camera into their evidence, and they'll hear everything for themselves. It's your call."

Her eyes flicker with defiance. "I have no idea what you're talking about. Your backpack is empty; you're bluffing."

Rage courses through me, pushing me to my feet. "Fine! Let the cops handle this. You'll be in a cell before you know it."

"Wait!" she pleads. "Let's talk."

I slowly sink back into my seat, a wicked smile playing on my lips. "Alright, spill it."

"But I need something in writing," she stammers in fear. "A signed document guaranteeing I won't end up in jail."

I scoff, my patience wearing thin. "You're dreaming, sweetheart. You've got three seconds to decide before the offer's off the table."

"Okay, okay, I'll talk," she whispers, trembling in fear.

I lean in, hungry for the truth. "When Dr. Scott received Erica's case, he forwarded it to our team for one of us to pick up. I chose her. I've hated Erica all my life. She was the reason I lost my mother, the reason I grew up an orphan. I wanted her dead, and for the past week, I asked the cafeteria to deliver rotten food, I denied her requests to call her family, and I made sure she suffered every second of her stay here."

"Wait, what the *hell* are you talking about?" I ask. "Erica doesn't even know who you are."

Myra snickers in a way that says she's about to prove me wrong. "I had hoped she would remember me, but it's been over ten years. She's probably forgotten what I used to look like. But I remember her. My mother, Chloe, used to be a tutor in Lake Town, the place where I grew up with my sister after our father abandoned us. Erica was one of the kids my mom tutored."

I loved my mom so much, even though she enjoyed torturing other kids and was obsessed with my little sister, always showering her with affection while neglecting me. It became unbearable. So, I made a twisted decision. I poisoned my sister's food, hoping that my mother's love would finally be directed towards me. I thought her death would go unnoticed, appearing as a natural occurrence. But when she was rushed to the hospital, the doctors suspected foul play. A postmortem examination revealed the truth, it was murder. My mother was charged, and Erica testified against her in court. The sentence? Forty years in prison for murder.

"A week later, I spotted Erica's mother, Sarah, at a late-night medical store. Without hesitation, I rammed my mom's pickup truck into her car and killed her. I disposed of the evidence by abandoning my car in a junkyard and fled the city. It was a struggle, but I managed to rebuild my life, becoming a psychologist and finding peace in this facility.

"And then Erica arrived. It was an opportunity I couldn't resist. I wanted to make her suffer, to see her in pain as I kept her captive here. But during one of our hypnotherapy sessions, she uttered those chilling words, she wanted to kill me. It made me furious. I brought her to the consultation room after lunch, determined to reveal the truth. I confessed that I'm Chloe's daughter, that I'm the one who killed Sarah. Until that moment, Erica believed her mother's death was an accident. But I wanted her to know the truth, to understand that it was murder and that I was the one responsible."

Dr. Scott's voice coldly cut through the air. "You're fired! Guards, get this murderer out of my facility."

Myra pleads, "Wait, please listen. You need me. Erica is in grave danger."

Curiosity piqued, I inquire, "What kind of danger?"

Myra's words spill out, painting a chilling picture. "When I revealed the truth to Erica, it dredged up memories of her torment during the days of bullying and her mother's tragic death. While I was detailing Sarah's accident, something snapped within Erica. She listened intently, but her body became stiff, and she tilted her head forward with hair covering her face and growled in anger. She began to claw at the wooden table relentlessly. Erica's battling with multiple personality disorder, and her alter ego, *Monica*, has been triggered by my words.

"This disorder must have taken root in her childhood and been lurking in the shadows ever since. I immediately ordered the guards to restrain her and return her to her room. I specialize in treating patients with dissociative disorders, and I know how violently they can be triggered, especially by reminders of past trauma like bullying. My theory is that, if Erica encounters someone who treats her like an animal, reminding her of her darkest days, Monica will emerge and seize control. You need me, Nolan."

Everything falls into place. Erica's eerie behavior is nothing but her alter ego taking control of her.

"I don't need you," I sneer. "Oh, and by the way, you were right. I was bluffing. My backpack is empty, and the cameras don't have backup batteries. But every word you just said is now recorded. I never called off the cops. They're on their way. Now, you'll be facing charges for Sarah's murder too. Guards, do your job and take her away."

Her eyes burn with a mix of rage and disbelief as the guards move in to arrest her.

I turn to Dr. Scott. "It's not over yet. I still need to know how Erica ended up at a crime scene."

I show him the picture I found that sent chills down my spine, the one of the two men lurking outside Erica's room.

"Do you know who these men are?" I ask.

Dr. Scott studies the photo, his brow furrowing in concern. "The muscular guy on the right is Hector," he says. "And the skinny guy beside him is Aaron. Aaron killed Hector."

My mind races, trying to piece together the puzzle. "Where is Aaron now?"

"After he murdered Hector, the guards caught him. We immediately transferred him to the Level-3 division."

"What's a Level-3 division?"

"It's the intensive division. It's where we keep people who can hardly be recovered. Most of the patients in this division are criminals who have served their time but are not yet clinically sane enough to live in society. It's a highly secured part of the campus with round-the-clock monitoring."

"I need to meet him," I declare. "I want to know what he knows about Erica."

Dr. Scott nods in agreement, and together we step out of the office. We hop onto a golf cart and zip through the sprawling campus.

Eventually, we arrive at a facility with imposing walls hidden beneath a thick blanket of creeping vines. The perimeter is fortified with wire fencing and bristled with security cameras, their unblinking eyes surveying the surroundings.

Stepping inside, we pass through the metal scanners. Once cleared, we venture down a dimly lit corridor leading us to the rooms where the patients are housed. Each room is bathed in sterile white light, their interiors visible through the glass windows that are adorned with a warning sign that reads "Keep away from the glass." Security cameras have been discreetly placed within the rooms and along the corridor.

As we walk, I can sense the patients' eyes on me, their gazes filled with a mix of curiosity and longing.

"Try not to make eye contact with them," Dr. Scott advises, his voice low and cautious.

I nod, understanding the importance of maintaining a safe distance. We continue our journey, passing by numerous rooms until we finally reach the one where Aaron is confined.

Before the guards swing open the heavy doors, Dr. Scott leans in close and warns me, "Listen, Aaron is cunning and prone to violence. Let's stay calm and ask our questions carefully."

"Got it," I reply.

As we step inside, a putrid stench assaults my senses. The room reeks of urine and is littered with decaying fruit. Aaron cowers in the corner, his body bound by chains. With the guards flanking us, we approach him and take our seats on worn-out chairs.

"I was hoping for some company," Aaron mutters, his voice trembling.

"We need your cooperation, Aaron. Can you help us with that?" Dr. Scott asks.

"Why should I help you after what you've done to me? Who's this guy?" he asks, his gaze fixated on me.

"I'm Erica's husband," I reveal. "You remember Erica, right? She was present when you murdered your friend, Hector."

"Ah, Erica." Aaron sneers. "She's quite the woman. From what I've learned about her during our time in Level 2, I can confidently say she belongs in Level 3. Compared to her, I'm the epitome of sanity."

I show him the picture of him and Hector outside Erica's room.

"How did you manage to leave the room undetected?" I inquire.

"I slipped out alongside Hector," he confesses. "There's a glitch in my room's lock that allows me to twist the knob in a specific way to open it. And I've fashioned a makeshift key from a metal spoon I carved from the dining hall. With it, I can unlock anyone's door within this entire facility. Surprisingly, this place isn't as closely monitored as you might think. They have cameras, but no one bothers to watch them."

My curiosity piqued, I press further. "How did you and Erica cross paths? And what was she doing at the crime scene?"

"We met during lunch," he reveals. "I introduced her to Hector, and we engaged in casual conversation. I shared with her the peculiar living arrangement my wife and I had in this facility. In return, she confided in me about Myra, her doctor. She hated Myra, and I can't blame her. All the doctors here deserve nothing but hatred. They forced me to sacrifice Hector, an innocent and mentally challenged man. I had no choice but to do it for the sake of my wife."

My brow furrows, confusion etching across my face. "For your wife? What do you mean?"

His eyes narrow, a dangerous glint flickering within them. "I've said enough. It's time for you to leave before I decide to kill you as well."

Dr. Scott, sensing the escalating tension, rises from his seat. "Nolan, we should leave before anything happens."

We exit the room and make our way back to the main building.

"So, it seems that Erica had a casual talk with Aaron and Hector during lunch," I remark. "It's no surprise, really. According to the camera footage from day four, Erica returns to the room with a smile on her face. But then Myra takes her for a consultation, triggering her multiple personality disorder. But what happened in the following two days that led her to end up near the site of Hector's murder?"

Dr. Scott ponders my question for a moment before responding, "I believe the answer lies within the camera recordings of the last two days."

We enter his office room and project the recording as I prepare to continue with the documentation.

Dr. Scott opens the video file titled "May 26, 2023: Day 5 of Admission to Oregon Regional Psychiatric Facility - Bedroom Camera."

Around two p.m., the faint thuds of footsteps comes from the hallway. Hastily, Erica makes her way to the window, only to find Aaron being dragged away by a doctor and a duo of guards. She waves at him with a smile, but her face changes as she witnesses Aaron turning back with tears streaming down his face.

"Where are you taking him? Hello?" she cries out, pounding the glass with her feeble arms. "Aaron, are they hurting you?" Her voice trembles as it dissipates into the air, unable to make its way to him.

The doctor and the guards, deaf to her pleas, take Aaron away. She keeps looking out the window once every half hour to see if they bring Aaron back, but they don't.

As the sun begins to set, Erica takes her place in the corner and awaits Aaron's arrival. The minutes drag on and ten p.m. passes without so much as a whisper. Then finally, there's the sound of his approach, but it's unaccompanied by Hector's presence.

Erica sprints to the window and urgently beckons to Aaron, pointing to where Hector usually stands. With tears streaming down his face, Aaron unlocks her door with the key he carved. He trudges into her room. The dread and grief are palpable in the air.

"Where's Hector?" she asks, her voice quivering, "Why are you alone?"

"They snatched her away," he splutters, his tears pouring. "They took my wife away."

"What? When did this happen?"

Aaron's sobs echo through the room as he continues, "I don't know! I woke this morning to find her gone."

"Where do you think they took her?"

"I went to the visitor room today, and my friends told me they had moved her to the Level 3 ward to hurt me."

"What is the Level 3 ward?" Erica inquires nervously.

"It's a building right next to this one. I think we should bust out of here and then break into Level 3. Will you help me?"

She asks with anxiety written across her face, "How would we even get there? Don't you think Myra and the other nurses will be mad if we try?"

"The nurses in this ward have no authority in the one beyond. I've heard that the doctors in Level 3 are quite compassionate. Why don't you join me and find out?"

Erica's eyes light up with excitement. "So, are you saying that if we head to the third ward, I can dodge Myra each and every day?"

Aaron responds with a slight nod, his warm gaze conveying his enthusiasm. "Yes. Would you like to come with me?"

Erica's smile broadens, her eyes twinkling with anticipation. "I'll come with you," she declares. "And we can meet your wife. How shall we get there?"

"We need to devise a plan to break out of here tonight."

"Break out? I'm sure this campus is patrolled twenty-four-seven. We can't dig a tunnel, that would take ages. How can we break out?"

Aaron ponders for a moment before responding, "We'll have to come up with something to distract them and make a run for it when no one's looking."

"What kind of distraction can we make? How can we make it happen?"

Aaron grins wickedly. "There's another way." He peers around the room before leaning in closer to her, his voice low and conspiratorial. "My buddy in the visitors room says we can get access to the third ward by... killing someone. Tomorrow night, I'll bring Hector, then we'll take the stairs up to the terrace and kill him. The doctors will have no choice but to move us to the third ward, and I'll be able to see my wife again. Considering Hector does whatever I command him to, he'll be an easy ticket to Level 3." He pauses, eyeing her intently. "What do you think? It's a great plan, right?"

Erica jumps back in shock. "Murder someone? Are you crazy? I'm mad at Myra, but killing someone? There's no way I could do it."

"It's the ideal solution," Aaron insists. "It's the only way you'll be able to escape Myra and her torturous bullying. I'll be right there with you. We can do it together."

"No. I can't. I can't kill a person." Suddenly, she presses her head hard and rolls her eyes. She tilts her head forward, her hair shrouding her face, and looks up at Aaron with her eyes rolled upwards. She's transformed into her alter Monica, and her thick, horrifying voice fills the air, "I can kill. I'll kill Hector. And then we shall go to Level 3 to see your wife, away from that bullying bitch Myra. I'll join you on the terrace tomorrow night."

Aaron cackles maniacally with glee, strutting from the room as though he owns the world.

End of Day 5.

Dr. Scott and I lock eyes, our expressions frozen in shock. Erica was not only present at the crime scene but was actively involved in Hector's brutal murder.

"It all makes sense now," Dr. Scott murmurs. "I finally understand why Erica was acting so strangely during our last consultation on day six."

Confusion gnaws at me. "What happened during that consultation?"

"On day six, Myra brought Erica to my office for a one-on-one meeting with me. Erica appeared terrified. At the time, I assumed it was just the stress of being separated from her family and the uncertainty of her future. Let me run the video and you can see it for yourself."

He opens the video, titled "May 27, 2023: Day 6: Scott - Erica One-on-One Consultation."

Dr. Scott gazes intently at Erica and softly asks, "Erica, tell me what's bothering you?"

She sniffs back her tears and whispers, "They took her away."

"Took her away? Who are you talking about?"

Erica responds, her voice trembling, "I'm speaking of Aaron's wife. He said the doctors here are wicked and that they snatched her away. He learned from his friends in the visitor's room that they had sent her to the third ward. These doctors and nurses are nefarious, and they separated a married couple."

"What? That's not true."

"No, you're a liar," she says.

Dr. Scott inhales deeply, fixing Erica with his steady gaze. "If we want to get you back home as soon as possible, Erica, you must have faith in us. Now the truth is, Aaron doesn't have a wife here. He's not married at all - he's simply delusional. His mind is playing tricks on him, conjuring up people who aren't really there."

"You're not telling the truth. I don't believe you. Aaron is a rocket scientist, an absolute genius."

Dr. Scott chuckles in disbelief. "Rocket scientist? Is that what he told you? He's a locksmith who has been implicated in a string of heists. He was eventually caught and thrown into this facility to get cured of his delusions. Once cured, he'll be sent straight to prison."

"I trust Aaron. He's a friend who lost his wife. I don't trust the doctors here."

"Erica, you need to trust us if we're to make any progress. Let me prove to you that he's delusional. Have you ever laid eyes on his wife?"

"No. She's always in his room. She didn't come to lunch on Monday."

"Let me show you something," he says, flipping on the display in the room and connecting his laptop to it. A video appears with Aaron sitting in the visitor room on one side of the table, talking animatedly to the empty air as if he's conversing with an invisible presence.

"Look," Dr. Scotts says, "Aaron believes he's talking to his wife, but there's no one there. He has no friends, no wife. That *is* the truth. Now, if you were to ask why he's unable to see his wife in his room, we believe this to be a result of our daily therapy. His delusions are slowly fading as our doctors provide excellent treatment, and he believes them to have taken his wife away. But he must understand that his wife is only a fabrication of his mind. This is our next step in his recovery.

"Now Erica, I have shared with you some of the most closely guarded information in the hope that it might engender your trust. Do you, now, place your faith in us?"

Erica slowly nods, her face pale as she watches the video and comes to the realization that Aaron is delusional. She mutters in shock, "Yes, Doctor. Aaron's pain felt so real, but the idea that a seemingly smart man is talking to thin air is baffling. My head is spinning. I need to take a break."

"Very well, Erica. Take some time to rest today, and we shall reconvene next week."

Recording ends.

"So, Aaron is delusional, and you told Erica about it on her final day here. And somehow, Erica actually believed you," I say. "But if that's the case, why did she still go along with Hector's murder?"

Dr. Scott leans in closer, his eyes intense. "Maybe it wasn't Erica who participated," he whispers. "It was probably her alter ego. We still have one video left and that will confirm if Monica was indeed part of the murder. This may just lead her to prison."

My heart sinks.

I shiver while I open the last video, titled "May 27, 2023: Day 6: Hector's Murder."

As the clock strikes nine p.m., the facility falls silent and the darkness settles in. Erica walks around the room, tapping her palm against her thigh. She strides to the mirror, her determined gaze meeting her reflection as she says, "I have to keep him from murdering Hector. I need to make him realize he's delusional."

Erica goes still for a moment, then her shoulders square and her jaw locks tight. Something shifts. Her voice, when she speaks, is low and rough, almost unrecognizable. "No, we must slay Hector and venture to the third ward. Away from Myra and her bullying."

Erica's voice comes through as she cries, "We can't slay Hector."

Monica resurfaces, her anger intensifying. "We must. If we don't take out Hector, we'll be eternally bound to this ward. Myra will continue to torture. We must go to the third ward."

Erica desperately tries to regain authority over her body and mind. "No. I'm not going to the terrace."

Aaron and Hector stroll up to Erica's room. Aaron unlocks the door and finds Erica switching between herself and her alter. He sidles up to her and whispers, "Hector awaits," gracing her with a knowing smile. Hector stands a few steps away, innocently surveying the scene.

Together, the three of them move forward, their steps measured and deliberate as they make their way to the stairs.

With stiff movements, Monica continues after her two male companions. Her hands suddenly lift and slap both her cheeks. Her semi-consciousness dissipates, and Erica comes back to reality. She turns around, her feet dragging her back towards her room, away from the stairs. "No, no, I can't do this. I can't."

As Erica attempts to stride back toward the room, Monica abruptly seizes control of her feet, propelling her back towards the stairs with a jerky movement, as if a magnetic force tugged her in the opposite direction.

Erica finally reaches the stairs and takes a step, straining to regain control of her thoughts and push Monica out of her mind with every ounce of strength she has. With a powerful determination, she starts walking away from the stairs again.

Monica delivers a mighty blow to her face, sending Erica hurtling out of control. Grasping the handrail, Monica begins her ascent.

They all trek up to the terrace. Aaron whispers that instruction to Hector to position himself at the brink of the roof, facing the campus. Then Aaron pivots to face Monica, who gazes up at him with a tilted head, her body quivering in what appears to be anger.

"Let's cut Hector by the throat and hurl him off the roof for our freedom from this ward, to get away from Myra and so I might join my wife in the third ward."

Twenty seconds later, the security guards at the bottom of the building gape in awe as Hector slams onto the pavement before them and oozes his lifeblood. They press the emergency alarm, unleashing a shrill siren across the campus that galvanizes the guards and doctors into immediate action. With urgency, they sprint towards the terrace.

Monica's presence evaporates from Erica's consciousness and she sinks to her knees, trembling and weeping, tears streaming down her sweaty face as she looks upon Hector's lifeless body.

The security guards and Myra arrive in time to witness Aaron guffawing with delight. Erica's cries of innocence echo through the terrace. "I didn't do it! I didn't do it!"

Aaron continues to laugh harder as he crows, "I did it! I did it! I've killed Hector and can finally join my wife!" The guards seize Aaron, clasping him in handcuffs as they drag him away.

Erica's anguish intensifies, her distress swelling to an unbearable level until she eventually succumbs to unconsciousness.

Dr. Scott sprints towards the building as the siren wails. He looks at Hector's body. He rushes up to the terrace and cries out, "What's going on? What's happening here?"

He looks at Aaron, who's chuckling. "I finally did it! I killed Hector! Now take me to my wife. I'm over the moon!" He cries out in joy, "Woohoo... I did it!"

The guards arrest Aaron and take Erica to the emergency unit.

Recording ends.

We both sit in silence, our eyes fixed on the monitor.

"We have to delete that last video," I suggest urgently. "Otherwise, Erica will be wrongly accused of a crime committed by Monica."

"But that's tampering with evidence, Nolan."

"Aaron already confessed to the crime. I can help close this case before an investigation begins. If not, you could be charged, too. Please, delete the last video."

Dr. Scott ponders for a moment, then we proceed to delete the video from both the original and duplicate drives.

"Thank you, Doctor."

"Nolan, you need to admit Erica back into this facility. People with multiple personalities can be highly unpredictable and often violent. Remember, Monica intended to harm Myra and anyone who emotionally tormented her. Alter egos are driven by a purpose, and they may linger until that purpose is fulfilled. Monica's purpose will only be fulfilled if all her bullies are dead. This means she will haunt Erica for the rest of her life. I can assist you with this."

"Thank you for the suggestion, Dr. Scott, but I don't need anyone's help right now. I'll handle Erica and Monica on my own. I'm a billionaire who built his own business from the ground up; I'm confident I can figure this out. I'll work with local politicians to ensure this case is closed. Thank you, and I hope to never have to contact you again."

"Before you go, Nolan, let me offer one last caution. If Erica wakes up and realizes that you're the reason she ended up in this facility and suffered at the hands of Myra, Monica will snap back into control. I just wanted to warn you about that."

I nod, absorb his warning, and exit the facility.

I start my journey towards Lake Town, the weight of the past twelve hours heavy on my mind. Erica could awaken at any moment, and I can't afford to let my guard down in case Monica wakes up in her place.

I can't believe I married a mad woman. A man of my intellect would never get deceived, but Erica had managed to do so. Since the day I met her, my life has spiraled out of control. The value of my company has plummeted by twenty percent, I've been consumed by endless visits to hospitals and psychiatric facilities during the week when my C.E.O. resigned, and worse, I'm doing all of this for sake of a murderer with selective amnesia and a multiple personality disorder.

I wish *I* could throw her in the Level 3 division with the other psychopaths where she belongs. But doing so would only prove my father and Myles right, that I am incapable of taking care of my own wife. I can't let them win.

I will cure Erica's selective amnesia and kill Monica. *Whatever it takes!*

Just as I'm lost in my thoughts, my phone jolts me back to reality with an incoming call from Myles.

"Erica is awake," he informs me.

My heart skips a beat. "When did she wake up?"

"About an hour ago."

An hour? I specifically instructed Myles to keep me updated. "What's her condition now?" I ask.

"Don't worry, Nolan," Myles reassures me, his tone relaxed. "She woke up screaming, drenched in sweat. Whatever happened at the facility triggered her selective amnesia. She has no memory of what happened there. I managed to convince her that she'd just had a terrible nightmare and it calmed her down."

"She has no recollection at all?" I inquire, my mind racing with possibilities.

"Not a single memory," Myles confirms. "Perhaps it's better this way, for her to forget the horrors she witnessed. The only shock she experienced upon awakening was the realization that six months had passed. I had to fabricate a story about her being in a coma for an extended period and dismiss the food poisoning incident. So, she's alright now. Come home, and we can discuss everything."

"Alright, I'm on my way. But it'll take some time. I'll have Kevin head to your home in case you need any assistance."

With that, I end the call and continue my journey.

What incredible news! She has no recollection of the facility, Myra, or Hector's murder. The only shock she has left to endure is the realization that she's married to me. For now, I'll let her believe she was in a coma until she fully recovers and then I'll reveal that she's my wife.

I urgently call Kevin and instruct him to meet me at Myles' home in Lake Town. I summarize to him over the phone what happened to Erica in the facility. I trust Kevin with my secrets; he's as loyal as a dog.

After about an hour, I arrive in Lake Town and step into Myles' home. From a distance, I observe Erica carefully enjoying a meal while watching the television in her bedroom. I walk to the living room and sink into the comfort of the reclining sofa, finally able to relax.

I hear Erica's voice from the bedroom. "Vincent, could you please bring me a glass of water?"

Vincent lets out an exasperated sigh, his response laced with annoyance, "Sure thing, Mad Sis. I'll get right on it." He takes the glass to her and returns to the living room.

"Vincent, out of curiosity, why do you refer to Erica as 'Mad Sis'?"

He chuckles, "It's just a little joke, you know? It's funny because, well, it's kind of true."

My gaze sharpens, my interest growing. "True? What do you mean?"

Vincent's smile falters slightly as he explains, "Well, don't take it too seriously. Growing up, there were nights when Erica would wake up and behave strangely. She'd stand by the window, talking to herself in different voices, her eyes wide and filled with an untamed energy."

"Like she was playing a role?"

"Exactly, like role-playing," he confirms. "Whenever I asked her to stop, she'd bark back at me furiously. So, I started calling her Mad Sis.' It's just a playful nickname, nothing more."

"When did this behavior stop?"

"The last time I lived with Erica was before she left for college. And she was always like that."

"Every night?" I probe, seeking to understand the extent of Erica's peculiar behavior.

"Not every night, just once every few months. Well, I have issues like sleepwalking. So, I guess everyone has a quirk," he says with a smile.

Huh, so Monica has always been there. I realize that during the few months Erica and I have been together, she must have been so happy that I never witnessed that side of her. I married her too soon!

Erica takes her medication and drifts back to sleep.

Myles approaches me, his eyes filled with anticipation. "Did you find out anything from the doctor at the facility?"

I can't tell him the whole thing. He would freak out if he knew the truth. He might just have a heart attack, and I *cannot* deal with another member of this insane family.

"Erica was found unconscious at a crime scene," I explain carefully. "Thankfully, she wasn't harmed or involved in anything. We don't have to take her back."

Myles nods, the weight of the situation settling upon us as we sit in silence in the living room. The tension is suffocating.

Suddenly, Kevin texts me that he's arrived. I excuse myself, step outside, and climb into his car.

Kevin turns to me, his eyes searching for answers. "What's our next move?" he asks.

I sigh, the weight of responsibility heavy on my shoulders. "Right now, our priority is ensuring Erica recovers. Eventually, I'll have to tell her the truth, that she's married to me."

Kevin's face contorts with concern. "Nolan, have you considered the consequences of that conversation? It could trigger amnesia or worse. If you tell her the entire truth, you would be triggering Monica."

"Well, there's no other option, is there? The only option I have for now is to reveal it to her and build a new relationship. In the meantime, I can keep working to devise a plan for a complete cure."

"But what if she gets stressed again in the future? It could trigger selective amnesia, erasing all her memories. Are you prepared to start over again and again?"

"Then what the hell am I supposed to do? Everyone has brilliant questions, but no one has given me a reasonable solution so far. Do you have a better idea?"

He clasps my hand tightly and says, "Listen, my friend. You mean the world to me; you're like family. It pains me to see you suffer like this. There's no easy way to say it, but I believe you should consider letting Erica go."

Does he think it didn't run through my mind a thousand times? Divorcing Erica might help her, but it clearly shows that I lost. What does he know anyway? He's just an assistant.

"How dare you suggest such a thing?" I snatch my hand away.

"I'm not the one who came up with the idea," he replies calmly. "Myles believes it's the only way to ensure his daughter's safety, and I'm inclined to agree. If you let her go, Erica can move on with her life as if nothing ever happened. Even if she learns the truth, Myles will take the blame upon himself, admitting her to a psychiatric facility. The only one who needs to heal from this pain is you. So, the decision is yours."

Of course Myles suggested this! I divorce his daughter and give her half my company? The barber seems to be smarter than I thought. Well played, Myles!

Fuck him! I'd rather let Erica suffer through selective amnesia and deal with Monica for the rest of her life than give her half of my stake in the company.

"I won't surrender, Kevin." I say, my voice firm. "I'm an entrepreneur; I never back down. She's legally married to me, so Myles has no say in this. As soon as she recovers, I'm taking her home."

"And then what?" he asks. "What exactly are you going to do?"

I keep thinking of a quote in silence.

"While I was at the facility, I saw a quote displayed on the wall, and it's been stuck in my mind ever since," I say. "It said 'The only way out is through.'"

"Okay, I'm not sure what that means."

"I have an idea!"

24

"You have an idea? An idea for what? To cure Erica?" asks Kevin, his voice tinged with hope.

"I believe I've found a way to resolve this," I say, "but I'm not sure if it leads to a total cure."

"How?" he asks curiously. "The doctors were unable to find a way; how can we do it without any expertise?"

We? He certainly thinks a lot of himself. It'll be me who's going to orchestrate this grand scheme to heal Erica. And all I need are some pawns.

"Get Abigail and Vincent to the conference room immediately," I command.

I step out of the car and stride back into the house, determined to show Myles that his feeble attempt to force me into a divorce won't succeed. I'll handle this in my style.

"Myles, I wanted to share something with you." I take a seat beside him on the couch. "I understand that you're afraid about what happens to Erica if she stays married to me, even if she gets through the current situation. Any father would feel that way. I get it. But I'd like to let you know, in the nicest way possible, that you can't make us divorce, and with all due respect, sir, you need to back off. I know I made the decision to put her in the facility, and it didn't go as planned. Now, I'm taking matters into my own hands. I will find a way to cure Erica, no matter the cost. All I ask is that you take care of her for a few days while I make some preparations, then I'll take her away. I hope you understand."

He looks at me with a pitiful expression, but I couldn't care less about what a coward like him thinks. I'm an entrepreneur, and I face my problems head-on.

"Nolan, are you sure this is the right thing to do? Just a week ago, you believed that putting her in a psychiatric facility would help, but it only made things worse. How do we know your new plan won't have the same result?"

"Honestly, Myles, I don't know if this will work either, but I have to try. If this plan fails, I'll come up with another one. And if that fails, I'll keep trying until she's cured."

"Son, I think you're approaching this issue like a problem you face at work. But this isn't a business. This is the health of a human being, and more importantly, my daughter."

Alright, I'm done talking with him.

"I wish I could spend more time discussing this with you, Myles, but I'm running out of time. I have to go now. I'll catch up with you later," I say, standing up from the couch.

Myles grabs my arm and looks at me desperately. "Wait, Nolan. Please, at least give me the details of your new plan. I'll be terrified every minute not knowing what's happening to her. Maybe I can help you."

Help me? That's actually not a bad idea. "Sure, Myles. I think you can be of help. First, I need you to take care of Erica for the next two days. After that, stay away from her for the next ten days. No calls, no messages, nothing."

Tears well up in Myles' eyes. I can't deal with him anymore. I need to leave.

"Please, Nolan, handle this with utmost care," he says.

"Will do," I say with a nod before I step out of the house alongside Kevin and Vincent.

Divorce my ass. I don't care if this kills Erica. I'm going through with it. It's do-or-die. Either way, she'll be doing everyone a favor.

As we drive back to Portland, I ask Kevin and Vincent to keep their mouths shut so I can focus on formulating my plan before sharing it with the group.

We arrive at the administrative building and climb out of his car.

As we walk to the conference room, I lean in close to Kevin and whisper, "Listen, I'm going to fill Abigail and Vincent in on everything that happened at the facility. But I won't mention anything about Monica. I don't want them getting spooked about Monica's involvement in this mission. Keep it to yourself, okay?"

"Are you sure about that?" he whispers back. "Wouldn't it be better to be transparent, so everyone knows who they're dealing with?"

"Kevin, just remember that you're an assistant to me inside this building. Just follow my instructions and stop being a pain in my ass."

He nods, and together we enter the conference room.

Everyone settles into their seats. I position myself at the front of the room and grip a pen tightly in my hand, ready to write on the whiteboard.

I recount the entire story to them, starting with my discovery of an unconscious Erica and leading up to finding her at a crime scene at the psychiatric facility.

"Now, here's the current situation: Erica's selective amnesia has resurfaced, wiping her memory of the entire time she spent in the facility. Myles suggests that I divorce her, but let's be realistic. Can anyone guarantee that Erica won't face stress for the rest of her life? She's been stress-free for the past ten years, but she still has at least fifty more to go. What's the point of divorcing her? She's going to face stress at some point anyway. So, my decision is to cure her, and I want the four of us to be part of this mission. Any questions before we proceed?"

Abigail speaks up. "What does Erica remember right now?"

"She has a hazy recollection," I explain. "As far as her current memory goes, she remembers having food poisoning and then waking up after six months, then waking up again a week later. Myles managed to convince her that she was in a coma and unwell, but she's fine and just needs a few days of rest before returning to work."

Abigail persists, her voice determined, "What if we give her time to heal and let the truth come out naturally? We can explain the selective amnesia and everything that has happened in the past six months. She may not feel the same affection for you as before, but we can start fresh and promise to protect her from any troubles going forward. Myles managed it for years, so why can't you do the same? Wouldn't that solve everything?"

"It's nearly impossible to avoid stress for the rest of your life," I counter. "And there's a chance that revealing the truth about our marriage could trigger her selective amnesia. She's not ready for it yet. Plus, what if telling her all the details triggers something even worse?"

"Like what?" Abigail asks, her curiosity piqued.

I pause, my gaze fixed on Kevin.

"Well," Kevin interjects, attempting to cover up the truth about Monica, "I think Nolan is speaking generally. He seems to have a better plan."

They all look to me for the divulsion of said plan. "First and foremost," I begin, "I want all of you to understand how stress triggers selective amnesia. It all started when Erica was just thirteen years old. She went through an unimaginable amount of pain, enduring bullying, the loss of her mother, and the murder of her friend — all within the same week. The doctors back then attributed her amnesia to stress and advised Myles to keep her stress-free.

"Myles did everything he could to protect Erica. He moved them to a new house, transferred her to a different school where she became friends with Abigail, and made sure Erica no longer received tutoring. Her life took a turn for the better, and for ten years, she lived without any stress. Sure, she had to face the usual challenges of being a student and finding a job, but she excelled academically and never felt overwhelmed. Then, out of nowhere, we have a fight, a common occurrence in any relationship, and her amnesia resurfaces simply because she believed I was dead after hearing my name on the news.

"But here's the thing: When Erica was confined to the psychiatric facility, she experienced extreme stress, yet her amnesia was never triggered. She was lonely, desperate for answers, subjected to terrible food, and constantly worried about her future. These were incredibly stressful circumstances, so why didn't they trigger her amnesia?"

Vincent says, "Well, maybe that wasn't stressful enough for her to get triggered."

The kid is smart.

"Exactly! The selective amnesia kicked in at the crime scene when Erica witnessed Hector's death. It was a shock more intense than our fight earlier before I stormed out of the apartment. Any questions so far?"

Kevin raises his hand. "I have a question. Didn't Erica participate in the murder?"

What the hell is he thinking? I explicitly told him to keep the Monica part a secret. Besides, Erica was merely a witness, not a murderer. Monica killed Hector and then vanished from Erica's body. Then Erica regained control and witnessed Hector's death. From her perspective, Aaron is the killer, not her.

"No, Kevin," I growl. "Erica didn't take part in the murder. She only saw Aaron commit the act and watched as Hector's body bled out. That traumatic experience triggered her selective amnesia."

"Got it," he mutters.

"To sum it up," I continue, my voice steady, "Erica's selective amnesia will only resurface if she faces a stress level far beyond witnessing a murder. That's her new *threshold* now."

"Wait," Abigail interrupts. "Something doesn't add up. Witnessing her own mother's death must have been more painful than seeing another patient pass away, right?"

"Absolutely," I respond. "But after that traumatic event, Erica was pampered for ten years, shielded from any real stress. It weakened her ability to cope with difficult situations. That's why triggering her amnesia became so much easier. The doctors failed to recognize this pattern because they never saw a pattern in the first place. They just saw a one-time event. If only Erica had lived a normal life, facing occasional stress like the rest of us instead of dwelling in Myles' fabricated world, she might have been okay today."

"Okay, so we understand the pattern and how her amnesia is triggered," Abigail acknowledges. "What's the plan to prevent it from happening again?"

"Prevention?" I question, a determined glint in my eyes. "No, I'm talking about a cure. I believe we can permanently heal Erica's selective amnesia."

The room falls silent. Everyone's gaze remains fixed on me, awaiting my idea.

"I call it Mission Gaslight," I declare. "This mission will be completed in three phases.

"Phase one: We let Erica recover with the fever and tiredness for the next few days at Myles' home. After that, she can go back to her apartment as if nothing happened and continue with her work. We let her believe that she got a leave of absence from my father, Mike. Then, I'll meet Erica on her first day back at work, acting like a new recruit. I'll develop my relationship again by going out on a few dates and making sure she's badly attracted to me. Then, I'll use one of her phobias against her to stress her mind. One of the biggest phobias she has is fear of heights. So, I'll take it up a notch and take her skydiving. I'm sure it'll stress her enough to trigger selective amnesia. Then we bring her back to the apartment, sedate her just enough to let her wake within a few hours and let her believe that the whole thing was a dream. Vincent, you'll have to live with Erica to make sure the plan stays on course. You'll need to make sure to update us in case of an emergency, but don't engage in any conversation that can jeopardize our mission.

"Next, phase two should be more daunting than phase one. What's worse than jumping out of sky? I'd say getting raped and murdered would be extremely horrifying for most women. So, when she gets back to work, I'll join again as a new recruit and get into the relationship with her, eventually making her believe that I'm a criminal who's about to rape and kill her. That'll trigger her amnesia again and push the limits of her stress. Once she falls unconscious, we repeat the same steps we did at the end of phase one. We bring her back home sedated and make sure she wakes up a few hours later, letting her believe that it was all a dream.

"The next time she faces another stress, it has to be worse than getting raped or killed. And I'm pretty sure, in relation to these horrifying events, letting her know that she's married to me during those six months wouldn't top that.

"That brings me to phase three. Once she's awake, I'll show up to her apartment and let her know that she's married to me. At that point, she'll be stressed, but not as much as her past limits. So, theoretically she should be able to take it. That also determines if the first two phases were successful.

"Your role comes into play only until I reveal to her that she's my wife. After that, I'll take care of the rest of the mission. Any questions?"

"Nolan, this all sounds like a theory based on patterns you've observed," Kevin says skeptically. "How can we be sure it'll work?"

"We never try, we never know," I reply confidently. "How did I know that I can build a good company? Because I tried hard. Same goes with this mission."

"Let's say your plan works," Abigail says. "After the skydiving event, what if Erica recognizes you from the so-called dream and tries to avoid you instead of date you again?"

"Good point, Abigail. That's where you come in. It's crucial that you ensure the plan stays on track. If Erica tries to distance herself from me, you need to pursue her and convince her to go on a date. That way the plan can continue."

"Isn't this all deceiving her?" she asks. "What if something worse happens?"

It's a do-or-die mission. If Erica dies during this process, at least she'll find peace. If not, she'll recover and continue living with occasional stress, just like everyone else on this planet.

"She'll understand, Abigail. Let's stay focused on the mission. Any other questions?"

"Yes," Abigail speaks up again. "I'd like to know about next steps. What do we do now?"

"Kevin and I are going to install micro cameras across Erica's apartment. We'll remove all the traces of our wedding pictures from the apartment and from social media, making sure Erica continues to believe that she's single. Vincent," I gesture to him "you need to get your clothes and video games and just be yourself. Just try to speak less while you're at her apartment and be attentive while your sister is sleeping. Of course, you can rest during the day. And Abigail, your job is the toughest. Erica's going to speak with you the most, and it's your job to make sure that the mission is going in the right direction."

Everyone nods, agreeing to the plan in its entirety.

PART III: THE CURE
Present
Abigail

25

June 25, 2023:

Phase two of the mission is complete, but the weight of deception is crushing me. I hope this is over soon. I can't deceive my friend any longer. Now in phase three, we must meet Erica today and reveal the truth. I can't wait to be by her side during the revelation that she's married, she lost her memory after receiving tragic news, and she witnessed a murder during her treatment at the psychiatric facility.

I'm not sure how Nolan plans to disclose all of this, but my role in the mission is done. I believe the best approach is to start by telling her that today is not June 19th but the 25th and to go from there. Regardless, I need to be there for her and ensure her well-being in the years to come.

It's 5:30 a.m., and I'm anxious that Erica might wake up soon, considering the sedation she's under should be wearing off. I message Vincent: "Are you awake?"

He replies instantly: "Yes, I am. I'm playing video games, just as instructed."

"Is Erica awake?"

"No."

Nolan and Kevin drive to my house, and we plan to head to Erica's apartment as soon as she wakes up. The rest of phase three is to just reveal and keep our fingers crossed.

The clock strikes 6:30, and Erica's call comes in. I answer it, trying to sound groggy as if I've just woken up. Erica starts crying on the other end, explaining her nightmare about Nolan trying to rape and kill her, just as we planned in phase two.

Tears well up in my eyes as I witness her unraveling. I have no choice but to stick to the plan. I instruct her to tidy up her home and prepare for our day of shopping and pampering at the salon.

After I end the call, Nolan, Kevin, and I exchange triumphant high fives, reveling in the success of our plan.

"What's our next move, Nolan?" I inquire.

"From your end, not much. We'll wait for Erica to call us once she's freshened up. It'll help calm her down before we head to her apartment for the grand reveal. You've done an exceptional job, Abigail. Erica is lucky to have a friend like you," Nolan praises.

"I'd do anything for her," I reply with a sincere smile.

I can't help but yearn for this ordeal to be over. The sense of accomplishment in our groundbreaking psychological experiment is overwhelming. The level of coordination required for this mission is astounding. Now, all that remains is to witness the outcome.

We settle into the living room and savor our coffee as we eagerly await Erica's call signaling her readiness.

An hour later, Erica calls, but she's sobbing even worse than before. Her voice trembles as she reveals the discovery of a hidden journal in her closet's secret vault. My heart plummets into my stomach, leaving me speechless and unsure of how to react.

I turn to Nolan, my voice barely a whisper as I seek guidance. "What should I say?"

"Say something and end the call quickly," Nolan advises, urgency lacing his words.

"Erica, I'll be there in ten minutes," I manage to say. "Just stay calm until then."

"No! I need answers now!" Erica's voice crackles with desperation.

"I'm on my way," I respond, abruptly ending the call.

"She found WHAT?" Kevin blurts. "Are you sure you heard her correctly?"

I turn to Nolan. "What does she mean she found a journal with pictures of you kissing her?"

Nolan falls into a contemplative silence before finally speaking. "Kevin and Abigail, I'll handle the rest of phase three alone. Stay here and wait for my message."

"No," I object firmly. "I'm coming with you. I can assist and try to calm Erica down, too."

"Fine, on one condition," Nolan concedes. "You must remain completely silent, no matter what happens. Please understand that this is the most complex psychological experiment I have attempted so far, and I don't want to ruin it right when it's about to conclude."

I nod, determination etched on my face. "I'll stay quiet and follow your lead, but I'm coming."

"Alright," he agrees. "But Kevin, you're staying here. Keep an eye on everything through Erica's living room camera. It's for the best. Trust me."

Kevin nods, his worry evident. "Sure, whatever you say. Just be careful."

We drive to Erica's apartment and wait on her doorstep for her to answer the door. She reacts to Nolan's presence with sheer madness, grabbing a knife from the kitchen and menacingly warning Nolan to stay away from her. I calmly urge her to listen to Nolan, and we all take a seat around the small dining table.

Hours pass as Erica reads through Nolan's journal, which becomes increasingly disturbing as he delves into entries about their date, the wedding, her amnesia, and Monica.

My heart sinks with each word of the story. I'm left in a state of utter shock as I absorb every detail. Erica is also diagnosed with multiple identity disorder? I can't believe I haven't noticed it all these years.

Nolan's plan remains a mystery to me, but I follow the instructions given, staying silent and observing everything closely.

He glares at Erica and his words cut through the air like a knife. "This is the whole damn story of what's gone down in the past few months. You're my wife, and you better get it through that messed-up brain of yours."

"Nolan, please, just be nice," I plead, my voice barely a whisper.

"Didn't I already tell you to shut up when we got here?" he bellows, his rage intensifying. "So, zip it and back off."

Fear grips me as I realize this is the first time he's ever been angry at me. I'm guessing his behavior is part of the experiment, so I fall silent and obediently sink back into my seat as he commands.

Erica sits in silence with her head bowed, her mind spinning with thoughts. After a few moments, her voice quivers as she gathers the courage to speak. "I have so many questions."

"Go ahead," Nolan replies, his tone harsh. "I'm gonna answer every damn one of 'em, no filters. And today, you're gonna listen without passing out."

"Why did you marry me?" Her tinny voice makes her sound so vulnerable. "Did you even love me?"

"I've never been in love before," he admits, his words laced with uncertainty. "Hell, I don't even know what it means. But I did enjoy seeing you naked every damn night, and I thought that was love, so I married you. And maybe you said yes because I'm a billionaire. I couldn't care less about why you decided to marry me. Your father turned out to be a gold digger, maybe you're one, too. From my point of view, I was just damn happy to have someone to sleep with when I get home from work."

Tears stream down Erica's face. I remain silent, observing Nolan's reaction to her questions.

"Did I ever mention wanting a honeymoon? Or did I ask you for anything, for that matter?" Erica asks.

"No, you never did," Nolan replies in frustration. "But I went out of my way to give you the best time, spending a significant amount of time and money. I did it all just to see you happy and to prove to your father that his daughter is content."

Erica's disbelief is evident as she continues, "I can't believe I fell for someone like you. Tell me the truth, are you really my husband?"

"Yes, I am," Nolan confesses while rising from his seat. "I married you, and that's the truth. I'm tired of pretending to be overly kind just to keep you satisfied, especially after everything you've put me through."

Erica's sobs echo through the room, her tears flowing uncontrollably.

"So, you're saying that my first dream was real? You actually pushed me from an airplane?"

Nolan meets her gaze, his eyes cold and calculating. "Yes, that wasn't a dream. It was my meticulous plan to cure you. I took you skydiving, hoping that the shock would render you unconscious once the blindfold was removed. But you surprised me. You were stronger than I anticipated. So, I had to improvise. I cooked up a story midair about a failed parachute and having to let you go. That worked and then we came down successfully in one piece."

Erica's brow furrows as she tries to make sense of it all. "But the next day, when I woke up, my journal was empty. How did that happen?"

"I hired a skilled calligrapher to create multiple copies of your journal. At the start of each phase, I replaced your journal with a professionally crafted forgery."

"You're the worst thing that ever happened to me," she seethes.

"Am I? Am I really the worst thing?" he yells, startling both Erica and me. "You're the worst thing that's ever happened to all of us. Do you know I had to use my company's resources to trick the network and make sure you never find out the real date? I spent so much — in the midst of recession, to cure your fucking brain."

"Then why did you do it?" she screams. "You could have divorced me and let it all go."

"And what? Let you take half of my wealth? You and your gold-digging family would love that!"

Erica glares at him, her anger intensifying. Her fist clenches tightly as if she's ready to strike.

"And you didn't feel any remorse when you found out about my painful stay at the psychiatric facility?"

"Remorse? You should be the one feeling remorse when this is all over. How dare you even ask me that? I sent you to that facility so I could finally have some peace and focus on my work. The only thing I missed during that time was your body. But you know what? I don't even enjoy your body anymore. I know I can do so much better.

"And now, thinking back, I understand why those kids bullied you when you were younger. They should have done more to teach you a lesson. I wish Chloe had stripped you naked and tortured you in front of the whole class. I wish your mother had taken you to the store the day of her accident so that Myra could have murdered you along with her."

Erica's tears abruptly cease. She tilts her head forward with stiff shoulders and her hair obscuring part of her face, she locks onto Nolan while he continues to shout at her.

I couldn't help but speak up, my voice trembling, "Nolan, you're losing control." I motion towards Erica.

Nolan's anger turns towards me once again, his voice filled with venom. "Shut the fuck up, Abigail!"

Nolan is completely unhinged. I'm not sure what he's trying to pull here. Wait. Oh god! Is he trying to trigger Monica?

He continues his tirade. "Do you have any idea what you've put me through? I wanted you to be completely cured so I could finally tell you everything without any filters. And this time, I need you to listen without triggering that damn selective amnesia. I want you to remember every single word I'm about to say."

His eyes burn with intensity and his words hit Erica like a barrage of bullets. "Do you know what I had to do after I rescued you from that facility? I had to spend millions of dollars and bribe the jury to throw Myra into prison for the rest of her life AND to get you out of it. Because apparently, that's the only way your alter ego, Monica, would be satisfied. You're the reason why so many people around you are suffering."

Erica's gaze remains fixed on him as she growls, "Did you put Myra in prison?"

"Yes, I did!" He closes the distance between them. His eyes lock onto hers, his expression twisted like that of a deranged psychopath. "What? You're not happy? You want me to do more for you? Enough is enough. You know what's going to happen next? You're going to live with me for the rest of your life. I'll lock you in the bedroom, never allowing you to leave this apartment. Your sole purpose in life will be to give me pleasure every night. That's what you deserve for causing me such pain. Do you understand? DO YOU UNDERSTAND?"

Erica snatches the knife from the table. Before Nolan can react, she swings it towards his throat. He falls, choking on his own blood, the room quickly becoming a gruesome scene. Blood splatters across her hand and face, and she keeps watching him, breathing heavily.

Vincent and I sit frozen, our bodies paralyzed by shock as we witness the horrifying events unfold before us.

As Nolan's movements cease, Erica suddenly snaps back to reality. She stares at Nolan's lifeless body, the knife still clutched in her trembling hand, his blood staining her skin. She realizes that she murdered him and collapses to the floor, slipping out of consciousness.

PART IV: THE TRUTH
Two Weeks Later
Kevin

26

July 09, 2023:

In one swift motion, I lost my dearest friend, Andrew Nolan ~~Kash~~ *Kerr*. I'll never forget the sacrifice he made to cure my wife, Erica.

I met Nolan in college. I grew up in Portland, Oregon, and had never strayed far from the Pacific Northwest. Suddenly, I found myself soaring across the country, headed for MIT. It was a whole new world.

As I entered my dorm on my first day, I was greeted by a geeky guy sporting thick-framed glasses and surrounded by a mountain of books. He approached me, extending his hand. "Hello, I'm Nolan. Are you my roommate?"

"Hi, Nolan, I'm Kevin. Yes, I'm your roommate. I'm here studying computer science. What about you?"

"Ah, welcome Kevin. I'm studying psychology," he replied, glancing around at his book collection. "Sorry about the smell. They're all used books, and sometimes they stink."

From that moment on, we spent the day getting to know each other. It was a memory I would never forget. Being thousands of miles away from home, I was feeling homesick. I had never been apart from my parents, Mike and Vivian, my entire life. The separation was tough, and I spent the first week at college in tears, pouring my heart out to Nolan about my longing for my family and my beloved hometown in Oregon.

Nolan comforted me for weeks and helped me find strength in my newfound independence from my parents. Little did I know, as I battled my own emotional turmoil, he was carrying his own burdens silently. He never felt the need to burden me with his pain.

It wasn't until several weeks later that I discovered the truth: His parents had tragically died in a car accident when he was just a child, leaving him to be raised in foster care. Yet, not once did he mention this while I poured out my heartache. He just listened, stayed present, and kept trying to lift me out of my own mess.

Overwhelmed with guilt, I finally mustered the courage to ask him why he hadn't shared his own story with me. His response was both heartbreaking and inspiring.

"When my parents died, I desperately sought emotional support. But everyone was too preoccupied with finding me a foster home. I hoped that once I found a new family, I would finally have someone to confide in, but the support never came. I cried for weeks until my tears ran dry. Slowly, I learned to move on. But from that moment on, I made it my mission to emotionally be there for every child who entered foster care. I wanted to be the shoulder they could cry on until they found their own strength. It brought me joy, and it gave me purpose. So, when you were missing your family, I didn't want to overshadow your pain by sharing my own loss. I believe that when someone shares their pain with you, trying to make them feel better by comparing it to your own and implying their struggle isn't as serious is not helpful. It's a form of narcissism that undermines what they're feeling. So, when you opened up to me, I didn't try to compare. I listened because I saw it as a chance to share in your pain and build a genuine friendship. That's why I'm taking psychology courses, to help as many people as I can before my time is up. Not just foster kids, but anyone facing phobias and disorders. That's what keeps me going."

In that moment, I held him tightly, realizing that I had found not just any friend, but an inspiring friend. Strong in mind, yet soft in heart.

I just wanted to repay him somehow, to show my gratitude.

"Please, let me do something for you as a thank you," I pleaded.

"I'm sorry, I don't expect anything in return," he replied. "It keeps me humble and grounded."

I realized that my desire to give him something was more for my own happiness than his. But Nolan wasn't someone who valued material possessions or money. He lived with just five pairs of clothes and his most prized possessions were his well-worn psychology books. He already owned majority of the best psychology books out there, so gifting a book of the sort would be difficult.

"Please, Nolan. Tell me what I can do for you. It's for my own peace of mind," I insisted.

"Alright, I guess there is something you could do. I want to pursue a doctorate in psychology. To do that, I need to work on real cases and create impressive reports that can help me secure a position as a doctoral candidate. If you come across anyone with psychological issues, no matter how small, connect me with them and help me work on their cases. Once I help them overcome their issues, I can ask for their consent to document their cases and publish them in scientific journals."

"Deal," I said with a surge of excitement.

It had seemed like such an easy request, especially since we were in college. I could easily find students struggling with breakups and drug addiction, and social media certainly opened a lot of gates for disorders.

I used to make friends with them and then introduced them to Nolan. And he used to work with those students and help them navigate their way towards being strong again.

Within two years, he had become *the* person to turn to. Word of mouth spread like wildfire, with many referring other students in need to him. Those who had their problems resolved by his help were so grateful that they began showering him with money and gifts as a token of their appreciation. Instead of keeping any of it for himself, Nolan selflessly donated everything to a nearby foster care center. He never sought personal gain. This inspired me to find a gift for him that he could truly cherish and use, something that wouldn't end up being given away.

So, I decided to create a small web application specifically designed to help him manage his student clients. This tool proved to be a game-changer, allowing him to efficiently work with them and provide the assistance they needed. It also helped him document these case studies. The satisfaction I felt from seeing him benefit from my application was indescribable.

Before he even had the chance to publish his groundbreaking psychological case studies, his reputation had reached the ears of esteemed psychology professors. One of them, impressed by his talent and dedication, offered him a fully funded master's degree followed by a Ph.D. program. It was an incredible opportunity that would propel him even further in his career. It gave me immense satisfaction to have played a part in his career growth. That app I designed eventually became the inspiration for Wise AI, the startup I built that helped millions launch their own careers.

The day those degrees were pitched to Nolan, I witnessed a rare sight, tears glistening in his eyes.

Curiosity consumed me as I inquired, "Nolan, you've accomplished your goal. What lies ahead for you now?"

With unwavering determination, he replied, "My goal? I haven't even scratched the surface. I'll construct an organization in Chicago, the very place where my parents tragically died. This organization will offer treatments to individuals nationwide, catering to a wide range of disorders. And with the profits we generate, we'll extend free therapy to foster children."

I had no idea how he was ever going to achieve such a monumental feat.

"Doesn't it cost like millions of dollars to start such organization?" I questioned, my voice tinged with skepticism. "Where will you raise such funds?"

His response was devoid of certainty. "I haven't mapped out every detail just yet," he confessed. "But this is my purpose in life."

I learned so much from him that he truly transformed me as a person. With his inspiration, I decided to create a company in my field, one that could truly make a difference in people's lives.

After graduating from college, Nolan pursued a master's degree at MIT, while I returned to my hometown of Portland to establish my own company. Witnessing the struggles of my college friends — burdened by student debt and unable to find employment, fueled my determination to create a business that could help recent graduates secure jobs with ease. My father, captivated by the idea, even withdrew money from his mortgage to support my startup, Wise AI. He, with his experience in business operations, dedicated countless hours each week to my venture.

During my entrepreneurial journey, whenever faced with a major decision, I would ponder what Nolan would do in that situation, ensuring that I made choices that would benefit both the organization and our customers.

Within a mere five years, Wise AI blossomed into a billion-dollar company, a reality we never could have imagined. It was on that day that I made a firm decision to fund Nolan's dream organization of psychological and behavioral sciences in Chicago as soon as he completed his doctoral program at MIT.

About eight months ago, we began receiving negative reviews regarding our customer support. Seeking guidance, I called Nolan for suggestions, knowing that his expertise in psychology would prove invaluable. He proposed that I immerse myself in a service-based job to gain insight into public behavior when faced with good or bad service. Intrigued by his idea, I took up a position as a waiter at a local ice cream parlor.

On my first day, I walked into the parlor and there she was, Erica. The moment our eyes met, I felt an instant connection. She was the kindest person I had ever come across, and her beauty was breathtaking. We started going out and as time went on, I couldn't help but fall deeper in love with her. I knew she was the one.

Eventually, I mustered up the courage to share my secret with her. I revealed that I was the co-founder of Wise AI, a company I had poured my heart and soul into. And then I asked her to marry me. It wasn't just about our love for each other, but also the way we respected each other's beliefs and values.

We enjoyed our initial few months of marriage with a trip to my Hawaiian island and few other places in Oregon. I wanted nothing more than to make all of Erica's dreams come true. She deserved every ounce of happiness.

Erica also became my partner in crime for driving and building our company.

But one day, everything changed. I'd received a phone call from my C.E.O., delivering the devastating news of a recession-induced loss of clients. If we didn't handle this crisis properly, our company could crumble by the end of the year. These roller coasters happen to me all the time. And stress had always been a constant companion in my life as an entrepreneur, but for Erica, it was uncharted territory.

As soon as the call ended, I explained the gravity of the situation to her, knowing that it wasn't just *my* company at stake anymore. It was *ours*. The weight of the impending consequences pressed heavily on her fragile state of mind. I held her close, promising to carry the burden on my shoulders. Of course it was my burden to carry. I appreciated her support in helping me run the company, but something as serious as a recession wasn't something I expected her to handle or take so personally.

Hours later, when I returned home from work, I found Erica unconscious. The cause remained a mystery, but it was clear that the weight of it all had stressed her out. I rushed her to the hospital and reached out to Myles, who helped me understand the history of Erica's condition. I was trying to reach out to Nolan, but he was off to a week-long conference in Europe.

With the guidance of the doctors in emergency care, Myles and I made the agonizing choice to admit her to a psychiatric facility under the watchful eye of Dr. Scott. Dr. Myra was assigned to Erica's case. Within a week, a call came from Dr. Scott, urging me to retrieve Erica immediately, as she had been found at a crime scene.

Leaving everything behind, I hurried to the facility to bring Erica home. I had no clear plan, but Nolan called just in time, returning from his conference. As soon as I heard his voice, tears streamed down my face. I poured out the whole situation to him, begging for his help. After all, that's what best friends are for, right? To rescue each other in the darkest of times.

Nolan had been working on a different case for his doctorate thesis, but he selflessly asked his professor to transfer it to a colleague so he could take on Erica's case instead. Without hesitation, he handed over two years of hard work to his colleague and caught the next flight to Portland.

As soon as he touched down, we shared all the information we had on selective amnesia with him. Nolan's mind was already racing, contemplating strategies to cure her. He figured out that every time Erica experiences stress beyond what she can handle, her amnesia is triggered and she loses an unpredictable amount of memory. That meant the solution was not to recover old memories, but to increase her ability to handle stress. If he could raise that threshold far beyond what most people experience, she could start fresh and live a stable, normal life.

The theory made sense, but it was still just a theory. Nolan needed to dig into every detail of what Erica had experienced at the psychiatric facility. So we visited the place together, and he worked closely with Dr. Scott to examine every part of her time there. That's when he discovered she was also struggling with dissociative identity disorder.

Through the security footage, we noticed a pattern. Erica switched to her alter, Monica, during moments of extreme mental torture. Monica was cold, violent, and entirely different from Erica's usual self. This discovery added a whole new level of complexity to Erica's preexisting condition. Dr. Scott suggested keeping Erica in the facility long-term, but Nolan knew that would mean a lifetime of confinement. There is no cure for dissociative identity disorder, and he didn't want her trapped because of it.

Nolan had a bigger vision, one where stress-induced amnesia and multiple personality disorder could be cured with a breakthrough method. But he couldn't tackle both at once. The only viable path was to first raise Erica's stress threshold and help her overcome selective amnesia without triggering Monica. Once that was achieved, he would work on a separate strategy to address the identity disorder.

Nolan devoted several hours to absorbing every bit of information about Erica. He sought insights from Myles, Vincent, Abigail, and anyone else who held a close connection to her.

With newfound clarity, Nolan created a three-phase plan to heal Erica once and for all. I was scared the experiment might fail, but Nolan is a true genius. If he couldn't solve the problem, it meant I would have to let her go. Not because I was giving up on caring for her, but because I loved her enough to want her to live in peace.

Nolan's methods were unlike anything most psychologists would consider. Every case he took on, he approached with unconventional thinking, and somehow, he always found a solution. He believed this plan would succeed.

The first phase was to cure her selective amnesia. Once he was confident she had fully recovered, the second phase would begin. That phase involved triggering Monica and using his techniques to make sure she never returned. Nolan explained the entire plan to all of us and received verbal consent from everyone before moving forward.

The first two phases were designed to push Erica's stress threshold to the max, helping her develop the resilience needed to prevent future breakdowns. The final phase focused on confronting Monica directly and ensuring that part of Erica would never come back.

This was the hardest time of my life. Not graduating from MIT, not building a company, but everything happening with Erica. It broke me in ways I didn't expect. I placed all my hope in Nolan, and he knew it. He understood exactly what was at stake.

We planned every detail of phases one and two with care. I cleared out an entire floor of employees in the administrative building and brought in hired actors who were fully briefed on their roles. Nolan and I joined as new employees and followed the plan down to the last detail. Nolan, being the perfectionist he is, made sure there were no flaws in the entire setup.

Phase one was a success. Erica even recognized Nolan's face afterward, which gave us a small but powerful sign that she might remember him again at the end of phase two.

The next day, Erica woke up, met Nolan, liked him, and eventually started dating him. Then, phase two began. Everything went exactly as planned. It was flawless.

Nolan believed that Erica was cured of selective amnesia at that point and all he needed was confirmation. He had planted a journal inside her closet, along with an AI-generated photograph showing him as her husband. That photo would be the test. If Erica saw the image and the shock triggered her amnesia again, the experiment would be considered a failure. But if she remained conscious and emotionally stable, it would mean the test had passed.

The moment Erica laid eyes on it, she managed to withstand the shock. This suggested that her ability to cope with extreme stress has proven effective, potentially preventing the reemergence of her amnesia. That was a breakthrough Nolan had been craving to present to the world.

I hugged him the moment we realized she was strong enough. For the first time in a long while, I could see a future with Erica again. I didn't care about starting over from the beginning. Explaining everything to her would have been possible, and she would have been able to handle it.

What's worse? Nearly dying in a plane crash, being assaulted by a criminal, or seeing a photo of herself kissing that same criminal and believing he was her husband? In comparison, learning the truth later would be easier. She would be angry, of course, but that would not be enough to trigger her amnesia. And she could never stay mad at her family and friends for too long. In the end, she would have understood. It all came from a place of love.

We were celebrating, but Nolan remained still and focused. He knew the real challenge was still ahead. Monica was the problem that needed solving. I knew he intended to trigger her and deal with her directly, but he never told me exactly how he planned to do it, or what he would do once she does switch to Monica.

He had studied Monica's patterns and concluded that she appeared as a defense against bullying and emotional abuse. By definition, bullies are fueled by arrogance and inflated egos. They tear people down by constantly undermining them. So he wrote a journal featuring a fictional version of himself, a character dripping with arrogance and ego, belittling Erica at every step.

Nolan was confident in the final draft. He told me that creating an obvious villain, like a murderer or a rapist, was easy. But in this case, he was limited to using only ego and arrogance, traits that exist in almost everyone. His goal was to show just how damaging they can be when taken to the extreme.

I have to admit, just hearing him describe the character made my blood boil. And that says a lot, considering I'm usually calm and composed and the fact that I knew it was fictional. If I reacted that way, there was no doubt Monica would be triggered, especially since Erica believed the journal to be real.

After phase two, Abbey asked Erica to clean the closet and wait until we arrived. But Nolan insisted that we all stay away from phase three, recognizing that none of us possessed the expertise to handle patients like Monica. But Abbey was determined to join him and support him wherever she could.

His plan was for me to stay home and observe everything through the camera in the living room. I had hoped to be by his side during phase three, but he was worried that Erica would remember him afterwards, making it difficult for me to rebuild a relationship with her. So, I followed his instructions and stayed home, watching him through the camera.

Once Nolan and Abbey arrived at Erica's home, she walked into the kitchen and picked up a knife. That was unexpected. Nolan had probably assumed he could handle any threat from her, but this moment caught him off guard. He sat in front of her and made her read the journal, essentially using *my* beautiful journey with Erica and replacing me with himself. He portrayed himself as a wealthy, arrogant, and egotistical monster at every twist and turn of the story.

I treated her to sweet ice cream dates, we marveled at the stars together, I spilled my secrets about work, I asked for her hand in marriage, we exchanged vows, and we escaped to Hawaii. And just like that, Nolan had seized my entire beautiful history and twisted it in ways I never saw coming. What a smart ass! Rather than crafting a fresh narrative with potential loopholes, he manipulated my own story, one that Erica would easily believe.

We all watched in astonishment as Erica read through the journal, but we obeyed his command and left him undisturbed throughout the narrative.

Erica *reading* the journal was the final experiment. Nolan observed her face to gauge her emotions as she read. He could have sat in front of her and narrated the entire past, but he was afraid that doing it on the spot might leave room for loopholes. Observing the shift in Erica's emotions as she read was the key. The journal was written to anger her, escalating her anger as she continued reading. He hoped that Monica would be triggered before Erica reached the end of the journal. However, Erica managed to read it all without triggering selective amnesia or Monica. I was amazed to see her mental strength, as those entries were unsettling even for me.

Even as the journal ended, Monica was never triggered. Turns out, Erica became a much stronger woman than she ever was. Determined to push the boundaries, Nolan began hurling painfully cruel words about Erica's life and family, hoping to ignite a reaction from Monica. Little did he know, things would take an unexpected turn. In a swift and decisive move, Monica ended his life with a single stroke, leaving him no time to react.

After Monica killed Nolan, she released her grip on Erica's mind. Erica came back to herself and stared down at her blood-soaked hands, the knife still dripping. The shock hit her like a tidal wave, the pain crashing so deep it could shatter a person completely.

A good person fears killing more than being killed. Death ends you, but killing someone stays with you forever.

The overwhelming trauma triggered her selective amnesia, pushing her to the very edge of what she could endure. An edge she would never reach again.

Once again, we sedated her and repeated the process of convincing her that it had all been a mere dream. Every trace of Nolan's blood was erased, and his body was buried beside his parents, forever hidden from the world.

Hundreds of people gathered at his memorial, traveling from all corners of the country. Many of the students battling drug addiction had recovered thanks to his guidance during their college years and gone on to establish respected organizations.

I stood before the crowd, delivering a heartfelt speech about his dreams and his unwavering commitment to humanity. Together, we pooled our resources, raising tens of millions of dollars to bring his vision to life.

Just days ago, I finalized the paperwork for a new psychiatric facility in Chicago, a fitting tribute to his legacy. It would bear the name "Dr. Kerr's Psychiatric and Behavioral Sciences." Additionally, I ensured that his groundbreaking case study of curing Erica's selective amnesia would be shared worldwide. His sacrifice would not be in vain.

When Erica awoke, fear gripped her and tears streamed down her face for hours. But Abbey, ever caring, reassured her that it was all just a bad dream, helping her find solace.

Erica, now liberated from her disorders, owes it all to one man: Andrew Nolan Kerr. Sadly, she would never know her hero.

***

Today is a pivotal day for me. Today I'm starting fresh. I'm going on a blind date with Erica, arranged by Abbey. Though she may sense familiarity, I will reveal my true identity and profession, explaining that she must have seen me somewhere at work. It won't be easy to reconnect with her, knowing she's the one who killed my best friend. But Nolan made a huge sacrifice for my marriage, and I owe it to him to make things right by marrying Erica once more and finding the peace I've been searching for.

Epilogue

Five Years Later
Abigail
December 22, 2028

Kevin and Erica tied the knot after just a few whirlwind months of dating. We all relived the moments, while Erica experienced it for the first time again. Their connection was so strong that waiting any longer simply didn't make sense. They were destined for each other, no doubt about it.

While Wise AI slowly regained its footing, Kevin's entrepreneurial journey continued to be a wild roller coaster ride. Erica, on the other hand, remained unaffected by the ups and downs. In fact, she stepped up to the plate and assumed the role of chief operating officer, tackling even bigger challenges within the company when Mike retired.

Nolan's groundbreaking thesis continues to be studied by doctors worldwide, exploring its potential to treat and possibly cure amnesia.

Today marks an extraordinary day. I just received a call from Kevin that Erica successfully delivered a baby boy and they decided to name him Andrew Nolan Kash.

Excitedly, I prepare a meal of Erica's favorite dishes and carefully pack them while keeping an eye on the news. As I'm getting ready to leave, I reach for the television remote to turn it off. However, my heart drops when I catch sight of the local breaking news story.

The headline flashes across the screen: "Dr. Myra, former employee of Central Oregon's psychiatric facility, escapes from prison and is on the run. Surveillance footage shows her leaving a hotel in Portland. Please be alert and report any suspicious activity to the local police."

Oh god, if she finds Erica, does that mean Monica will...

Author's Note

I want to take a moment to explain why I felt compelled to share this story with you, the readers.

Some of the events from Erica's childhood are based on my own experiences growing up. The torment inflicted by the tutor Chloe and the relentless bullying from other children are all rooted in real-life events. Unfortunately, there are countless children around the world who face even greater challenges as they navigate their way through life. This poses a grave danger to humanity.

One of the reasons for this danger is the widespread ignorance surrounding mental health. We live in a time where people are easily triggered by the smallest things. The sensitivity towards personal choices, self-identity, opinions on climate, religious ideologies, and more is starting to take a toll on the mental well-being of the younger generation. Social media only amplifies these issues, as people must navigate a minefield of potential triggers when communicating with others.

It's crucial for everyone to prioritize their mental health by confronting their fears and becoming resilient to the world around them. Instead of constantly being triggered and manipulated, we must build our mental fortitude. Erica's journey through stress serves as an example in this novel, but it can be applied to the many other weaknesses that humans face.

I hope that reading this novel has brought you both pleasure and a deeper understanding of the importance of mental health.

Remember: "The only way out is through."

Acknowledgements

This story lived in my mind for nearly five years before it found its way to the page. It all started in early 2023 when I casually shared the plot with my wife, Harika, who's a thriller enthusiast. She was instantly hooked and encouraged me to turn the idea into a novel so others could experience it as well. As an entrepreneur and scientist, becoming an author was never part of my life plan. But sometimes, all it takes is a little push. To quote the Joker, "Madness is like gravity... all it takes is a little push." Harika not only supported this journey, but also beta read multiple versions of the manuscript, helping shape it into what it is today. I owe this leap to her, and I hope readers are ready because this is just the beginning.

A special shoutout goes to the star proofreaders and copyeditors of this novel, David Aretha and Danny Raye. Your incredible feedback and support have been invaluable as I start this new journey.

And I can't forget to thank my friends Arun, Kalyan, Preetham, Praneeth, and Prachi, who provided unwavering support by beta reading this work.

Q&A with Akash

1. What was going on in your mind while writing the toxic character Nolan (specifically in the journal)?

   ○ I keep seeing thrillers and murder mysteries rely on villains defined by murder or rape. It's the easy route; make someone a killer, a rapist, or a human trafficker and readers will hate them instantly. But I felt there had to be a more nuanced way to portray toxic characters. What if we used traits we actually see around us every day and just pushed them to the extreme? Think about it: How many people in your life struggle with egotism or arrogance? Probably most of them, to varying degrees. So I saw an opportunity. I built Nolan's character around these common traits and dialed them up to a level that would make readers' blood boil. It also fit perfectly with the story, since he needed to reflect the traits of a manipulative bully. Writing him was honestly a lot of fun. Some of my beta readers disliked him so much that they were glad Nolan died. I even had to tone down his toxicity a bit! A few readers started judging me as a person, and I had to gently remind them that he's just a character.

2. Nolan (in the journal) was a jerk and then slowly starts to show love towards Erica. But just when we thought he was starting to become a nice person, he becomes a jerk again after marriage. Why did you write it that way?

- It was definitely intentional. How many times have you heard a woman say to her husband, "You're not the same person I married"? Truthfully, they didn't change; their real selves just resurfaced. When people date, they often wear a mask, presenting a version of themselves that's affectionate, attentive, and agreeable. But after the wedding, that mask eventually slips off. What's underneath can feel so different that it seems like the person they fell in love with has disappeared. I used that exact human behavior in Nolan's journal. At first, Nolan comes across as judgmental, egotistical, and arrogant. But his attraction to Erica causes him to put on a mask, to act in ways she finds lovable and charming. Once they get married and he feels his goal is achieved, that mask slowly starts to come off. His true self, a condescending jerk, returns. Of course, all of this is part of Nolan's journal, which isn't a reflection of reality, but is a carefully crafted narrative. The real Nolan, a psychology expert, made sure this part felt disturbingly realistic. I suppose it also serves as a dating tip: Be your true self while dating so you never have to hear, "You're not you anymore."

3. The novel has some core psychology factors behind it. Do you think this would reach most thriller readers?

- I think so. Well... I hope so. A lot of readers I've talked to are getting bored with the same old thrillers. They're craving something original. And it's not just about the plot; it's about the emotions they experience while reading. Sure, there are plenty of thrillers that build tension and lead you anxiously towards a big twist or reveal. Some even do a great job blending romance and suspense. But with my first novel, I wanted to create a fully emotional roller coaster ride, including sympathy by the end. I think that helps bring a sense of originality back to the genre and gives readers a true glimpse of my writing style.

4. What was the biggest challenge during your publishing journey?

- "You're not a celebrity, so I can't give you a shot at getting your work in front of big publishers." Ugh. I'm so sick of hearing that. Writing a story is all about turning an idea into something real, something people can feel. But the publishing industry? Honestly, it's brutal. The biggest problem I've encountered has been with landing a literary agent. If you're just a regular person with a great story, you can't just send it to a top publisher. Nope, you have to go through an agent. And agents? They care about one thing: money. If you're not famous or haven't already written a bunch of books, good luck getting their attention. Even Freida McFadden talked about how hard it was to get her first book out there. So for me, the hardest part wasn't writing the book; it was finding a way to publish it and bring it to you, my beloved reader.

5. How many versions did you write?

- Well, there were quite a few iterations, probably seven or eight. But the biggest change happened a couple of years ago. I originally wrote the novel in a third-person point of view. It was solid, but one of my beta readers suggested switching to multiple first-person perspectives. I'm so glad she gave me that feedback. Now, readers can connect with the characters on a much deeper emotional level. Of course, that meant rewriting the entire novel line by line — all 75,000 words of it. It was a lot of work, but honestly, it was fun. As a debut author, it's good to make mistakes and learn from them. That's part of the journey.

6. Will Erica come back in part 2? Because in the epilogue you gave a hint that Monica might be back.

   ○ Probably not. My next novel will definitely focus on a different type of mental disorder and will explore some creative ways to cure it.

7. If this is made into a movie, who would you cast for Nolan and Erica?

   ○ I definitely think this story would make an interesting movie. I'd probably choose Penn Badgley to play Nolan and Elizabeth Lail for Erica.